Running for it

When the eight-second whistle blew, Clay felt like he'd been on the bull's back for two hours. He waited for Gargantua to move to the left, then grabbed the rope and threw himself to the right. He hit the ground and came up running as the huge beast turned and caught sight of him. The bullfighters moved in to distract Gargantua's attention, but the bull didn't waver. It was as if he only wanted to get at the man who had ridden him.

Clay looked over his shoulder and saw that Gargantua was quickly closing the distance. It was at least twenty feet to the safety of the chutes, and the bull was charging full-steam ahead. A bullfighter ran to the bull's side and slapped it, but the massive animal only glanced at him and continued after Clay.

Clay had time to peek back once more—all he saw was bull. There were ten feet left to go when he felt Gargantua's massive head slam into his back, launching him into the air. . . .

Rodeo Riders #2

RIGGED TO RIDE

Mike Flanagan

A SIGNET BOOK

Dedicated to Sam and June Hutchinson, for the help and support they have given me.

I would also like to give special thanks to Jan Branch and Donna Whipkey for their professional advice.

SIGNET
Published by New American Library, a division of
Penguin Putnam Inc., 375 Hudson Street,
New York, New York 10014, U.S.A. Penguin Books Ltd, 27 Wrights Lane,
London W8 5TZ, England
Penguin Books Australia Ltd, Ringwood, Victoria, Australia
Penguin Books Canada Ltd, 10 Alcorn Avenue, Toronto, Ontario, Canada
M4V 3B2
Penguin Books (N.Z.) Ltd, 182–190 Wairau Road, Auckland 10, New Zealand

Penguin Books Ltd, Registered Offices: Harmondsworth, Middlesex, England

First published by Signet, an imprint of New American Library,
a division of Penguin Putnam Inc.

First Printing, June 2000
10 9 8 7 6 5 4 3 2 1

 REGISTERED TRADEMARK—MARCA REGISTRADA

Printed in the United States of America

PUBLISHER'S NOTE
This is a work of fiction. Names, characters, places, and incidents either are the product of the author's imagination or are used fictitiously, and any resemblance to actual persons, living or dead, business establishments, events or locales is entirely coincidental.

BOOKS ARE AVAILABLE AT QUANTITY DISCOUNTS WHEN USED TO PROMOTE PRODUCTS OR SERVICES. FOR INFORMATION PLEASE WRITE TO PREMIUM MARKETING DIVISION, PENGUIN PUTNAM INC., 375 HUDSON STREET, NEW YORK, NEW YORK 10014.

Prologue

Early in April, a meeting took place in a suite at the Sands Hotel in Las Vegas, Nevada. It was a meeting that would drastically impact professional rodeo and the national finals for the remainder of the year. It involved two men of imperial wealth, Tom Larrs and Harmon (Hank) Tallridge. Tom had made it big in the building boom in California in the late seventies, then increased his holdings through wise investments and careful planning. His greatest passion in life was gambling, but only if the stakes were high and the odds were great.

Hank Tallridge accrued his vast fortune in the electronics industries. After four failed marriages and numerous bad relationships, he had found solace in the casinos on the Vegas strip. It was there he'd met Tom Larrs. Their shared passion for gambling forged an alliance that kept them both looking for new ways to test their luck and feed their appetites for excitement. They bet large sums of money on Lady Luck, and waited to see which way she would turn. They had long tired of the normal games available in the casinos, though each would occasionally enter a high-stakes poker game. They bet on every baseball, basketball, football, hockey, volleyball, and soccer game played. They wagered on every event of the Olympics, and on every kind of race there was. In any given week, each of them had somewhere between a hundred and fifty to three hundred thousand dollars out in bets. Like two junkies, they needed more and more to satisfy the fire within. Now, as they sat in the plush room at the Sands, looking at the two separate sheets of paper spread on the table before them, they knew that they were about to embark on what would be one of the largest gambles of all times. One sheet of paper listed the top thirty national contenders in each of the rodeo events. On the other sheet of paper was listed fifteen of the wealthiest people in the United States, all known for their passion for gambling.

"Did you contact all the people on your list?" Hank asked.

"Yep. How about you?"

"Every one of them—and they're all in."

"All of mine too," Tom said. "Each one will wire five hundred thousand to the bank account in the Carribean by the close of business tomorrow."

The idea for this gambling extravaganza had come to Hank while he sat watching the Professional Rodeo Cowboy's Association National Finals the year before. As he thought about what it took for each of the cowboys to qualify for the finals, and how many times the leaders changed during the year, he realized what a long shot it was for anyone to finish in the number one spot. An injury, bad draws, financial problems, family problems—anything could impact the odds of making it to the finals. The odds would change constantly, and as far as Hank could see, no one could determine what those odds were. What a gamble!

Tom and Hank worked out the details over a period of two months. They compiled the list of the men and women who would be invited to their game, then they made a list of the top thirty contenders in each of the six events: barebacks, saddle broncs, bulls, calf roping, steer wrestling, and team ropers, both headers and heelers. They decided not to include women's barrel racing, mainly because of Hank's bad luck with women. He thought having them on the list would jinx him. Though Tom thought that the event would add another degree of excitement to the game, he agreed to its omission. A gathering of all fifteen participants was then planned for the following week in the very same room the two men sat in now. Tom had reserved the room for a month at a time. The meeting was timed to coincide with the release of the latest standings. All of the contestants' names would be placed in various bowls. Those in first through third place would be put in one bowl, fourth through eighth in another, and so on. There would be fifteen participants, because that was the number of top contestants that worked more than one event. Each of the fifteen would be allowed to draw names from each of the bowls in turn, until all names had been drawn. The names each person drew would comprise his team for the season. Each team would be ranked by the amount of prize money it won. The contest would last through the finals, with the winner of the pot being the holder of the team that won the most money. The winning amounted to a staggering seven and a half million dollars.

Neither Tom nor Hank realized what they were creating, nor did they know how it would affect the rodeo world. "Just think, we have eight months to watch the game and see how Lady Luck plays her hand," Hank said, the excitement gleaming in his eyes.

"And we won't know until the end which way she'll go. It's solely in her hands," Tom said. He had no idea how untrue those words would be.

Chapter One

Clay reined in the dapple gray he was riding and waited for Jack Lomas to ride up beside him.

"How many did you count?" Jack asked.

"One hundred and seventy-four," Clay answered.

"I counted one fifty-five. That makes three hundred and twenty-nine head. There's only one missing, and we probably just overlooked her," Jack said, removing his hat and wiping the sweat from his forehead.

They had been riding since daylight, checking the cattle in the north section of the Lazy L Ranch, the spread that Jack Lomas owned near Roswell, New Mexico. It was the place that Clay had called home for the past two and a half years, ever since his brief run-in with the law.

"The calves are looking good, but if we don't get some rain soon, the cows are going to start dropping weight," Clay said, surveying the cows standing around the tank by the windmill.

"Yep, and the grass ain't gonna hold out much longer. It's been two months since we had any rain to speak of," Jack said, frowning through the dust stirred up by the cattle milling around.

Looking at the sky, Clay sighed. "And it don't look like we're gonna get any today."

"I reckon not," Jack replied. "Let's head back to the house. I'm hungry, and I saw Julie rolling out piecrusts this morning. I'll bet she's making some more of her apple pies."

"I wish you hadn't told me that," Clay said, groaning.

"Why not?"

"Because it's still an hour to the house and I'm starving. If it weren't for the fact that it's bad to run horses to the barn, I'd race you back for the first piece of pie."

"I'd take you up on the challenge, but as it is, I reckon we'll have to hit a fast trot and get there as quick as we can."

The ground-eating trot was also a bone-jarring one if you happened to be riding a rough horse, and Clay was definitely riding one today. The dapple gray was a stout quarter horse that Clay had trained himself. He loved the performance the horse gave when it came to roping and cutting cattle. In fact, he loved everything about it. Everything, that is, except its trot.

Jack smiled as he watched Clay's backside bounce in the hard seat of the saddle. Moving his own horse up beside him, he asked, "You ready for your rematch this weekend?" Jack was talking about the saddle bronc horse Clay had drawn at the upcoming Salina, Kansas, rodeo. It was a horse called Outlaw, a top bucking horse that had been to the National Finals three years in a row. Clay had drawn it two months before in Tombstone, Arizona. Outlaw had won the battle, throwing Clay six seconds into his eight-second ride.

"I'm ready. I should have ridden him last time," Clay said in a voice that reflected the anger he still felt at his performance.

"You should have," Jack said, "but you didn't. Now you have to put your mind to it and ride him this time. Don't let that move he's got throw you off again."

Clay chuckled. "It sure is a sneaky one. He throws his head to the right, then ducks left. The only horse I've ever seen do that."

"He's good, all right. That's why he's made it to the finals three years in a row."

"How do you ride a horse that moves his head one way, then turns the other? You've always taught me to watch their heads in order to follow the direction they're going to turn."

"That's true on most horses, but I reckon there's always an exception to the rule. You'll have to tighten your seat and keep your rein a little more and not anticipate which way he'll go."

"Oh, that ought to be easy," Clay said, smiling.

"That's the only thing I can tell you. You might talk to Billy Ettinger. He won the Ft. Worth rodeo on him," Jack said.

"Yeah, I know," Clay sighed. Billy Ettinger was in first place in the standings, while Clay was sitting third just behind Ron Bowers. Both men were great guys, but the competition among the three was fierce as they vied for that coveted first place title. "If I see him in Salina, I'll ask him what he did to cover him."

"He'll sure tell you," Jack said.

"I know, that's what hurts," Clay said, rolling his eyes. "And if I make a qualified ride on him, he'll never let me forget it was him that made it possible."

Jack broke into laughter. "If you make a qualified ride on Outlaw, you'll probably win the saddle bronc riding, and that will more'n likely move you into second place in the standings. You can throw that back at him. That should take most of the sting out of it. You got to learn to look at the bright side of things."

"Believe me, I try that all the time when I'm working with you. The only problem is, I can't find any bright sides," Clay said, laughing.

Without batting an eye, Jack responded, "Well, I guess you won't be wanting any of that apple pie then, since that sure isn't a bright side to this day."

"Well, maybe there are one or two bright sides," Clay said, grinning, "but they're few and far between."

The two carried on their easy banter as they covered the distance to the ranch house where Julie had a late lunch waiting for them.

As they unsaddled their horses, Jack thought back to the time when he had first met Clay. The boy had gotten into trouble with the local sheriff on a trumped-up charge of grand theft auto. Ben Aguilar, the Chaves County sheriff, had seen potential in Clay, and rather than let the judge send him to juvenile hall, he had asked Jack to take the boy in for a year. Reluctantly, Jack had agreed. It had been a stormy start, since both possessed a streak of stubbornness. Neither had been willing to give an inch in the beginning, but each had a love for rodeo, and through that they had found common ground that had forged a friendship. It was a friendship that had survived some of the most trying times imaginable.

Clay had served his one year of county time on the ranch, and had stayed on with Jack helping on the ranch and traveling to rodeos. It was a situation that had suited them both.

Clay was now participating on the professional rodeo circuit. His first year as a professional had been a learning experience for both him and Jack. Clay had finished in eighteenth place in the saddle bronc riding, twenty-second in the bareback riding, and seventeenth in the bull riding, just two places out of the finals. Though it had been disappointing, he had vowed to work harder and make it in all three events this year.

As Jack and Clay unsaddled their horses and turned them into the large corral by the barn, Terry Stevens came driving up in the ranch's old Dodge pickup. Terry was Julie's husband. Jack had hired them both to take care of the ranch while he and Clay traveled from rodeo to rodeo. Terry was just coming in from working on a windmill, and stopped at the barn when he saw Jack and Clay.

"How's the calf crop doin'?" he asked, stepping out of the pickup.

"They're lookin' good right now, but if we don't

get some rain soon, we're going to have to start feedin' 'em," Jack said, looking again at the sky as if he could somehow will rain clouds to appear.

"It *is* dry," Terry agreed. "But there's still plenty of grass in the north pasture, and the east pasture looks pretty good too."

Jack nodded, his mind mulling over the options they would have to face if it didn't rain soon. "Clay and I'll be gone for about two weeks. We're going to rodeos in Oklahoma, Missouri, Kansas, and Colorado. We'll take a look at things when we get back and see what we need to do."

"We should get at least one cutting off the hay field," Clay added.

"It won't be much of a cutting," Jack said. "I doubt we'll get four hundred bales."

Clay pointed to the large dirt tank that served as a watering place for the barn stock and the cattle during gathering time. "I was thinking the other day, if we could find some way to use the water from that tank to irrigate the hay pasture, we might be able to get enough hay to hold us over until it rains."

Jack looked at the tank, then at the hay pasture. The tank was almost three acres wide and about twenty-five feet deep. "If we use the water out of there, we won't have anything to water the stock with," he said, though his mind, seeing Clay's logic, was already trying to conceive ways to get the water into the field.

"If we don't get some hay, we won't have any stock to worry about watering," Clay responded. "We could use the gasoline pump to flood the hay field. It'll take a little work directing the flow to get an even cover, but it should work."

"A little water on that field right now would make a lot of difference in the amount of hay we get," Terry said.

"It sure would," Jack agreed.

"I'll get everything working while you two are gone. I'll water it in the evenings so the water won't evaporate. With two weeks of water, we'll have hay ready to cut by the time you two get back."

Jack nodded. "Sounds like a plan. Now let's get up to the house and get something to eat. My stomach is rubbing my backbone."

Julie and Terry were young, in their early thirties, but Julie took care of Jack and Clay as if they were her children. Cooking and cleaning for them was only part of her responsibilities, as she saw it. She also made sure they ate right, doctored them when they were hurt, and if one of them so much as sneezed, she was there instantly with cough syrup and a thermometer. Jack once made the comment that he wished she and Terry would have some kids of their of own so she would quit mothering him all the time. But the truth was, he loved the attention she paid him, and her constant worrying was comforting. So when she scolded all of them for coming home late and fussed about the lunch she'd prepared having turned cold, Jack just chuckled and patted her on the arm. "Now, Julie, you know when we're out working cattle we can't quit until the job is finished. Besides, you're such a good cook it tastes good even when it's cold."

Julie slapped his hand away in mock anger. "You're so full of bull, Jack Lomas. Now go wash up while I finish heating up ya'lls lunch." Though she acted upset, it was easy to see Jack's compliment pleased her immensely. Clay and Terry exchanged winks as Jack left the kitchen grinning.

Jack and Clay left early the next day. The Ford four-door pickup they drove had a cab-over-camper that served as their motel on wheels, complete with shower, bed, and a small refrigerator that could run on either propane or electricity. There was a rooftop air conditioner that was powered by the small generator they had installed on the bumper of the truck. Julie had packed their clothes in the camper's small closet, and had stocked the refrigerator with snacks and as many prepared meals as she could fit into the confined space. She constantly admonished them about their eating habits on the road, and made them promise they would eat wholesome meals.

Jack let Clay do most of the driving while he navigated, getting them lost on a few occasions, much to Clay's teasing delight.

The first rodeo Clay was entered in that week was in Oklahoma City that night. "I can remember when the national finals were always held in Oklahoma City," Jack said as they crossed the Texas/Oklahoma border. "I know the finals have grown and done better since they moved them to Las Vegas, but there was something about having them in a cowtown like Oklahoma City that can't be replaced."

"They may miss something," Clay said with a grin, "but money isn't one of them. The payoffs have quadrupled since they moved to Las Vegas, and you have to admit it's a heck of a lot more exciting there than it is in Oklahoma City."

"Maybe," Jack responded sullenly, "but there's still something missing that can't be found in Vegas."

"I don't care if they're held in Podunk, Rhode Island, as long as I make 'em," Clay said.

Jack smiled at him. "I reckon I felt the same way."

"What was the greatest thing about making it to the finals?" Clay asked, glancing over at Jack.

Jack thought for a moment before answering. "There were a lot of great things about making the finals. Of course, the first thing is the fact that you beat out a lot of good people to get there. Then there's the knowledge that you're going to get a shot at the best stock there is. But if I had to pick the best thing about going to the finals, I guess it would have to be the excitement I saw in Marie's eyes when we got to Oklahoma City. I guess that's probably one of the reasons why I love this city so much."

Clay felt a lump rise in his throat at the mention of Jack's deceased wife. "You made it to the finals four times, didn't you?" he asked.

"Four times in seven years, and every time was just as exciting as the one before. Marie was just as excited to be going too. The year I won the saddle bronc riding she was on cloud nine. You would have thought she was the one doing the riding, the way she carried on," Jack chuckled as the memories flooded back to him. "And I guess in a way, she did make every ride. Sometimes it's harder to sit in the stands and watch than it is to actually ride. I've learned that myself since I've been watching you."

"I just hope I have someone, someday, to share my victories the way you had Marie," Clay said.

"You got me," Jack said, looking at him and grinning.

"That's true," Clay said, "but I don't think it's quite the same. I'd like to have someone give me a big kiss when I make a good ride—and I sure don't want it to be you."

"You don't know how happy that makes me," Jack said.

The rodeo grounds were a buzz of activity as they drove through the contestant gate. The rodeo wouldn't start for another hour, but both Jack and Clay liked to arrive early in order to talk to the other cowboys. It was one of the few times they got to socialize and catch up on the news of what was going on elsewhere on the circuit.

Since Clay had turned pro, he was able to call in and find out what stock he'd drawn, so he knew ahead of time which bull and horses he'd be riding. And like the other cowboys, he knew most of the stock either by experience or by reputation. He had drawn number X7 (Red Rocket) in the bull riding; number 28, Double Trouble, in the barebacks; and number 315, a horse called Doctor Death, in the saddle broncs. Double Trouble was the only animal Clay had reservations about. The sorrel horse didn't have the reputation of being one of the top bucking horses in the Ray Carrie bucking string.

Ray Carrie was one of the top stock contractors on

the pro circuit. His stock was consistently voted into the finals. The top fifteen cowboys in each event that made it to the finals voted on the stock they wanted to ride, which insured that the year's best stock was at the finals.

The Oklahoma City rodeo kicked off with the grand entry, followed by the invocation and the National Anthem. Then the bareback riding began.

Clay was slated to be the fifth rider in bareback riding, so he settled in to watch the first four riders. Cory Hickman, the third rider, scored a seventy-four to take the lead. Jack helped Clay set his rigging and gave him words of encouragement as he eased down into the chute and worked his hand into the handle, rotating it to heat the resin on his glove, and making the leather handle sticky. Easing onto Double Trouble's back, he set his feet on the chute over the points of the horse's shoulders. Reaching up, he pulled his hat down tightly on his head and nodded to the gate man.

Double Trouble pivoted on his hind feet and lunged into the arena. Clay's spurs remained over the points of the horse's shoulders as his front hooves hit the ground, satisfying the mark-out rule.

Double Trouble spun right and leapt into the air, coming down stiff-legged and hard. The jolt shook Clay's body, but he kept his hold and maintained his balance, all the while raking his spurs along the horse's shoulders as it leapt forward.

Double Trouble bucked straight down the fence of the arena. Head down and kicking high, the horse gave

Clay a good ride all the way to the eight-second whistle.

The pickup men moved in as Clay worked his hand from the rigging handle. Grabbing the man on his right around the waist, Clay slid easily to the ground.

The judges gave Clay a score of sixty-nine. It was not good enough to place and Clay knew it, but he had also learned that that was how a rodeo event went. Sometimes you draw well and sometimes you don't. He smiled as he walked back to the chutes to get his bareback rigging, knowing he'd done the best he could. There was a time when he would have been upset, but Jack had convinced him it was futile to worry over a ride that had already taken place. It was much better to focus on the rides yet to come.

Jack was waiting for Clay behind the chutes. "You put on a good ride," he said as Clay climbed up on the platform with his bronc saddle.

"Would have been better if I'd had a better horse," he said, then held up his hand as Jack started to say something. "I know, I know, that's rodeo; you pay your entry fees and you take your draw, but it doesn't hurt to want the best horses."

Jack chuckled. "No, it doesn't hurt, as long as you know it's not always going to happen and accept it when it doesn't."

Clay laughed. "I've learned that lesson already."

"I guess you have," Jack said. "Let's get something to drink."

"Good idea. I think I swallowed half the dust in this arena."

They watched the calf roping and steer wrestling while they waited for the saddle bronc riding to begin. As they were walking back to the chutes they passed an area where several young ladies were sitting on their horses. Clay glanced at them and smiled, and was turning his attention back to the chutes when a female voice called out to him. "Hi, Clay." He turned and looked in the direction of the voice and instantly recognized Tamara Allen as the one who had spoken. "Hi, Tamara," he said with a wave of his hand.

Clay had always thought Tamara was the best-looking woman on the rodeo circuit and had said so to Jack on several occassions. She had long blond hair that hung almost to her waist and swung from side to side as she walked. She had a figure that would make professional models jealous—a slim waist and long legs. Her high cheekbones suggested she might be of Indian descent and her emerald green eyes, which held Clay captive, sparkled when she laughed.

"Good luck on your ride," she said, smiling brightly at him.

"Thanks," he said, grinning back, then hurried to catch up with Jack, who had continued toward the chutes. As Clay caught up with him, Jack gave him a bewildered look. "What?" Clay asked, surprised by the look.

"You got at least twenty minutes before you have to start getting ready for your ride. Why didn't you talk to Tamara? She's definitely interested in you."

"Uh, she's just being nice," he stammered.

"She's bein' nice, all right, and she especially likes being nice to you. I've seen how she looks at you and I've seen how you watch her. The chemistry is there; all you have to do is add the ingredients."

Clay grinned in embarrassment. "And what are the ingredients?"

Jack cocked an eyebrow at him, then said, "Conversation is the first one. Start there and everything else will fall into place."

Chapter Two

Standing behind the chutes waiting to ride, Clay talked to Ray Jones, a fellow saddle bronc rider who was sitting fifteenth in the standings. "Did you hear about Steve Cannon?" Ray asked. Steve was another saddle bronc rider who, last time Clay had checked, was sitting seventh in the standings.

"No, what about him?" Clay asked.

"He was on his way to a rodeo in Arizona, and stopped to get gas. While he was paying for it, someone slashed all four of his tires and put sugar in his gas tank. He missed the rodeo and had to spend almost a thousand dollars getting his truck fixed."

"Did they find out who did it?" Clay asked.

"They have no idea. The police figure it was just some kids who did it for kicks."

"That's tough," Clay said. "I hope they catch 'em."

"Somebody did that to my truck, I'd kill 'em," Ray said.

Doctor Death was already in the chute and Jack helped Clay set his saddle and put his halter on. By the time the first two competitors had ridden out, Clay was in the saddle and ready to ride.

The arena director called his name and Clay pulled

his hat snug on his head. "Let him out, boys," Clay said, and the gate swung open.

Doctor Death was a large black horse with lots of power, and he used every bit of it as he swung on his hind feet and pushed off in an upward lunge.

Clay gripped hard with his thighs and held tightly to the braided rope rein, fighting against the force of the horse's movements. At the peak of Doctor Death's leap, his feet almost cleared the top of the chute gate. When gravity pulled him back to earth, he landed with a jolting crash, sending shock waves through Clay's body. There was no time for Clay to think about the pain as the black horse coiled himself and shot into the air again.

Though Doctor Death's bucking style was hard to get in time with, Clay used his spurs to the best of his ability. He raked them from the points of Doctor Death's shoulders to the cantle of the saddle, then back to the shoulders when the horse's front feet hit the ground again. Clay held on tightly to the buck rein and shifted his weight to keep his balance. He kept a watch on the horse's head to try and determine which direction he was going.

Doctor Death hit the ground and shifted to the right before lurching forward. Clay was ready for the move and tightened his grip with his right thigh, and was ready when the horse suddenly shot in the opposite direction on its next jump.

At the end of eight seconds, the whistle blew and Clay dismounted with the help of the pickup man. Smiling, Clay began walking back to the chutes. He knew he'd made a good ride and was elated as the judges' score was called out.

"Clay Tory's score is a seventy-nine, moving him into first place in the saddle bronc riding," the announcer called out, and Jack grinned from ear to ear, knowing this would help move Clay up in the overall standings.

After retrieving his saddle and putting it in the camper, Clay walked back to the stands to find Jack. Walking past the gate leading into the arena, Tamara Allen was sitting on her horse waiting to run barrels. "Great ride, Clay," she said as he walked by.

Changing his course, he walked up and smiled broadly at her. "Thanks," he replied. "You tear 'em up in the barrels."

"I'm gonna try," she said, returning his smile with a dazzling one of her own. Clay felt his knees go weak. "Where you up next?" she asked.

"Springfield tomorrow, and Salina, Kansas, Saturday," he replied.

"Hey, me too," she responded. "Then I'm going to Lincoln, Nebraska."

Clay tried not to look disappointed as he said, "I'm going to Colorado Springs." He was secretly pleased to see the look of disappointment on her face. "Where'll you be staying in Springfield?" he asked.

"At the Holiday Inn," she answered. "If you need a place to take a shower, you can use my room."

Clay blushed as he stammered, "Th—thanks, but the Hightowers have us a room at the Howard Johnson." He hurried to change the subject. "Are you leaving tonight?"

"As soon as the rodeo's over," she said. "I thought I'd stay and watch you in the bull riding, though."

"Good, I need all the cheering I can get."

She laughed. "I guess I better start warming up my horse. If I don't see you again tonight, I'll see you tomorrow in Springfield."

"Good luck on your run. I'll be rooting for you."

"Thanks," she said, and smiled at him again, making him feel like a lovestruck schoolboy.

Clay turned and walked toward the stands, humming silently to himself. He didn't notice Jack watching him or see the grin on his face. Jack had been watching the two of them, and was pleased to see them together. He had known Tamara's father for many years, and though they weren't close friends, he thought highly of Cliff Allen. Cliff had been on the circuit back in the days when Jack was rodeoing, but had quit a long time before Jack had. He had taken over his parents' ranch in San Angelo, Texas. With his keen business sense, Cliff had turned it into one of the most successful ranches in the state. Of course, striking oil didn't hurt any either, Jack thought to himself, but in spite of that, he genuinely liked Tamara, and thought she and Clay were a great match. Both were good kids.

Clay stopped in front of Jack, noticing the smile on his face. "What are you grinning about?" he asked.

Jack's face held an innocent look as he shrugged. "Nothing, I was just enjoying the rodeo," he said.

"Uh-huh," Clay said suspicously as he took a seat next to him. Jack turned back to watch the first barrel racer enter the arena.

They watched each of the barrel racers in turn, commenting on how each of the horses worked, but when the announcer called Tamara's name, Jack noticed that Clay sat forward and waited with a little more anticipation for her to enter the arena. She and her horse entered at full speed, her auburn hair flying loose beneath her Stetson, checking just before the first barrel. She spun around the metal barrel with little room to spare between it and her horse. As the big sorrel came around the barrel, he accelerated to full speed in two strides, covering the distance between the first and second barrel in short order, then checking to make the turn. Tamara spurred him to the third barrel and came around it clean, racing toward the timer. She finished with a 16.3-second run, good enough for second place.

As Tamara disappeared from the arena, Clay picked up his gear bag and turned to Jack. "They're loading the bulls."

Jack nodded and stood up. "She made a good run, didn't she?"

"Who?" Clay asked, grinning.

"Yeah, who indeed," Jack said, returning his mischievous smile.

Each chute was now filled with thousands of pounds of strapping bovine flesh, each bull ready to challenge the cowboys who chose to strap themselves to their backs and attempt to conquer them for a total of eight seconds.

The bull riding always drew the largest crowds, and many of the top bull riders were also riding on the PBRA, Professional Bull Riders' Association, where they rode for larger purses.

Clay had been riding bulls since he'd started rodeoing at age fifteen, and had suffered his share of injuries from what was considered the most dangerous sport in America. The old saying went, "It's not *if* you get hurt riding. It's *when*." Clay's injuries so far consisted of bruises, sprains, and concussions. He was luckier than many, who lost whole seasons of riding to debilitating injuries, others had even lost their lives pursuing the sport.

Clay's draw, Red Rocket, a red bull whose breeding was undetermined, was loaded in chute number four. He had the reputation of being hard to ride, and getting real nasty once he had you on the ground. Clay had drawn him in Gladewater, Texas, but had missed riding him by two seconds when the bull had pulled a lightning quick reverse and moved Clay off his rope, jerking him down. This time, Clay hoped to even the score.

Jack helped Clay get his bull rope set as the first of the bull riders nodded for his ride. Clay sat on the chute gate and watched, making mental notes of the way each bull bucked for future reference.

The current rider was Jay Kemp from Kansas, who had drawn a large black bull called Ground Shaker. Jay was trying his best to stay with the fierce bucking bull, and it looked like he might make it to the whistle. But in a surprising move Ground Shaker planted his front feet and quickly pivoted into a left spin that moved Jay off his bull rope. The cowboy was soon airborne and landed hard in the arena, three seconds before the whistle blew.

The next three bull riders didn't fare any better. Brock Weisman hung up four seconds into his ride on Air Time. Pulled beneath the hooves of the bull, he was stepped on several times and knocked unconscious. It took all three bullfighters risking their lives to free Brock's hand from the death trap. The paramedics rushed to his side even before the angry bull was run from the arena. The crowd, with quiet reverence, waited as the paramedics strapped a head-and-neck brace on the injured man then eased him onto a stretcher and carried him, still unconscious, from the arena. The spectators watched in grim silence as the rider was carried out to the waiting ambulance, many of them whispering amongst themselves about their predictions regarding his injuries.

Clay eased down on Red Rocket's back, and placed his hand in the braided handle of the bull rope. Jack pulled on the tail of the rope, which was run through a loop at the other end, and the handle pulled down tightly on Clay's hand, securing it inside the handle. Clay nodded when he felt the rope grow tight enough. Jack kept the tail pulled tight as he laid it across Clay's open palm. Closing his fist on the rope, Clay wrapped the tail around his hand. He then laid it in his palm and worked the end between his little finger and ring finger, then closed his hand, hammering his fist tightly closed with his other hand. He moved up over his rope and nodded for the gate to be opened.

Red Rocket didn't stand around patiently. Seeing

the gate move, he lunged against it, knocking the gate man backward. The bull exploded into the arena. His first move was a quick turn to the left, making the cowboys in the arena scramble for the chute gates to get out of the way. Red Rocket immediately shifted and turned right.

Clay dug in with his spurs, leaned back, and pulled hard on the bull rope as Red Rocket tried his best to throw him off balance. The huge red beast went into a right spin, making three complete turns, during which it seemed his nose almost touched his tail in midair. He suddenly changed direction and leapt into the air in a high kicking leap, twisting his body to the left.

Clay was still up on his rope and sitting in the middle of the bull's back, waiting for the impact when Red Rock landed. Leaning back, he braced himself as the angry bull came back to earth and suddenly ducked to the left. The move was intended to pull Clay down into the well, the point between the bull's head and shoulders, but he was prepared for it, and dug into the bull's tough hide with his left spur, remaining upright as the big beast went into a tight bucking left spin. Clay got in time with the spin and began spurring with his right spur while maintaining a solid hold with his left spur.

The whistle blew just as Red Rocket came out of the spin. The bullfighters moved in to draw the animal's attention away. Clay grabbed the tail of his bull rope, pulling it loose from his hand. Red Rocket shifted to the left, and went after one of the bullfighters. Clay used the diversion and let go, swinging himself to the right, landing on his feet, and making it to the safety of the chutes in two rapid strides. He was high on the adrenaline rush, having evened the score with the bull. He waited as the judges totaled his score, his heart still racing from the excitement of the ride.

The announcer called out Clay's score over the speaker system; an eighty-five, moving him into first place. Clay broke into a huge triumphant smile as Jack slapped him on the back. "You got the best of that bull that time."

"It was great," Clay said, moving out of the chute as the next rider came out for his ride. Standing behind the chutes, he looked around the arena until he spotted whom he was looking for. Tamara was standing on the arena fence close to the side exit.

"I'll be back in a minute," Clay said to Jack, stepping across the chute and jumping into the arena. Making his way to the gate, he exited the arena and walked up to Tamara, who was now on the ground smiling brightly at him.

"That was fantastic," she said excitedly.

"It felt good," Clay admitted, then stood there, lost for words. He had intended to ask her to have lunch with him the following day, but now that he was face-to-face with her, he lost all courage. The silence grew awkward until Tamara mercifully broke it. "I'll bet your score holds. I don't think anyone will beat it."

"You never know," Clay said. "There's still some good bull riders in tomorrow night's show."

"Yeah, but I'd put my money on your ride," Tamara said, smiling sweetly.

"Uh . . . I was wonderin' if you might like to get some lunch tomorrow?" Clay asked, feeling incredibly shy and uncomfortable.

"Well, I *was* planning on getting lunch sometime tomorrow," Tamara said teasingly.

Clay looked at her, surprised by her response until he realized she was playing with him. "What I meant—" he began, but she cut him off.

"I know what you meant, silly. Of course I'd like to have lunch with you. I have to feed my horse at about twelve o'clock, so why don't you meet me at the Holiday Inn around one?"

"Why don't I meet you there around eleven-thirty and help you feed?" Clay asked, finally finding his courage.

"I don't know," she said hesitantly. "I planned on sleeping until eleven and then getting cleaned up after I got back from feeding. I'm not sure I want you to see me before I've had a chance to get my makeup on."

Clay smiled. "I reckon you'd look beautiful anytime," he said, and was pleased to see a flush come across her high cheekbones.

"You haven't seen me first thing in the morning."

He grinned again. "No, I haven't, but it sounds like something I could look forward to." His smile broadened as she blushed even further.

"I didn't mean it like that," she stated.

"Like what?" he asked innocently.

"You know like what," she said sternly, trying to

sound upset, but her mouth couldn't help but smile as she said, "I'll see you at eleven-thirty tomorrow morning, and I may or may not have my makeup on. It'll serve you right if I don't."

Smiling back at her, Clay responded, "I'll be there and looking forward to it either way."

"See you tomorrow," she said, and walked away with a wave of her hand. Clay watched her lithe, supple form sway as she walked back to her pickup with the gooseneck trailer in tow. Turning, he started back toward the chutes, but Jack's voice stopped him.

"You ready to go?" he asked, standing by the gate.

"I reckon," Clay answered, noticing that the bull riding was over and people were leaving. "Did anyone beat me?"

Jack burst out laughing. "That's the first time I've ever known you not to finish watching the bull riding. There must have been a good reason."

Clay grinned. "A real good reason," he said, but didn't elaborate. "I'm hungry, how about you?"

"Starved. You buyin'?" Jack asked.

"Yeah, I'm buyin'. I hear there's a good steak house on the way out of town. I think I could eat a whole cow right now."

"I never knew bull riding could build such an appetite," Jack said, elbowing him gently in the ribs.

"Oh, but it does," Clay said with a grin. "I burned a lot of calories out there and now I have to replace 'em."

Jack tossed Clay the keys to the truck. "Well, let's get those calories replaced and get to Springfield. I'm anxious to see Will and Dottie, and spend the night in a hotel rather than sleeping cramped up in that camper with you. Besides, it's starting to smell like your feet in there again."

"I don't think those are my feet you're smelling," Clay shot back as he unlocked the doors. "I saw buzzards circling your boots yesterday."

"Very funny," Jack said, climbing into the pickup. "I just hope Tamara can overlook your stinkin' feet and bad sense of humor."

With a smile on his face, Clay turned to look at him. He put the truck in gear and drove away from the Oklahoma City rodeo grounds.

Chapter Three

Will and Dottie Hightower were old friends of Jack and Clay's. Will, Dottie, and their two boys, Carl and Terry, owned Running H Stock Contracting. Clay had started out riding at rodeos put on by the Hightowers before they started producing rodeos for the PRCA. He had continued with them after he'd gone pro. Clay and Jack always tried to make as many of their rodeos as possible, working their schedule around Running H shows. Not only were the Hightowers good friends, but they also had some of the best stock on the circuit.

Crossing the Oklahoma/Missouri border, Clay was lost in his thoughts as Jack dozed in the seat beside him. Clay was looking forward to seeing the Hightowers. He always enjoyed visiting with them, but this time he had an ulterior motive for being glad they were there. If he was going to spend the afternoon with Tamara, he wouldn't feel bad about leaving Jack in the company of his good friends. He looked over at Jack, who was snoring softly. Jack Lomas was more of a father to him than his own father had ever been, but he was also his best friend. They shared a lot; a love for rodeo, for the ranch, and an appreciation of good horses.

Ever since Jack had lost his wife and son years ago, he had been alone. But only when he'd agreed to take on Clay in order to keep him out of juvenile hall, had he found out how truly lonely he'd been. Clay had become his closest companion, and in a sense replaced the son he'd lost. Clay wondered if Jack would ever be interested in another woman again, and had even asked him as much once. Jack had skirted the issue and refused to talk about it again, though Clay had harassed him unmercifully. Of course, Will and Dottie Hightower always tried to pick out women they thought would make a good mate for him, but Jack ignored their attempts, saying he was too old to be changing his ways for another woman.

It was close to two o'clock in the morning when they pulled into the Howard Johnson in Springfield. Clay went in and registered, giving Jack a chance to stretch his legs and get their clothes bags pulled to the back of the camper. Clay got a wake-up call for ten o'clock and returned to the camper outside.

"We're in room one twenty-six, right next to Will and Dottie," Clay said as they got back into the truck.

"I hope they let me sleep late and don't come barging in at some ungodly hour."

"I've got a ten o'clock wake-up call," Clay said sheepishly.

"Ten o'clock!" Jack exclaimed. "What in the world did you do that for?"

"I've got a date with Tamara and I don't want to be late," Clay said.

"Oh," Jack said, caught by surprise. "Where are you going?"

"To help her feed her horse, then we're going to eat. I reckon after that we'll just play it by ear."

"I guess that means you're going to leave me at the mercy of Will Hightower?"

Clay smiled. "I figured I could trust you two alone for a little while. Besides, Dottie will be there to keep an eye on you."

"Hmmph," Jack snorted. "I may just take off with Dottie and leave Will somewhere on the edge of town and hope he gets picked up by some migrant workers heading back to Mexico."

Clay grinned. "Well, let's get to bed. I'm tired after driving all night, and your snoring all the way here has given me a headache."

"I don't snore," Jack said indignantly. "I stayed awake all night one time just to see if I did, and sure enough, I didn't snore at all."

Clay chuckled and shook his head as he pulled up to the room and cut off the engine. "I'm going to buy a recorder and tape you sometime. I bet I can match your snoring against the best chain saw around and you'd win."

"Be a waste of your time and money," Jack said, grabbing the clothes bag out of the camper. "Like I said, I don't snore."

"Yeah, well, I'm going to bed and see if I can get to sleep before your lack of snoring keeps me awake," Clay said, hanging his clothes in the small closet. He took the bed closest to the door and sat down to remove his boots. "I'll try not to wake you when I leave."

"That would be nice," Jack said as his second boot hit the floor. "What time will you be back?"

Clay stopped removing his jeans and rubbed his chin, thinking. "I guess that depends on how well my date goes. If it goes as well as I hope it does, I reckon I'll be back before the rodeo starts."

"I won't wait for you then," Jack said as he crawled under the covers. "I'll just hitch a ride to the rodeo grounds with Will and Dottie."

"Say hello for me, and tell them I'll see 'em tonight," Clay said as he turned out the light. "Good night—or I guess I should say good morning."

"Good night. Have fun tomorrow. I'm sure Tamara will be a whole lot better company than Will Hightower."

Clay laughed as he turned over and pulled the covers around him. In ten minutes he was asleep.

The ringing of the phone sounded miles away to Clay as he fought to wake up. Finally he rolled over and grabbed the receiver off its cradle and brought it to his ear. "Hello?" he mumbled.

"This is your ten o'clock wake-up call," said a strange female voice.

"Oh, yeah," Clay said, and hung up the phone. He felt as if he'd just gone to sleep. The curtains were pulled over the window, and the room was still dark. He pushed off the covers and sat on the edge of the bed, looking over at Jack. The gentle snoring assured him that Jack was sleeping peacefully.

After a long shower and a shave, Clay felt a little less tired. He walked to the hotel office and got directions to the Holiday Inn. It took him fifteen minutes to drive the short distance to the hotel. He drove up to the front office, went in, and asked which room Tamara Allen's was.

"I'm sorry, but we can't give out that information," the young lady behind the counter told him. "If you want to use the house phone," she said, pointing to a white phone at the end of the counter, "I'll be glad to connect you to her room."

Clay nodded and picked up the phone. He could hear the phone ringing and his heart leapt into his throat as he waited for her to pick up. "Hello," he heard her say and his mind just froze. "Hello?" her voice came again.

"Tamara," he managed to say.

"Clay, is that you?" she asked.

"Yeah, I'm here in the lobby. Are you ready to go?"

"You're early," she said. "I just got out of the shower and I still haven't dressed."

"I'll wait for you down here," he said. "I can't wait to see you without your makeup."

"You may run away when you see me," she replied.

"I doubt it. I've got a feeling you'll look just as good without it."

"Boy, are you in for a big surprise. I'll be down in ten minutes. Don't run off with the desk clerk before I get there," she said with a laugh.

"Well, you better hurry," Clay said, "she is cute."

He saw the girl behind the counter blush as she looked up at him, apparently eavesdropping on his conversation.

"I'll be there in five minutes," Tamara said and hung up the phone.

True to her word, Tamara came through the elevator door five minutes later. Clay was sitting in one of the large overstuffed chairs in the lobby thumbing through one of the magazines. He threw it on the table and hurried to stand when he saw her, his heart increasing its tempo. She was dressed in an old pair of blue jeans that were faded from wear and a loose fitting T-shirt tucked in loosely at the waist. Her hair was still damp, and she wore a ball cap perched on her head, but to Clay she looked better than any woman he'd ever laid eyes on.

"I told you I looked terrible in the morning. This is your chance to turn and run," she said, wrinkling her nose.

"If all women looked as good as you do in the morning, there'd be a whole lot fewer divorces," he said without the trace of a smile.

Tamara giggled at the compliment. "You must need glasses."

"Nope, I've got twenty-twenty vision and I'm enjoying the best sight my eyes have ever seen," he said.

"We better go feed my horse before you become delusional."

Stepping to her side, he took her by the elbow and ushered her outside, holding the door open for her and playing the gentleman, delighted by the smile it brought to her face.

They walked to Tamara's pickup, a new Ford four-door. She unlocked the passenger door, then walked around to the driver's side. Clay didn't know why, but suddenly he was feeling extremely nervous. He had dated before and had never felt this way. The girls he'd gone out with in his hometown of Roswell had never affected him the way Tamara did. And then there were the girls that hung out at the rodeos just to pick up cowboys. He'd gone out with a couple of them, but had found them shallow and self-centered. They had treated him as if he were some sort of trophy to be shown off to their friends.

Clay's good looks and boyish charm made him attractive to the opposite sex, but his road schedule on the rodeo circuit didn't give him a lot of time to socialize. That was one of the reasons he was so excited about being with Tamara. Besides the fact that he found her mentally stimulating and physically attractive, their busy schedules found them at the same rodeos on a regular basis.

Tamara drove to a small farm on the outskirts of town. It belonged to some friends of hers, she explained, and they had let her board her horse there for the night.

Taking the horse out of the stall, they led it to a small trap outside where it could run for a few hours before the rodeo. Clay helped carry the feed and hay outside. "How many horses do you have?" he asked her. "I've seen you ride three different ones."

"I don't own a single horse," she said, a hint of

anger in her voice. "All the horses I ride belong to my father. It's his way of keeping me in line. If I don't behave myself, he takes the horses away. Of course, I've got five to choose from. Charger there is my favorite."

"Can't you buy your own?" Clay asked, surprised by her answer.

"I could, but I wouldn't have anyplace to keep it. Don't get me wrong; I get along great with my father, but I'm his only daughter and he wants to keep me under his control for as long as possible. It's just that sometimes I feel like I'm being suffocated. I guess that's why I love to barrel race so much. It gives me a chance to get away and be on my own."

"How does your dad feel about that?" Clay asked.

"At first he wasn't crazy about the idea, so I threatened to marry Robert Dolton. That changed his mind in a hurry."

"Who is Robert Dolton?" Clay asked, an unfamiliar jealousy welling up in him.

"Oh, he's my father's accountant. A real wimp. He's allergic to horses and can't stand the sight or smell of them. My father would rather die than have me marry someone like him."

"So would you have married him?" Clay asked, wondering just how far she'd have gone to get her way.

"No way, but I convinced my father I would. He finally gave in and bought me the pickup, the trailer, and five of the best barrel racing horses in Texas. Of course, he threatens to take them away from me every time I don't toe the line, but then I threaten him with Robert and he backs off."

"Sounds like there's a real war going on," Clay said.

"In a way there is. It's the kind my father likes to play, and I have to admit I enjoy it some myself."

"Hmmm, I just wonder if I'm up to playing that kind of war," Clay stated.

"Oh, I think you'd be able to handle yourself," Tamara said with a smile. "But I don't see any reason why we would ever have to wage a war like that."

"Good," Clay answered, returning her smile. "I can think of a lot of things I'd rather do than fight."

"Oh? Such as what?" she asked innocently.

Looking back later, he could not fathom what had possessed him to do what he did then, but he didn't regret it. "This," he said, taking her in his arms and kissing her. He was pleased to feel her arms glide around him and her lush, soft lips returning his kiss.

Leaning his head back he stared into her brilliant azure eyes. "I like that a lot better," she said breathlessly, and leaned forward to kiss him again.

Clay felt his head spin as he held Tamara tightly in his arms. Nothing had ever made him feel like this. He was intoxicated by the feel of her body pressed against him, the aroma of her skin, and the taste of her lips. He wished this moment could last forever, but he knew if it continued his heart would explode from the sheer joy of the moment.

Finally breaking away, both of their hearts racing, Clay said, "I could stay here doing this the rest of the day, but I imagine your friends would begin to wonder what we were doing down here."

"Knowing Howard and Margaret, I'm surprised they're not down here already. How about we go back to the hotel and let me put on some makeup, then you can take me out to lunch like you promised. I'm starving."

"I guess if I can't stay here and hold you in my arms all day, that's the next best thing. Besides, I'm starving too."

Tamara linked her arm in his as they walked outside. "How come it took you so long to ask me out?" she asked.

"I guess I'm out of practice," he said. "Being on the road all the time doesn't give a guy much of a chance to build his social skills." He didn't tell her the main reason was because he thought she was different than any other girl he'd gone out with, and that he'd planned on asking her out a thousand times, but lost his nerve every time he was around her stunning beauty.

"Well I'm glad you finally did. I was beginning to think I was going to have to ask *you* out."

"Hey it's the nineties. That sort of thing is acceptable nowadays," he replied with a grin.

Laughing, she handed him the keys to the truck and waited for him to open the door for her. She slid up close to him and slipped her arm through his. "I know it's acceptable, and usually if I saw someone I wanted to go out with I'd ask him, but for some reason it was different with you. I was afraid you might say no."

Clay was in the process of starting the engine, but stopped to turn and stare at her. "You were afraid I might say no?" he asked incredulously. Tamara nodded, and he laughed, saying, "I was afraid *you* might say no! That's why it took me so long to ask you."

They were both smiling bashfully as they drove out of the farmyard. It looked like it was going to be the start of an interesting day.

It was twenty minutes before the rodeo started when they drove up to the arena, Tamara pulling her trailer with Clay following behind in his pickup.

Clay grabbed his gear bag from the camper, and after giving Tamara a quick kiss, he promised to meet her in the stands after the bareback riding event, then headed for the bucking chutes.

"Where have you been, young man?" a voice asked as he tossed his gear bag on the ground.

Turning around, he saw Will Hightower sitting on his horse in the arena. Climbing up on the platform that ran behind the bucking chutes, Clay reached over and shook hands with him. "I've been out seeing the sites of Springfield," he answered.

"I saw the sites you were seeing," Will said with a knowing smile, looking in the direction of Tamara's pickup. "Jack tells me you left this morning, and you're just now getting back?"

"What can I say, there's a lot of sites to see around here," Clay responded with a sly grin.

"Well you better get your mind off the sites and get it on Laramie, or all you'll be seein' is the arena dirt," Will said, referring to the horse Clay had drawn.

"He's all I'll have on my mind. I promise."

"You better run on over to the trailer and say hi to Dottie before the rodeo starts, or she'll never forgive you. She was expecting to see you earlier today."

"I'm on my way right now," Clay replied. "Where are Terry and Carl?"

"They're down at the roping chutes getting the calves and steers ready. Both are anxious to see you. They can't wait to rib you about being out all day with a young lady."

"They're just jealous," Clay said.

"I'm sure you're right," Will said, "especially when you consider who the girl is. Her father and I are old friends, so you better take good care of her or I'll use a bullwhip on you," he jested.

Clay glanced toward Tamara's trailer and saw her brushing her horse. He couldn't begin to describe the feeling that welled up within him, but he knew he liked it. It was almost the same feeling he got from riding bulls and broncs, but at the same time it was totally different and he wanted to keep it for the rest of his life. "You don't have to worry about me. I plan to take real good care of her," he responded, giving Will a wink.

Will chuckled. "You just heed my warning, young man. Now get yourself over to the trailer before Dottie calls the police on you."

"I'm as good as there," Clay said, jumping off the platform.

Will watched him go, a smile on his face. Jack Lomas could be proud of the young man he'd helped bring to adulthood.

Chapter Four

Dottie Hightower was sitting at the desk in the small travel trailer the Hightowers used as an office. It was a new trailer they'd had custom built to store all their records and files while providing a comfortable work place for Dottie. It was a drastic improvement over the ancient rusted trailer they'd had before going pro.

Clay opened the door and stepped quietly inside. Dottie was busy writing in a ledger. "I'll be with you in a moment," she said without looking up.

"I figured with all the money you were making, you'd have hired you a secretary by now," Clay said.

Dottie looked up in surprise. Coming quickly to her feet, she embraced Clay in tight hug. "I want to hear all about your day," she said excitedly, then stepped back and looked him in the eye. "And it better be clean."

Giving her a look of mock surprise, Clay said, "Dottie, I can't believe you'd think it wouldn't be."

"I know men," she said. "And what's even worse, I know cowboys. Tamara has a special place with me, young man, so you better treat her with the utmost respect."

Clay gave her a hurt look again. "Your husband has already threatened to use a bullwhip on me, and now you're after me. What kind of person do ya'll think I am?"

Dottie, seeing the look of anguish on Clay's face, felt remorse for her admonishment and hurried to right the situation. "I'm sorry, Clay," Dottie said, giving him a motherly look, "it's just that I've known Tamara since she was a little girl. I think of her as one of mine. I guess I'm just acting like a mother. I know you won't do anything to hurt her, and I'm thrilled to see you two together. You make a perfect couple. Now tell me all about your day."

Clay gave her the highlights of the day in a few short sentences, leaving out the part where he'd kissed her. "Sounds like you two had fun," Dottie said.

"We did," Clay agreed.

Dottie smiled. "Well you better get out to the arena. The rodeo is about to start. We're all going out for supper after the rodeo. Why don't you invite Tamara along?"

"I'll do that," Clay said, smiling. "I better go. I'll see you later."

"I think I'll go find Tamara and get a woman's perspective of the day's events."

Clay smiled at her and left the trailer. The grand entry was just beginning.

Jack was waiting behind the chutes when Clay got there. "I was beginning to wonder if you were going to make it," he said as Clay got his bareback rigging from his gear bag.

"I've got plenty of time. I'm the sixth rider."

"And how was your day?" Jack asked nonchalantly.

Clay looked at him, trying to determine if he was genuinely interested or just asking to see what kind of response he'd get. Figuring he was sincere, he answered, "It was fun. I had a great time."

Jack smiled. "I'm glad. It's about time you started showing an interest in the opposite sex. I was beginning to wonder about you."

Clay gave him a surprised look, then smiled as he saw Jack was pulling his leg. "Well, if you ever have any doubts, just ask me," Clay said.

"I will, providing you don't go off and leave me alone with Will again."

"You better get used to it," Clay said. " 'Cause I plan on seeing a lot of Tamara Allen."

"Well," Jack said, rubbing his chin in thought, "I don't see why I can't go along with you instead of being stuck with Will."

Clay knew he was just joking. Jack loved nothing better than spending time with his old friend, talking about the old days when they were on the rodeo circuit together. The one Clay felt sorry for was Dottie. She had to put up with the two of them.

Jack said, "You better get ready, they've already bucked out two horses and Laramie is in the alley waiting. There's two more before him."

Clay had been working more resin onto the handle of his rigging and his glove when Cory Laird walked by. "Hey, Cory," he said, expecting a greeting in return, but he got a baleful look instead. Shocked, Clay called out to him again. "Hey, Cory, what's up?"

This time the man turned back to him. "Sorry, Clay. It's just that I'm so mad, I could bite nails right now."

Puzzled, Clay asked, "What happened?"

"I almost missed the bareback riding because some idiot stole the battery out of my car, and left me stranded at a roadside park thirty miles from nowhere. If it hadn't been for Carl Stamford and Dave Hampton coming by when they did, I wouldn't have made it. Now I got to go buy a battery and get a ride back to my car."

"That's rough," Clay said sympathetically. "Any idea who stole it?"

"No, but if I ever find out, I'm going to take my payment out of their hides."

"Probably someone who was stranded and needed a battery. I imagine they're long gone by now," Clay responded.

"They better be, if they know what's good for them," Cory replied bitterly.

"At least they didn't slash your tires and put sugar in your gas tank like they did to Steve Cannon," Clay said in the way of solace.

Cory looked at him in surprise. "Who did that?"

"They don't know. It happened at a gas station in Arizona. He missed the entire rodeo because of it."

"I reckon I'm lucky getting by with just a stolen battery. But it still makes me mad."

"If I can help, let me know," Clay said, seeing

Laramie in the chute. He handed the rigging up to Jack and climbed up on the platform.

Laramie was a large black horse with a flowing mane and tail. He came off a ranch in Laramie, Wyoming, which was how he got his name. He was one of Will's best bareback horses. Clay had drawn him twice before and placed both times. Jack set the rigging on the horse's withers and dropped the latigo down the side, waiting for it to be hooked by one of the chute hands. Clay supervised the tightening of the cinch and tested the rigging's set until he was satisfied it was just right. He put on his chaps, which buckled on his legs just above the knees. The flapping of the leather and fringe showed off the spurring action of the rider.

Clay stood astride Laramie's back, one foot on either side of the chute. When the fifth rider began his ride, he eased down on the horse's back and worked his hand into the rigging handle.

The pickup men moved in to help the previous rider off and herded the horse out of the arena. Clay moved into position, placing his feet on the rails on either side of the horse's shoulders, tightening his grip on the rigging handle as the gate man moved into position. "You're up, Tory," the arena director called.

"Outside, boys!" Clay called out.

Laramie bunched up as the chute gate opened. He leaped up and out at the same time. Clay made sure his spurs were over the points of the horse's shoulders marking out in perfect form. At the peak of his skyward lunge, Laramie kicked out with his back feet. Clay leaned back and raked the horse's shoulders with his spurs. The black horse hit the ground hard with a crash before bunching and rocketing skyward again, repeating his kick out and descending to the hard earth of the arena. Clay's hat flew off his head as Laramie launched into the air repeatedly.

Clay's back ached from the impact of hooves and earth meeting. His backside felt as if someone had used a jackhammer on it and his right arm felt as if it were going to be jerked from the socket, but he remained in time with the horse's jumps.

Laramie changed tactics suddenly, going from high-leaping, bone-jarring bucking to a series of twists and cutbacks that had Clay gripping hard with his thighs and pulling tightly on the rigging in a valiant effort to remain aboard the demon's back. His spurring action failed to stay in time with the horse's moves, but points added up as he kept his balance and stayed in control.

When the eight-second whistle blew, Clay grabbed the rigging with both hands and waited for the pickup men to move in. Once on the ground, he retrieved his hat, and walked the length of the arena as he waited for the judges' score. It was a seventy-seven, putting him in first place.

"Good ride, Tory," a cowboy congratulated Clay as he climbed over the chutes to stand beside Jack.

"Thanks," Clay replied, removing the glove from his hand and turning to Jack. "How'd I do coach?"

"It was a fine ride. I don't think anyone will top it," Jack said proudly.

"Thanks," Clay said. "He's a good horse. I didn't expect him to turn it on as much as he did. He kind of surprised me with that leap out of the chute."

"That's a new move for him, all right," Jack said, "but you didn't let him shake you. You stayed with him and made a heck of a ride."

Clay looked into Jack's eyes. It was hard for him to tell this man, who was so much more of a father to him than his own father had ever been, how much he appreciated and needed his approval. "I couldn't have done it without you," he said. "I guess moving all that hay into the barn really worked."

Jack laughed at the reference to his training tactics. He'd had Clay move hay from one side of the barn to the other in order to help develop his muscles. He'd also set up balance beams for him to walk across to improve his balance. It may not have been the most up-to-date training practice, but it had done the job. "And you thought I was crazy when I first introduced you to my training plan."

"Oh, I still think you're crazy," Clay said. "But you did have some good ideas."

"I may be crazy, but I think I see a young lady looking this way, and I doubt she's looking for me. But if she knew the truth, she'd be a whole lot better off with me. She doesn't realize what a hardheaded, hot-tempered, person she's getting involved with."

Laughing, Clay threw his glove into the gear bag, "Yeah, you're such an even-tempered, easygoing person, and so easy to live with."

"You got it right, Junior," Jack said with a grin.

"Well I guess I better get my riggin' and get over there before she realizes what a catch you are and loses interest in me."

"Probably a good idea," Jack said with a sincere

face. "I'm going to go give Will a hard time. I'll see you back here before the saddle bronc riding. Make sure you don't run off somewhere."

"I'll see you right back here," Clay said with a grin. "Don't be giving Will too hard a time now."

Jack waved as he climbed down from the platform and made his way to the back of the arena.

Clay got his bareback rigging and put it in his gear bag, then slinging the gear bag over his shoulder, he walked to where Tamara stood waiting.

"Not bad," she said as he came up and put his arm around her.

"Thanks," he said. "I'm real glad it didn't last any longer than it did."

"It looked like you had him just about broke to ride," Tamara said, handing him a soft drink.

Smiling his gratitude, he asked, "How did I ever get along without you?"

"Apparently not very well," she responded with a smug look.

Clay gave her a sideways glance. "Oh I don't know, I had Jack to take care of me, and he's as good as anybody's mother."

Tamara laughed. "It looks like I've got some stiff competition."

"It's going to be close," he said. "I think a couple of back rubs, a few well-placed kisses and maybe a home cooked meal or two would assure you of taking the lead."

Tamara looked thoughtful. "That doesn't seem like too much. But then again, if Jack offers the same things

I might stand to lose. So maybe I better bow out now and save myself the shame of coming in second."

"But taking the chance is what makes it exciting," Clay answered. "And besides, I happen to know the judge. I'm sure I can sway things your way."

Holding her hand to her chest, Tamara looked aghast. "What, you mean cheat? Why, I couldn't do that." Sighing, she said, "I guess I better just drop out of the race and take my losses."

"Boy, you give up easy," Clay said as they started to walk toward his camper. "I was sure you'd at least put up a good fight. But if you're afraid of the competition, I reckon maybe we ought to just settle for a few kisses and let it go at that." He threw his gear bag into the camper and pulled her close to him. "I think one here," he said, kissing her on the neck. "And one here," he said, brushing his lips against her ear. "And one here for good measure," he said, giving her a long kiss on the lips.

Breathless, Tamara pulled back. "I'm going to have to watch you, Clay Tory. You're sneaky."

"You can watch me anytime you want to," Clay said, kissing her again. When they finally parted, he asked, "You want to go watch the rodeo?"

"I think that would be a great idea," she said, her cheeks flushed and her breathing heavy.

Clay carried his saddle and bronc halter to the chutes, then he and Tamara sat in the stands with Jack, Will, and Dottie to watch the calf roping and steer wrestling. Jack and Will told her stories about Clay, and tried to impress upon her the mistake she was making by taking up with the likes of him. She took their remarks with good humor and added a few of her own in Clay's defense.

When the steer wrestling was over and the specialty act was coming in, Clay stood up. "I guess I better go get ready."

Jack said, "It's about that time, I reckon."

"I guess I better get over there and make sure the boy's getting the horses loaded right," Will commented.

Dottie snorted in disgust. "They can do a better job than you can, old man. Why don't you leave them alone and let them do it?"

Will patted her on the shoulder. "You know they can do it better and I know they can do it better, but they don't know it, and I don't want them to. They might figure they can run this show without me, and then where would we be?"

"I got news for you, Mr. Hightower. They already know they can do it better without you," Dottie said. "They just let you hang around because they feel sorry for you. But one of these days they're going to run you off."

"And when they do, you and I will take a cruise to the Caribbean. But until then, I guess I better keep an eye on things and make sure everything runs smoothly," he said, smiling at her and walking away.

As the three men walked away, Dottie turned to Tamara. "That old man is so hardheaded, they couldn't drive a tenpenny nail into his forehead with a sledgehammer." Tamara smiled and kept her eyes on Clay as he walked toward the chutes.

Chapter Five

Most professional rodeos try to have at least one specialty act during the performances. These performers travel from rodeo to rodeo the same as the contestants, thrilling the crowds with animal acts, rope tricks and riding skills. Tonight's act was a team of trick riders that entertained the crowd with their special riding abilities. Riding four matching white horses Roman style, each one standing on two horses, they performed intricate maneuvers with precise synchronization. They turned somersaults at a full gallop, changed horses while jumping a three-foot hurdle, and jumped all four horses through a burning hoop. While they were strutting their stuff, Terry and Carl were busy sorting and loading the saddle bronc horses in the chutes, getting the flank straps in place and making sure everything was ready for the saddle bronc riding.

Clay had drawn Warrior, a red-and-white paint Will had bought at a bucking horse sale in Texas. Clay had never been on the horse, but had watched him buck on several occasions. Warrior usually came out of the chute hard, running two to three lengths before bucking, but once setting his mind, he bucked hard, varying from the right to the left.

Warrior was now standing in chute number two. Jack took Clay's bronc saddle and placed it on the horse's back. He then cinched it down while Clay buckled on his bronc halter and measured the buck rein. By the time the trick riders were through, all the horses in the chutes and the cowboys riding them were ready for action.

The first rider out was Toby Wills from North Dakota. Toby was a top bronc rider who had made it to the finals for the last three years in this event. He'd drawn a large gray called Ground Shaker, a good horse in anybody's book, and made a qualified ride, scoring seventy-two points to top the previous night's top score of seventy-one.

Clay was in the saddle while Ground Shaker was run out of the arena. Pulling his hat down tight on his head, he nodded for the gate to open.

Warrior left the chute on the run, making two strides before burying his head between his front legs and bellowing in anger. From then on, it was a battle between man and horse. Kicking high with his back feet, Warrior kept his head between his front legs. He turned first to his left, then to his right. He snorted loudly each time his front feet hit the ground. Clay raked him with his spurs, making the rowels sing as they went from the points of Warrior's shoulders to the cantle of the saddle. The whistle blew at the end of eight seconds and Clay grabbed the saddle with his free hand, waiting for the pickup men to move in.

Safely on the ground, Clay waited to hear his score as he walked the distance back to the chutes. The judges' score was a seventy-one. Aghast, Clay stopped in mid-stride. He knew it was a better ride than that. Passing by the judge, he stopped as the next rider prepared for his ride. "That was a little low on the score wasn't it, Gregg?" Gregg Trent was one of the two judges who scored the rides.

"It was a good ride, Clay, but Warrior wasn't turning it on like he normally does. I scored it thirty-eight."

"That means Harvey only scored me a thirty-three. That's too low and you know it."

"I can only take care of one side. You'll have to talk to Harvey about it. Maybe he saw something I didn't." Clay nodded and walked away. The next rider came out and Clay moved over by the chute to wait for the ride to end. As soon as it was over, he moved next to the judge, waiting for him to write his score and call it to the rodeo secretary before speaking.

"Harvey, why did you score me so low on Warrior?" Clay queried.

Harvey Daniels had once been a saddle bronc rider himself and he knew what it was like to receive a score that was lower than you felt you deserved, "Warrior wasn't giving you his best effort tonight, Clay. I scored your riding high, but I didn't feel he earned any more than what I gave him."

"Gregg scored me higher than that," Clay argued.

Harvey gave the same answer Gregg had given. "I only score one side," he said, then moved away without saying another word.

Clay felt himself growing angry, but he checked

his temper. Getting into an argument with the judge could result in a fine, and he didn't need that. Turning, he stomped away, knowing there was nothing he could do.

Jack watched Clay come toward him and knew by the set of his jaw that he was angry. It had been a long time since he'd seen that look. When he and Clay had first started traveling to rodeos, Clay would get angry whenever he made a bad ride or drew a bad horse, but over time Jack taught him there was no use getting mad. This time though, Jack agreed with Clay; he had gotten a bad score, and from the way the other cowboys avoided meeting his look, apparently they thought so too.

"I don't believe that Harvey has enough brains to be a judge," Clay said, climbing over the chutes to stand on the platform next to him.

"You may be right, but unfortunately he's the judge and you can't change the score he gave you."

"I just wonder what he's got against me. You and I both know that ride was better than a seventy-one. Gregg scored me a thirty-eight. Harvey's score should have been close to that!" Clay said.

"We'll lodge a complaint with the PRCA and let them deal with it. If they get too many complaints, they'll pull his judge's card."

"I guess that's all we can do," Clay admitted. "But it still makes me mad to think about it."

"I know, but you've got to put it out of your mind and start thinking about the bull riding."

"I know. I'm going to get my saddle and put it up," Clay said, jumping down off the platform.

"I'm going to the little boy's room," Jack replied, "I'll meet you back here in a few minutes."

Clay nodded and headed for the de-rigging chute to get his saddle.

"That was tough luck, Tory," said a voice behind Clay as he pulled his saddle off the fence. Turning around, he saw Floyd Davis standing a few feet away. If there was anyone Clay could honestly say he didn't like, it was Floyd Davis. He was a loud-mouthed, foul-talking, know-it-all who drank too much. He was also a poor excuse for a bull rider as far as Clay was concerned. It was beyond him how Floyd had ever gotten his PRCA card. Clay could see the slippery smirk on Floyd's lips and it made the hair on the back of his neck stand up.

"That's the way it goes sometimes," Clay said as he started to walk around him, but Floyd moved to block his way.

"Yeah, that's the way it goes—and sometimes it can get worse."

Clay's eyes narrowed as he read the barely veiled threat behind Floyd's words. "And just what does that mean?" he asked.

The look on Floyd's face turned to one of total innocence. "Why, it don't mean nothin' 'tall," he said. "It's just that things have a way of occurin', and you never know when somethin' worse might happen."

Clay let the saddle drop to the ground in front of him. "If that's some kind of threat, then let's find out right now just how bad things can get," Clay said, stepping around the saddle and staring straight into Floyd's eyes.

Floyd's eyes darted in different directions, looking around, seeking support. He hadn't expected this reaction from Clay, and now he'd talked himself into a jam. Like a rat trapped in a corner, he was looking for a way out. "I wasn't threatin' you," he stammered. "I was just commentin' on your bad luck was all, and I've been hearin' about some of the other fellas havin' bad luck. I was just thinkin' about how bad things happen, that's all."

Clay eyed him suspiciously. He didn't believe him, but knew there was no use pursuing it further. Reaching down, he picked up his saddle and walked past Floyd, saying, "Don't get in my way again. Next time I'll walk over the top of you."

Floyd watched Clay walk away, anger burning inside him. He'd always had a dislike for Clay Tory, envying the success he'd achieved. He'd been approached earlier in the day by a man in a business suit wearing dark sunglasses. The man had offered him a large sum of money to see that Clay Tory finished behind two other riders and Floyd had eagerly accepted. It hadn't been hard to bribe Harvey. Floyd had finally gotten him alone after the bareback riding, and offered him two hundred dollars to score Clay low on his rides. Since it was common knowledge that Harvey had financial problems, Floyd knew a little money would help a lot. But now he just wanted to rub it in. When Clay had challenged him, he'd grown weak and Floyd hated himself for it. But more than that, he hated Clay Tory, hated him for being good, hated his confidence, hated him for being a winner. One way or another he'd see Clay Tory fall, and when he did, he'd make sure Clay knew he had something to do with it.

Clay's anger slowly subsided as he watched Tamara from atop the arena fence. She was warming up her horse outside the gate, and when her name was called she charged the barrels. Turning the first two with exact precision, she pivoted around the last barrel to race out of the arena at top speed. Once again, she had the winning time. Clay smiled as she pulled her horse to a stop and looked over at him. He gave her a thumbs-up sign and was rewarded with a bright smile.

Clay was behind the chutes as the bulls were run in, his rope and glove resined, his bull spurs and chaps on. His mind was on the considerable task before him. The bull he'd drawn was a huge brindle bull called Gargantua. This bull was known for his size and agility. Though he was one of the biggest bulls in the string, he could move fast and change direction in the blink of an eye. Once he had a cowboy on the ground, he was trouble in every sense of the word.

Gargantua stomped and kicked the chute gate as it closed behind him, then lunged forward, butting the gate in front of him with his massive horns. As Clay eased his rope down, Gargantua kicked out, lunging in the chute. It took Clay several minutes to get the tail of his rope run through the loop at its end, and get the handle set properly. Gargantua con-

tinued his lunging and fighting as the next three riders tried their bulls in the arena. So far the bulls were
winning the battle. There had been no qualified ride
yet. Clay watched as Paul Dansworth from Houston,
Texas, came into the arena aboard a big Hereford
bull named Lambchop, a name that didn't do the
rank bull justice. Lambchop was a money bull at any
rodeo if a qualified ride was made.

Paul stood a good chance of making it to the whistle. Four seconds into his ride, he was still in the
middle of Lambchop's back as the red white-faced
bull used every trick he knew to unseat him. At six
seconds, Paul Dansworth was using his spurs to gain
extra points, and was still in the middle when the
whistle blew. His ride earned him a score of eighty.

"Looks like Paul might take the whole purse home
with him," Jack said, "unless you ride the hair off
this brute."

"I hope to do just that," Clay replied.

"Good, 'cause we're all going out to eat after the
rodeo and you're buying, so you better pick up a
paycheck."

Clay laughed as he slipped down on the bull's
back and put his hand in the bull rope. Jack pulled
the rope tight until Clay nodded, then laid the rope
in his hand. Clay wrapped it behind his hand and
brought it back over his palm, pounding his fingers
into a tight fist. Pushing himself up on top of the
rope, he nodded to the gate man and dug his spurs
into the bull's tough hide. Bull riders' rowels are
wired down to prevent them from turning. This

allows the sharp points to hold to the bull's hide without turning and slipping off.

Gargantua turned into the arena and immediately shot to the right. He continued a right turn for two leaps, then abruptly turned back to the left, twisting his body hard. He kicked high with his back feet, then turned into a left spin as his feet touched the ground. Gritting his teeth, Clay strained against his rope and dug in with his left spur. He knew he was in time with the bull's spin, and began using his right spur to rake the beast's side.

Gargantua came out of the spin and lunged upward, throwing his head back as he did. Clay felt the change coming and leaned back, digging in with both spurs now. When the bull came to the ground, it was with a shocking jolt that shook Clay all the way to the top of his head. The next four jumps were a series of twists and turns that had Clay digging in and gripping his rope for all he was worth.

When the eight-second whistle blew, Clay felt as if he'd been on the bull's back for two hours. He waited for Gargantua to move to the left, then grabbed the tail of his rope and threw himself to the right. He hit the ground and came up running as the big brindle bull turned and caught sight of him. The bullfighters moved in to distract Gargantua, running between him and Clay to draw his attention, but the bull didn't waver. It was as if he only wanted to get at the man that had ridden him, and no other would do. Clay glanced over his shoulder and saw that Gargantua was quickly closing the distance. There still remained twenty feet to the safety of the chutes, and the other cowboys were yelling encouragement to Clay. One bullfighter ran to the bull's side, hollering and waving his arms, trying to distract him. But Gargantua only glanced at him and continued after his quarry.

With ten feet remaining to the chutes, Clay felt the bull's massive head come in contact with his backside. The next instant he was off his feet as Gargantua lifted him and threw him into the air. Hitting the ground hard behind the bull, Clay felt the breath knocked from him, but he knew he had to move. Regaining his feet, he saw the bull turn toward him and Clay started to run. Gargantua charged again just as Clay bolted toward the chute. The distance closed between them and Clay suddenly changed direction to move away as the bull passed by him. Gargantua's horns barely missed him, and both bullfighters moved in. Clay didn't hesitate. Sprinting the last few feet, he gained the safety of the chutes.

"You all right?" Will asked as Clay stood on the chute gate breathing fast, his heart pounding like a bass drum.

"I got the breath knocked out of me, but other than that I'm all right," Clay answered.

"Well, turn and wave to that young lady standing over there by the fence, before she comes in here and butchers that bull."

Clay looked in the direction Will was pointing and saw Tamara standing on the fence, an anxious look on her face. He smiled and waved at her and saw her smile back, though she looked a little pale.

"Looks like you got some bull snot on your

britches," Jack commented as Clay climbed across the chute and stood on the platform.

"I think I got the whole load," Clay remarked, leaning against the top rail.

"Did he hurt you?" Jack asked with relaxed concern.

"Nope, but he sure scared the daylights out of me."

They waited for the announcer to call out the score, and when he did, Jack and Clay turned and looked at each other, neither believing what they'd heard. His score was only a seventy-eight. It was a low score for the ride and the crowd agreed, hissing and booing the judges.

Clay looked at Harvey Daniels and caught the man turning away. "That's a crock!" Clay said to Jack angrily. "I'm going to have a talk with that sorry son of a horse thief." He started over the chute, but Jack grabbed his arm and pulled him back.

"That won't accomplish anything," Jack said.

"It'll make me feel better," Clay replied, trying to pull away from Jack's grasp.

"And it'll get you a fine and a possible suspension as well," Jack said heatedly.

Clay finally relented and stepped back down on the platform, glaring at Harvey.

Will Hightower climbed up on the chute in front of Clay. "I'll file a protest against Harvey. That ride was at least an eighty-one or two. Gregg scored you a forty-one, which means Harvey only scored you thirty-seven—and there's no way there could be that much difference in the two scores. He did the same thing to you in the saddle broncs."

"Harvey's never scored Clay low on his rides before. Why do you think he's doing it now?" Jack asked.

"I don't know, but I'll tell you one thing: If I have my way, he won't be judging any more of my rodeos. I won't have him pulling that sort of thing with any rider. I want you to file a complaint too."

"We will," Jack replied.

Clay had been listening to Jack and Will, but now he glanced up and saw Floyd standing on the fence a few feet away from Tamara. He was looking at Clay, smiling as if he was enjoying the whole spectacle. Clay threw him a menacing glance and turned away. The bull riding was over. Clay had received a low score, but he was still sitting third, though he didn't expect it to hold through the next performance.

"Let's get your bull rope and find Dottie. I'm hungry enough to eat a horse," Jack remarked.

"I'll go get my rope," Clay said. "Why don't you tell Tamara to meet me at the pickup."

"Sounds like a plan," Jack agreed.

Clay found his bull rope hanging on one of the chutes. As he was pulling it down, someone walked up behind him. He whirled around expecting Floyd to be there, but instead it was Gregg Trent. "I'm sorry about the score in the bull riding," Gregg said sincerely. "It was a good ride and it deserved a higher score than you got."

Clay nodded. "Thanks, Gregg." He started to turn away, then stopped. "Gregg, you got any idea why

Harvey gave me such low scores in the saddle broncs and bulls?"

Gregg paused in thought. "I can't think of any," he answered. "I've judged a lot of rodeos with him and he's always been fair. This is the first time I've ever known him to do anything like this."

"Have you seen Harvey hanging around with Floyd Davis any?" Clay asked.

Gregg gave him a curious glance. "Yeah, as a matter of fact I did see them together, right after the bareback riding. Why do you ask?"

Clay started to tell him about his run-in with Floyd, then decided against it. If Harvey and Floyd were teaming up against him, he didn't want them aware that he knew. "Oh, no reason, I was just wondering."

"Look, Clay, if there's something going on here, I want to know about it. I don't like having things like this happen."

Clay shook his head. "I don't know that there is anything going on. And until I do know, I don't want to start spreading rumors that might not be true."

Gregg nodded but Clay could tell he still wasn't convinced. "If I find out anything, I'll let you know," Clay said.

Gregg nodded again. "Good enough. I'll be keeping an eye on things as well."

Clay walked out of the arena, his bull rope thrown over his shoulder. He found everyone gathered by the pickup. Tamara came up to him and took his bull rope. "That was a bum deal," she said, opening the camper door and pulling his gear bag out.

"Jack always says that's rodeo, but it's not. That's not what it's about."

"No, it's not, but unfortunately it does happen. As long as men are judging the rough stock events, it will always be open to that kind of scoring. I don't know what the answer is, but I'm thankful it doesn't happen more often."

Chapter Six

After a late supper at the Red Barn Steak House, Jack, Clay, and Tamara said their good-byes to the Hightowers and headed for Salina, Kansas.

It was three weary travelers who pulled into town in the early-morning hours. Tamara checked into a motel after boarding her horse, while Jack and Clay slept in their camper in the motel parking lot. Tired as they all were, they slept until noon. After caring for Tamara's horse, they ate a hearty lunch, then lounged around the motel swimming pool until it was time to leave for the rodeo grounds.

Clay felt the excitement build as he parked the pickup and looked at the buzz of activity taking place in and around the rodeo arena. He helped Tamara unload and tie her horse to the trailer, then the three of them walked together around the arena, talking to acquaintances and catching up on the latest news.

Tim Sullivan and Cody Boone were telling them about a rodeo they'd come from in Nebraska, when Cody asked, "Did you hear about Billy Dodd?"

"No, I didn't," Clay answered. "What about him?"

"Someone knocked him cold and carried him about ten miles out of town right before the rodeo."

Clay was astonished. "No kidding. Any idea who did it?"

Cody shook his head. "He never saw 'em. They hit him from behind as he was coming out of his motel room. The police couldn't find any witnesses."

Clay went on to tell them about Cory Laird and Steve Cannon. "It's beginning to sound as if there's a conspiracy to keep cowboys away from rodeos," Clay remarked.

Cody gave Clay a look that plainly said he didn't believe it. "You're starting to get paranoid, Tory."

"Maybe," Clay responded. "It just seems a little too coincidental that this is the third rodeo I've been to this week, and I've heard of three different instances where some accident has caused someone to miss, or almost miss, a rodeo."

"But that's all it is, coincidence. If you're not careful, you'll go crazy looking over your shoulder for boogeymen," Cory said. "Come on, I'll buy you a Coke."

"You're probably right," Clay said, but he still wasn't convinced.

Clay had drawn Timberwolf in the barebacks, a charcoal-gray horse with black mane and tail. He was small for a bucking horse, but with his quick moves and unique bucking style, he had proved to be one of the best. Clay had drawn him twice before and placed on him both times. He planned to do the same tonight.

Timberwolf stood patiently with Clay's bareback rigging cinched down on his withers. Jack and Clay stood with the other cowboys behind the chutes and watched the first four riders in the bareback competition. When Clay's turn came, he climbed down on the horse's back and worked his hand into the handle of the rigging. When he was ready, he nodded to the gate man and dug his spurs into Timberwolf's shoulders.

Timberwolf pivoted out of the chute and jumped into the air, kicking out with his back feet. When his front feet hit the ground, Clay made sure his spurs were over the points of the horse's shoulders. Hitting the ground stiff-legged, the small gray horse ducked first to his left and sprang into the air, only to duck right the next time his feet touched the dirt in the arena. It was this very bucking style that made him one of the harder horses to ride, but Clay stayed with him. His right arm locked tight as he gripped his rigging and spurred upward with each jump throughout the eight seconds.

The pickup men moved in to assist Clay off and drive Timberwolf from the arena. The announcer's voice boomed over the PA system, calling out Clay's score. "The judges have given Clay Tory a score of seventy-eight, moving him into second place in the bareback riding."

Clay retrieved his bareback rigging from the de-rigging chute and joined Jack behind the chutes. "Good ride," Jack commented as Clay came up beside him.

"Thanks," Clay responded. "He's a good bronc."

Clay's score held through the remaining rides. Feeling good, he carried his gear bag to the camper and checked over his bronc saddle, a habit Jack had instilled in him. Tamara was waiting for him by the chutes when he returned.

"You done good, cowboy," she said as he put his arm around her.

"If I can make as good a ride on Outlaw, I'll be happy," he said with a smile

"You'll ride him," Tamara responded with confidence.

Clay smiled but said nothing, hoping she was right.

Tamara had seats for them in the stands where she, Clay, and Jack watched the calf roping and most of the steer wrestling before Jack and Clay left to get ready for the saddle bronc riding.

Outlaw was already in the alley waiting to be run into the chutes. A large, stout black horse with a white blaze running down his face and three white stockings, he looked more like somebody's roping horse than a saddle bronc.

Clay stood on the platform behind the chutes, studying the horse and remembering the last time he'd attempted to ride him. He was lost in his thoughts when someone moved up beside him. Clay glanced around, immediately recognizing Billy Ettinger. "Hey, Billy," he said, pleased to see the cowboy. "I was wonderin' if you'd be here."

Billy smiled at him. "I got here in time to see you on Timberwolf. Impressive ride."

"I'm glad you didn't miss it," Clay said with a wry smile.

"Everyone gets lucky every now and then." Billy grinned.

"I reckon you'd know more about that than I would," Clay chided.

Billy chuckled. "I'll take luck over skill any day," he responded.

"Well, now I've got Outlaw to contend with. I see you drew Midnight's Bandit."

"Yep, a good horse. But he's not Outlaw. I'll trade horses with you," Billy said good-naturedly.

"Nah," Clay responded. "I've been waiting for this rematch."

"Well, I hope you ride him to the finish," Billy said, and Clay knew he meant it.

"I'm going to try, but this time I'm going to ride him different. I'm not going to watch his head."

"That's the best way to ride him. He's real tricky. He'll turn his head to the right, then buck left. I found out that if you just sit in the middle and keep a tight seat, you'll stand a better chance of riding him."

Clay nodded. "Thanks, I'll remember that."

The horses were run into the chutes. Outlaw was in number two and Jack placed the saddle on the horse's back. Clay cinched it down and buckled on the bronc halter. Billy helped him into the chute and stood by to assist, giving words of encouragement as Clay adjusted his buck rein and set his stirrups.

The first horse and rider were in the arena when Clay placed his feet over Outlaw's shoulders. When the ride ended and the horse was run out, Jack leaned down close to Clay's ear and spoke softly. "You can ride this horse. Just stay focused and stay in the middle."

"Right," Clay responded, thankful for Jack's calming presence. The gate man moved into position and Clay leaned back, pulling his hat down with his free hand. Then he nodded for the gate.

Outlaw bolted from the chute, ran two lengths, and ducked his head between his legs, stopping stiff-legged on a dime before bunching himself and jumping into the air. Clay's spurs were in time with the horse's lunges. The large horse moved quickly to the right, then sprang to the left and back to the right again like a tightly wound spring out of control. Clay willed himself not to look at the horse's head, instead concentrating on the point just past the pommel of his saddle.

Outlaw lunged skyward and twisted himself in midair, then came back to earth, grunting as he hit the ground. He pushed off with all four feet, cork-screwing his body and kicking hard.

Clay felt the exhilaration of the ride, knowing he was going to make the whistle. His spur rowels were ringing as he spurred from shoulder to cantle and back again. Outlaw twisted his head to the left and moved hard to the right, then spun around and leapt forward. Normally Clay would have been watching his head and leaning left in anticipation. But this time he was concentrating only on staying centered and he remained in the saddle.

Clay was so intent on the ride that he didn't hear the whistle blow. Only when the pickup men moved in beside him did he know he'd completed the ride. On the ground he listened to the applause of the crowd and lifted his head to smile at them as he walked by the stands, giving Tamara a special wink. She threw him a kiss and smiled at him.

"You finally made a good ride, Tory," Billy Ettinger said as Clay climbed back over the chutes.

"The score's even now," Clay said. "And I can't wait until the next match."

Billy laughed. "Spoken like a true bronc rider."

Jack slapped him on the back. "Now that's the kind of ride I taught you to make."

Clay grinned at him. "I'm glad you approve." He listened as the announcer called out his score of eighty-five. "I'll take one of those any day!" Billy said, and Clay's grin affirmed his pleasure.

Clay and Jack helped Billy saddle his bronc and wished him luck. Midnight's Bandit gave a good performance and Billy rode him to the whistle, turning in a score of eighty-one. Clay congratulated him when he returned, but couldn't help ribbing him. "That was a good ride for a man of your age." Billy had just turned twenty-two.

Smiling, Billy grabbed his back. "I'm getting so old I may have to have a wheelchair to get to my pickup. But then, I guess I can always hire some kid like you to carry my gear bag and push me around. Since you can't ride that good, you're going to need a job."

Clay laughed. "I'll be glad to do that for you, old-timer." Jack smiled at the two of them, enjoying the banter. They might be competitors, but that didn't mean they weren't friends.

"Where you headed to next?" Billy asked.

"Colorado Springs," Clay responded. "How about you?"

"Same," Billy said. "You aren't going back to New Mexico first, are you?"

"No. We're gonna look around and see if we can buy some hay. Things haven't been as dry in Colorado as they have in New Mexico."

Billy nodded. "I've got some friends around Colorado Springs and Lamar. They might be able to help you."

"We'd appreciate it," Jack said.

Billy took a pen and pad of paper from his gear bag and wrote the names and phone numbers of his friends. Tearing the page out, he handed it to Jack. "These folks should be able to help you. They're all in the cattle business. If they don't have any hay, they should be able to help you find some elsewhere."

"Thanks, Billy," Jack said, folding the paper and putting it in his shirt pocket.

Jack helped Clay carry his gear to the camper. "I thought we'd get us a room at the hotel tonight and leave for Colorado tomorrow," Jack said. "Since you placed in both the barebacks and saddle broncs, I figure you could afford a room."

Clay shook his head in wonder. "I reckon I can, but it sure is gettin' to be a burden, carryin' you all the time. You're gonna have to start pullin' your own weight a little."

Jack guffawed. "You sure are gettin' big for your britches, youngster."

Tamara came up just then, leading her horse. "Oh," she added. "I got the impression he's always been too big for his pants, but then, all rough stock riders are pretty much that way, aren't they, Jack?"

Caught by surprise, Jack could only stand staring at her with his mouth open.

Clay broke into laughter. "She's got you there, Jack. What you got to say to that?"

"Out of respect for your gender, young lady, I'll refrain from further comment on the subject and leave you two alone."

Tamara smiled sweetly at him as he made his exit. "You gonna watch me run the barrels?" she asked, turning to Clay.

"I wouldn't miss it for the world," he replied, throwing his gear bag in the camper.

Tamara knocked over the third barrel on her run and received a five-second penalty, putting her out of the money.

"Tough luck," Clay said as she brought her horse under control.

"I was trying to trim a little time off my run," she said, "and I cut it too close."

Clay stayed with her while she walked her horse out and cooled him down, then left to get ready for the bull riding. He had drawn Coal Train, a large Brahma with banana horns, the kind that droop down and hang loose on the side of the bull's head. The leading score in the bull riding was turned in by Steve Ballinger the night before. He had ridden a small black bull named Dolittle to a score of eighty-one. Second place was a seventy-four, followed by a seventy, and a sixty-three.

Clay rode Coal Train to the whistle and scored a

seventy-nine, the top score of the night and good enough for second place.

It was after midnight by the time Clay, Jack, and Tamara got Tamara's horse settled for the night and grabbed a bite to eat. They decided to sleep late and leave for Colorado around noon. While they slept, others were planning events that would change the course of their lives.

Stan Dickson sat in his high-rise office looking over the report that had just been delivered to him. At age forty-eight, he had amassed a considerable fortune through shrewd investments in the stock market. Up until now he had enjoyed the lifestyle that had come with such success. Recently, however, a few bad investments and untimely downturns in the market had taken their toll. He was mortgaged to the limit with nowhere else to turn. If things didn't change by year's end, he knew he'd be bankrupt. He had only one chance to stave off financial ruin, and he was looking at it now.

It was eight o'clock Sunday morning, and normally Stan would have been at home with his family enjoying the only day of the week he took off. But a phone call the night before had alerted him that a fax would be sent to his office early this morning. He was poring over the figures on the fax before him, a deep frown creasing his brow. The letterhead bore the name of an accounting firm in Chicago; however, were anyone to look in the business registry, they would not find any such firm listed. The name signed on the cover sheet was fictitious as well.

The only real things were the results from the pro rodeos for the past month, and those were what Stan paid dearly for. Picking up the phone, he dialed the number written on the bottom of the page. The phone was answered by a desk clerk at the Hilton Inn in Denver, Colorado.

"Room six-twelve, please," Stan said politely and waited for the connection to be made.

"Hello, Mr. Dickson," came the voice on the other end. Stan wasn't surprised by the fact that the man knew it was him calling. "You saw the report?"

"Yes, I did," Stan replied.

"Are you satisfied with the results?" the voice asked.

"Things are looking better, but I'm still fourth—and only by a small margin," Stan stated impatiently.

"We have to do this slowly. If we move too fast, it will look suspicious. We've already had to take measures that are somewhat risky," the man replied. "We still have several months to go and plenty of time to achieve the results you expect."

"You've done a good job so far," Stan lamented. "There's a lot riding on this and I can't afford to lose."

"Don't you worry, Mr. Dickson, I know how to proceed. I'll take care of things on this end, you just make sure the money's there when the time comes."

Stan gritted his teeth, hating to continue but knowing he had to. "I noticed Clay Tory is moving up in the standings. You assured me he wouldn't be a threat!"

"That's right, Mr. Dickson, I assured you he

wouldn't be a threat." The voice held a hint of anger and Stan recoiled slightly "And he won't be!"

"That's all I wanted to know. When will I hear from you again?" Stan asked, relieved that the conversation was almost over.

"When I call," the voice said. "Same as before. Good day, Mr. Dickson." The phone went dead.

Stan Dickson stared at the receiver in his hand, then gently placed it in its cradle. Standing slowly, he placed the report in the wall safe and spun the combination lock. Taking the elevator to the garage, he pressed the keyless entry button on his key chain and heard the familiar beep come from his Jaguar as the locks opened. Sliding behind the wheel, Stan allowed himself to smile. Things were going to work out, he thought as he drove home to his wife and daughter. They were going on a picnic at the zoo this afternoon and he didn't want to be late.

Chapter Seven

Jack, Clay and Tamara sat at a booth in *Denny's* restaurant, enjoying their last cup of coffee. Jack looked up and motioned to someone, drawing both Clay's and Tamara's attention to the person walking toward them.

"Larry Benton!" Clay exclaimed. Larry was a bull rider, and a pretty good one at that. Both Tamara and Clay knew him well.

Larry walked up to the booth and slid in beside Jack. "Have you eaten?" Jack asked him.

"I ate earlier," Larry answered, "but I could sure use a cup of coffee."

Jack waved over the waitress, who smiled and brought an extra cup without having to ask. Clay gave Jack a questioning look. "Larry's riding to Colorado Springs with us," Jack stated.

Both Tamara and Clay were caught by surprise. "Great!" Clay responded, recovering from the shock.

"Jack was askin' if anyone needed a ride," Larry explained. "My truck's been in the shop for the last week, so I've been hitchin' with Terry Gould. But he's got to go back to Missouri, and since my folks live in Canon City just south of Colorado Springs, and I have to borrow their car, I thought I'd take Jack up on his offer."

Jack had been watching Clay's and Tamara's faces, noting their surprised looks. "I figured if I had someone to ride with me, you two could ride together."

"Oh," they said in unison, his motive suddenly clear to both.

"Where's your truck now?" Clay asked.

"In a shop in Sand Springs, Oklahoma. Jeremy White is checking on it for me. As soon as it's ready we'll figure out where to meet and he'll drive it there." That was life on the rodeo circuit. You never knew what might happen next, but you could always count on your friends to help.

They pulled out of Salina before noon. Clay and Tamara led the way as they traveled west on Interstate 70. Clay was telling Tamara about Jack's ranch in New Mexico when suddenly a ringing sound in the cab of the pickup made him jump. Tamara laughed as she reached down and picked up the cellular phone that had been lying on the console by her feet.

"Hello," she answered, still giggling.

Clay tried not to listen as she talked to the person on the other end, but it was impossible in the confines of the pickup not to. He realized she was talking to her father and was surprised when she mentioned his name.

"He's driving right now and Jack is following in their truck," she said as Clay gave her a startled look. "No, I don't think I am going to Nebraska. I think I'll go to Colorado Springs with Clay and Jack, and enter in Raton and Santa Fe." She was silent for a moment, then answered, "I should be home about a week from tomorrow. Give Mom a hug for me. I miss you too. Bye."

Clay looked at the phone, then at her. "Handy device," he said.

"Uh-huh," she answered, returning the cell phone to its place by her feet. "It's a good way for Daddy to check up on me."

Clay arched his eyebrows in a questioning look, not sure how she meant that.

"It's one of the small concessions in our ongoing battle, and I really don't mind. Besides, it lets me keep in touch with my friends, and helps make the miles go by faster. It also lets me call in and enter rodeos without having to stop and find a pay phone."

"Uh-huh," Clay said. "I thought I heard my name mentioned in there somewhere. How did your dad take that?"

"He was pleased," Tamara responded. " He usually gives me the third degree about who I'm with and what they're like. But when I told him you were driving, it was as if he was actually happy about it."

"I've never even met your dad," Clay said. "Why would he be happy to know I was with you?"

Tamara smiled. "He knows Jack. He even asked if Jack was with us. And he knows Will and Dottie Hightower. I wouldn't be a bit surprised if he hasn't called the Hightowers and checked on you. I think he already knew who I was with."

"And he's all right with that?" Clay asked, still bewildered.

"Oh, I think he's more than all right with it. I think he's delighted."

Clay's look was one of puzzlement. "I don't follow," he said.

"My father knows all about you. He follows rodeo like other men follow football or baseball. He knows who the top riders are and who will make it to the finals. He knows where you are in the standings right now. And like I said, he knows Jack. They used to rodeo together, so that already puts you in his good graces."

A cloud crossed Clay's face. "He doesn't know everything about me," he said.

Tamara gave him a puzzled look. "You say that as if you have a deep dark secret," she said.

Clay looked out at the Kansas prairie and thought about his past. About how he'd come to know Jack Lomas and how because of him Jack had almost been killed. Taking a deep breath, he turned back to her. "Tamara, there's some things you need to know about me. I wish I didn't have to tell you, but I want everything with us to be on the level."

She moved away from him a little, not from fear, but so she could see his face. "What is it, Clay? You didn't kill somebody, did you?" she asked jokingly, trying to break his solemn mood.

"No, but I almost got somebody killed," he responded. He went on to tell her everything, beginning with the reason he'd been arrested and how he'd come to live with Jack. He told her about his father and the cattle stealing. He told her how his father had kidnapped him and Jack and was going to ship them with a load of stolen cattle to Texas. He told her how his father had been killed by the sheriff and that his brothers were now serving time in the New Mexico state prison. When he finished, he glanced over at her, expecting to see an expression of shock on her face. Instead, he saw her lips turn up in a smile.

"Clay Tory, I swear, I thought you were going to tell me you were an ax-murderer, or you had three wives in different cities, or you'd robbed a bank or something. I've known all about that since it happened. You think we don't get the papers or watch TV in Texas? Dad even knew the man in Texas that was behind it all. As a matter of fact, he called Jack right after it happened and talked to him. I remember him asking if you were all right and if you'd be back to riding soon."

Clay sat dumbfounded. He had been dreading telling her for fear she'd think badly of him, yet she'd known about it all along.

"I can't believe you'd think it would make a difference how I felt about you," Tamara said.

Clay was blushing by now. "How was I to know you already knew all about it? Anyway, it's not something I'm proud of, and I just wanted to make sure you knew about it before we went any further."

Tamara scooted closer to him and put her arm through his around his biceps. "I can understand why you wanted me to know. All I'm saying is, it doesn't matter. Even if I hadn't known, it wouldn't change anything. I've been waiting a long time for you and I wouldn't let something like that scare me off now."

Clay smiled at her, grateful that all his worrying had been for naught. "I still don't understand why your father is so pleased," he said. "If I had a daughter as pretty as you, I sure wouldn't want some cowboy like me chasing after her."

"That's exactly the reason why he's pleased," she said with a sly grin. When he gave her a questioning look, she explained. "You're a cowboy just like him. He sees himself in you, except that you're going to the finals, and he never did."

"Correction; I'm *trying* to make it to the finals. I haven't made it yet, and there's still a long way to go."

"You'll make it," she said. "We both have confidence in you."

They continued to talk about the finals and their dreams of qualifying. The tension of the last few miles slipped away behind them.

By the time they reached Colorado Springs, the sun had already set. Clay and Tamara took Charger to a small farm owned by another barrel racer. Tamara had made prior arrangements to keep her horse stalled there. Jack went on ahead and got motel rooms for them at a Hampton Inn and Larry called his parents to come pick him up.

When Clay and Tamara got to the hotel, they found Jack on the phone with Terry, discussing conditions back on the ranch. They discussed Jack's plans to buy hay in Colorado. "We'll be home in about a week," Jack said into the phone. "Yeah, he's been winning a little but not enough to cover his costs yet. Maybe he'll get there one of these days. We can only hope."

After Jack hung up the phone, Clay asked, "How are things at the ranch?"

"Terry's been watering the hay field from the tank. It's starting to green up pretty good, but it still hasn't rained, and he says there's not much chance of it for the next couple of weeks."

Clay could only nod as he heard the news. He could see the worry etched on Jack's face. "I'm starved. Where are you buying supper?" he asked, trying to take Jack's mind off of his troubles.

Snapping from his reverie, Jack snorted, "Where am *I* buying? The question is where are *you* buying? It's about time you started carrying your weight."

Tamara had been sitting on the edge of the bed, but now she stood. "Come on, you two, I'll buy supper. I have a hankering for a T-bone steak."

Clay and Jack both looked surprised by her invitation. "Now look what you've done," Clay admonished. "You've shamed her into buying us supper, all because you're too tightfisted to pay for it."

Jack picked up his hat and started for the door. "It was you that shamed her. If you'd start doin' your part and quit relying on poor folk like Tamara and me to carry you all the time, we wouldn't have these problems."

Tamara rolled her eyes. "Would you two quit your silly chattering and come on, or I'm going to change my mind and go by myself."

Jack and Clay exchanged grins and raced to the door, rushing past Tamara and leaving her to close the door behind them. "I hope one of them got the room key," she said to herself, and couldn't help smiling.

The Colorado Springs Rodeo didn't start until Thursday, which would give Jack four days to find the hay he needed and make arrangements to have it shipped to the ranch. He called the people on Billy Ettinger's list on Monday morning. Each one told him of places where he might be able to buy hay. While he was busy making phone calls, Clay and Tamara lounged around the pool, taking some time to relax in the warm sun.

By lunchtime, Jack had found six possible places to purchase hay. He had drawn crude maps to each of the six farms, and with an area map he obtained from the hotel, they were ready to begin their quest. It was Wednesday morning before they were able to locate, purchase, and make arrangements to have the hay trucked to New Mexico. Jack bought twenty-four hundred bales of prime alfalfa hay, which would require six tractor-trailers to haul. Fortunately he was able to find a trucking company to do the job for a reasonable price.

Jack lay on the bed in his room, tired but satisfied, after talking to Terry at the ranch. Jack let him know when to expect the hay and made arrangements to hire extra hands to help unload the shipment. Stretching his arms and stifling a yawn, Jack was thinking about taking a nap when Clay and Tamara came barging into the room.

"Get up, you lazy bum," Clay said, grabbing Jack's foot and shaking it. "We're going to the Rodeo Hall of Fame."

They spent the rest of the afternoon walking through the museum, taking in the history of rodeo. "I rode with several of these fellas," Jack said, entertaining them with stories from his past. He told them about Casey Tibbs, the best saddle bronc rider there had ever been, and Jim Shoulders, seven-time world champion bull rider. But they were enthralled by his rendition of Freckles Brown's historic ride on the famous bull Tornado. By the time they had toured all the exhibits, Tamara and Clay were ready for something to eat and Jack was ready to turn in. They ate a quick meal at a family restaurant across from the hotel.

"I'm turning in for the night," Jack stated as they walked across the street. "What are you two going to do?"

"I don't know," Clay answered. "We might go see a movie. Sure you don't want to come along?"

"No thank you," Jack said. "Hay hunting has plumb wore me out. Lou Daniels invited me over tomorrow to look at his Limousin cows. I've been thinking about buying a bull." Lou was one of the farmers Jack had bought hay from. "You two want to come along?"

"As much as I love to look at good cattle, Tamara and I are planning on taking a drive and seeing the sights. No offense, but we've been running around

looking at hay for the past three days and I'm ready
to see something besides fields."

"No offense, but so am I," Tamara added.

Jack chuckled. "You two go on and have a good
time. I'll see you tomorrow afternoon."

Clay and Tamara left early the next morning in
Tamara's pickup. They planned a leisurely drive
through the mountains and a sight-seeing trip in Gar-
den of the Gods National Park. They stopped at a
local market before leaving town and picked up sup-
plies for a picnic. At noon they stopped and ate at a
roadside park before walking one of the many na-
ture trails.

They had been hiking for half an hour when they
came to a point overlooking a broad valley. The trees
were swaying lazily in the afternoon breeze as the
sun warmed them. A small stream wound its way
through the valley and the rays of light danced
across the shimmering ripples of water as it cascaded
over time-smoothed stones.

"I don't think I've ever seen anything as serene as
this," Tamara said in a near whisper, as if by talking
she would disturb the pristine beauty before her.

Clay looked out over the picturesque scene, letting
a sigh escape from him. "It's so beautiful!"

"I don't think anyone could look at this and not
know there is a creator," Tamara said, then turned
to look at Clay. "You believe in God, don't you?"

Clay hesitated, reaching down to pick up a small
rock, then rolling it in the palm of his hand. "There
was a time in my life when I wasn't sure there was

a God. Especially back when I lived with my folks and things were always tough. My father drank all the time, my mother just sat watching soap operas and smoking her cigarettes, and my brothers were always stealing. I didn't see how there could be a God. I always thought if He really existed, He would strike our house with lightning and kill us all. But after I went to live with Jack and saw the faith he had and how he trusted God, I started to believe. Jack's taught me a lot about the Bible and how God works. And now I know one thing for sure.'' He paused and looked her in the eye.

"What's that?'' she responded.

"God likes cowboys!''

Laughing, Tamara asked, "And what makes you think that?''

"Well, you stop and think about it. If you look back at the time of the big cattle drives and large ranches, it was an era that only lasted a couple of decades. But there's been more written about that period of time than any other in history. And look at what's come out of it. There's more rodeos, horse shows, ropin's, jackpot barrel racin's, bull ridin', and a bunch of other things going on every weekend than you can count. I figure if God didn't like cowboys so much, all that wouldn't be goin' on. And I'll tell you something else; cowboys aren't made, they're born. I've seen men come from big cities in the East where they'd never seen a horse before, but because they were born with the spirit of a cowboy, they answered their calling.''

Tamara had been listening intently to all that Clay

had to say, surprised by the force of his voice and the passion with which he spoke.

"And if you look at the Bible," Clay continued, "it says that when Jesus comes back, He's coming on a white horse. Just goes to prove He's a cowboy too."

Tamara laughed again. "You make a good point," she responded, looking out over the valley once again. "We probably ought to start back down. It's almost four o'clock."

"I guess you're right, but I sure hate to leave this peace and quiet. It's the same as when I'm out riding pastures on the ranch."

Tamara smiled knowingly. "I know what you mean. Some of my best times are when I'm riding Charger on Daddy's ranch and there's not another soul in sight. I love the peacefulness."

Clay took her by the hand, and they both took one more lingering look at the valley before they started back down the trail. Clay was thankful he'd worn his tennis shoes instead of his boots as they negotiated their way around rocks and trees.

They had left the pickup in a roadside parking area at the beginning of the trail. Rounding the final curve, they both stopped and stared, unable to believe what they saw. All four tires had been flattened. Clay could only stare at the scene before him, his brain refusing to comprehend what his eyes were seeing. Slowly he started forward in a dazed stupor, Tamara following close behind. "Who would have done this?" he asked, walking around the pickup, looking at each tire and shaking his head in disbelief.

"Every one of them's been cut!" Tamara cried. "How are we going to get back?"

"It doesn't look like they broke in," Clay said. "Your phone is still in there. Let's see if it works out here."

Tamara took the keys from her pocket and unlocked the door. Taking the phone from its cradle, she held it up and looked at the digital display where the No Service light blinked at her in red. Searching the glove box, she found the hotel receipt and quickly dialed the number listed on it and pushed Send. But as expected, there was no response. She threw the phone back in the pickup. "We're out of range!" she said in despair. "What are we going to do now?"

Theirs was the only vehicle in the parking area. Looking back down the road, they saw not a single car. Clay turned to Tamara. "It's about two miles back to the county road and another three miles from there to Highway 67. If I run, I can make it in about an hour. There's bound to be traffic this time of day. I'll flag down some help and come back for you," Clay said.

Tamara shook her head, the fear plain in her face. "You don't mean to leave me here? What if the people that did this come back?"

"I don't think they'll be coming back. I suspect that whoever did this did it to keep one or both of us from making it to the rodeo tonight. If I can get us a ride, we'll still make it, but the only way I can do that is if I run. Lock yourself in the truck and don't open the door for anyone."

Tears welled up in Tamara's eyes. "Why don't we

just wait, maybe someone will come along in a little while.''

"Tamara, if we wait any longer, we'll miss the rodeo.

"Then let's both go for help," she argued.

Clay sighed. He understood why she was scared, and wished there was something else that could be done. "Tamara, I can make it a lot faster if I go alone. I hate leaving you by yourself here, but I'll be back as fast as I can. You have to trust me."

Tears flowed unchecked down her cheeks as she listened to him. "I'll stay," she sobbed, "but you'd better not be gone long, or I won't wait for you."

He smiled at her attempted humor. "I'll be back before you even know I'm gone."

She smiled weakly. "You be careful," she said.

"I will," he answered, pulling her to him and holding her tightly. Kissing her cheek, he pushed her gently away, though she tried to cling to him. "Everything's going to be fine," he said. "Now get in the pickup and lock the doors." He opened the door and ushered her in. "And don't start the engine," he continued, remembering what had happened to Steve Cannon. "They might have put sugar in the fuel tank."

Tamara's eyes widened with fear and Clay hurried to reassure her. "Don't get alarmed, it's just a precaution. I'll be back soon," he said, then kissed her quickly and closed the door. Stepping away from the pickup, he turned and started jogging down the road. Tamara watched him until he rounded a curve out of her sight. Leaning back and closing her eyes, she uttered a silent prayer.

Chapter Eight

Clay set a pace for himself that would allow him to cover ground without wearing him down. He estimated he could run a mile between twelve and fifteen minutes, but he knew he'd eventually have to slow and rest. He focused his mind on Tamara's face and ran.

There was a dull ache in his side by the time he got to the county road. Looking both ways, he saw no sign of a car. Gritting his teeth, he picked up the pace. As he ran, he thought about another time when he'd had to run, only that time he'd been running for both his and Jack's life after his father had kidnapped them. That time he'd run across the southwestern prairie in boots. This was a piece of cake compared to that, Clay thought as he ran along the blacktop road.

The pain in his side subsided after the fourth mile, and he ran on, glancing at his watch. It had been forty minutes since he'd left Tamara. By his estimate he had two more miles to go before he reached Highway 67. He was now in a runner's trance, his feet moving on their own accord as he trained his eye on a point ahead of him. In his trance, he didn't hear the pickup coming from behind until the driver honked his horn. Looking around, Clay saw the pickup only a few yards behind him and realized he'd been running in the middle of the road. Stumbling to a stop, Clay doubled over, gulping in deep breaths of air as he tilted his head to watch the pickup slowly roll toward him.

Clay held up his hand, hoping the driver would stop. The pickup came forward at a crawl, then braked just before reaching Clay. The driver's side window rolled down a few inches as Clay walked to the side. "What's the problem?" said a gruff voice from inside the pickup.

"I need some help," Clay stated, walking up to the window. He could see a lone man, perhaps sixty years of age, sitting behind the wheel. The door was locked and the window was down only far enough to allow conversation.

"What's the problem?" the old man repeated his question.

"Someone slashed our tires back up the road," Clay said, pointing back the way he'd come. "My girlfriend is back there with the pickup."

"What do you want me to do?" the man asked.

"Mister, we're both entered in the rodeo tonight and need to get back to town as soon as possible. All we need is a ride. I'll be glad to pay you for your trouble."

Clay could see the man was looking at him suspiciously. "How do I know you're not trying to lure me up there so you can rob me?" Looking at the old pickup the man was driving almost made Clay smile at the question. It was an early seventies model, its tires almost bald. Black smoke belched out the exhaust pipe, indicating bad rings.

Clay reached for his wallet and opened it up, exposing an assortment of bills. Pulling out a fifty, he stuck the end of it through the small opening in the window. "Here's fifty now if you'll let me ride in the back until we get to where my girlfriend is. I'll give you another fifty when we get to town."

The old-timer licked his lips as the fifty dangled in front of his face, his mind struggling with the decision. Then he reached out and grabbed it, his greed apparently winning out. "Jump in," he said, motioning to the back of the truck.

Clay yelled out directions as the pickup rattled along. Anticipation gripped him as they turned on the road leading to the hiking trail. In a few moments they rounded the curve and Tamara's pickup came into view. As the old man braked the truck to a stop, Clay jumped from the back, yelling out Tamara's name.

Tamara, exhausted from worry, was dozing when she heard Clay's yell. Waking with a start, she threw open the door and jumped out of the pickup, relief flooding over her as she flew into his arms. "I told you I'd be back before you missed me," Clay said, hugging her to him.

"I'm just so glad you're back. Who's this you're with?"

"I don't know his name. He's not very friendly but he's got a truck and he'll take us to town," Clay said, reaching into Tamara's pickup and grabbing her cell phone. "You still have the number to the hotel?" he asked.

She reached in her shirt pocket and pulled out the receipt. "Right here," she said, holding it up.

"Good. Let's go," he said, locking the doors.

Tamara started toward the pickup, looking suspiciously at the man sitting inside. As she approached it, the door opened and the old man stepped out, removing his hat and smiling at her. "Howdy, miss. Sorry about your problems. I can see somebody did a job on your tires there. I wasn't inclined to believe your boyfriend. He looked kinda wild and crazy, but I can see he was telling the truth. Ya'll can ride up front here with me."

Clay looked at his watch. It was a quarter after six, only forty-five minutes until rodeo time. Jumping in beside Tamara, he asked, "Any chance you can get us to the rodeo grounds in forty-five minutes?"

"If old blue here'll hold together, I'll give it my best," the old man answered with a smile. "My name's Emmett Claybourn, by the way."

Tamara and Clay introduced themselves, smiling at each other as the old truck bounced over the road, belching smoke.

They hit Highway 67 with tires squealing. Clay winced, expecting one to blow out at any moment. Watching the speedometer, he saw it climb to eighty and felt his nerves tighten. If they blew a tire at this speed, it could be disastrous.

When they passed a road sign that said Colorado Springs 20 miles, Clay pushed the power button on Tamara's cell phone. It came on with a strong signal indicator. Tamara took the receipt from her pocket and held it while Clay dialed and pushed Send. When the receptionist at the hotel answered, Clay asked for Jack's room. Jack answered on the first ring. "Where are you?" he asked before Clay could say a word.

"How'd you know it was me?" Clay asked, surprised.

"Never mind. Where are you?" he demanded, anger and worry clearly evident in his voice.

Clay briefly explained what had happened to them. "We're on our way now, but we need someone to haul Tamara's horse and tack to the rodeo grounds. Can you find someone to take care of that? We'll meet you there."

"I'm on my way!" Jack said, hanging up the phone.

Clay smiled at Tamara, who was looking nervously at the speedometer. They were barreling into Colorado Springs and Emmett hadn't slowed his speed.

"I think we're gonna make it," Emmett said, as if sensing Tamara's nervousness.

Clay looked at his watch; it was ten minutes before seven. The rodeo started promptly at seven and he was the fourth rider. They would be cutting it mighty close. He knew that Jack would have his rigging ready and he might just make it.

Emmett careened around another corner with tires screeching and smoke boiling out the tail pipe. Clay gripped the door with one hand and held Tamara with the other, praying the pickup would hold together until they got to the rodeo grounds. One more corner and Clay could see the arena's lights. "Pull in at the second gate," he said to Emmett. "That's the contestant's gate. I need to get as close to the bucking chutes as possible."

"What event do you work?" Emmett asked.

"Barebacks, saddle broncs, and bulls," Clay answered, looking anxiously ahead.

"A three-event man, huh? I used to do a little rodeoin' back in my younger days," he mused. "I was a bronc rider. Won a little here and there, but never really went at it that hard. I had a ranch to work and spent most of my time building it up. I had me some good rides though. Hold on, we're there," he said, turning the wheel hard left. Clay gripped the back of the seat as Tamara was thrown against him.

Emmett stomped on the brakes, sliding to a stop beside the gate attendant. "I got a couple of contestants here that need to get in," he yelled out of his window.

Struggling to right themselves, Clay and Tamara pulled out their contestant cards and showed them to the shaken gate man. He gulped and nodded, motioning them through. "Hot dog! I got in free!" Emmett exclaimed, smiling as he headed for the bucking chutes.

The national anthem was already playing as Clay jumped out of the truck. "I'll give you your other fifty after I ride," he shouted over his shoulder as he ran for the chutes.

"Forget it!" Emmett shouted after him. "I was comin' in to the rodeo anyway."

Tamara leaned over and kissed the old man on the

cheek. "Thanks, Emmett," she said with a smile. "I hope I'll see you again."

Emmett's face reddened as he stammered, "Aw, it weren't nothin'. I was glad to do it. I ain't had that much fun in years."

Tamara slid out the door and closed it behind her and, giving Emmett a final wave, she hurried after Clay.

Jack was anxiously pacing the ground when Clay came running up. His horse, Daisy Chain, was loaded in the chute with his rigging in place.

"You all right?" Jack asked, concern evident in his voice.

"I'm fine," Clay responded. "But if I ever find out who slashed those tires, I'm going to do me some proper butt whippin'."

"How's Tamara?"

"She's shaken up, but other than that she's fine. Did you get someone to bring her horse?"

"Cassidy Lane brought him. He's over there by her trailer," he said, motioning to a pickup and horse trailer. "There's Tamara now. I'll go tell her. You go on and get ready."

Clay laid his gear bag up on the chute platform and unzipped it. Inside he found his boots, the bronc spurs already buckled on. Changing these for the tennis shoes he wore, he buckled on his chaps and pulled on his glove, smiling as he noticed the new resin already burned on. Clay silently thanked Jack.

When the bareback riding began, Clay was standing over the chute. He didn't see the scowling black look given him by the man sitting in the third row of the stands. The man was dressed in a corduroy shirt, blue jeans, and boots, with a new straw hat on his head. He wore a light blue windbreaker against the chilly evening air. A casual observer would have taken him for a business man dressed for the occasion. But if one looked closely, they might see the slight bulge of a shoulder holster under his jacket. The cold gray eyes boring into the cowboy standing on the chutes were the eyes of an angry man, a man not used to his plans going awry. He watched the bareback riding with special interest. The first three riders each received their score, the highest being a seventy-six given to Bert Halstead.

Clay was now mounted on Daisy Chain, a brown mare with two white stocking feet. She had been to the finals twice as a top bareback horse.

The man watched as Clay nodded to the gate man, hoping to see a flag fall as the mare came out of the chute and jumped into the air. The flag would indicate Clay had failed to mark her out, not having his spurs in her shoulders when her feet hit the ground on the first jump. But there was no flag, and the man cursed silently under his breath, pushing a fist into his other palm.

Daisy Chain tried every trick she knew to throw the rider on her back, and as the man in the stands watched, he couldn't help admiring the athletic ability of the rider.

Though Clay had run a four-mile marathon already that day, the adrenaline coursing through his body and the thrill of riding gave him the strength he needed. He was in perfect time with the mare beneath him. His spurs were in her shoulders each time her front feet hit the ground. He raked them upward each time she lunged, his rowels singing with each jump.

When the whistle blew, no one needed to tell the man in the stands that Clay had moved into the lead. His shoulders sagged as he sat back in his seat and watched the cowboy walk back to the chutes.

"Folks, we have a new leader in the bareback riding," the announcer's voice blared out over the PA system. "The judge's score for that ride is an eighty-two."

The applause and whistles from the crowd only fueled the ire the man felt, and he swore under his breath again.

Clay retrieved his rigging and gear bag before finding Jack and Tamara. They were standing outside the arena at the end of the bucking chutes. Tamara was smiling as he walked up. "I wasn't sure you'd be able to do it after the run you took today."

Clay smiled for the first time since the ordeal began. "I wouldn't have been able to if it hadn't been for the training program I've been on."

Jack smiled, knowing that he was referring to the hard regime he'd had Clay doing. "You two want to tell me what this tire slashing is all about?" he asked, looking at the two of them.

Clay shrugged his shoulders. "Your guess is as good as mine," he replied. "I don't have any idea, but it's not the first time it's happened." He went on to tell him about the other mishaps that he had heard had taken place at other rodeos.

"Hmm, I don't like the sounds of that," Jack mused. "I reckon we better call the authorities and report this."

"What about my truck?" Tamara asked. "I don't like the idea of it sitting out there all night."

"Why don't you two sit down and relax for a few moments," Jack said. "I saw a sheriff's deputy here earlier. I'll tell him what happened and make arrangements to get Tamara's truck brought in."

"Tell them not to start it until they've drained the fuel tanks," Clay reminded him.

Jack left in search of the deputy while Clay and Tamara put Clay's gear bag in the camper, then went to find Cassidy Lane and check on Tamara's horse.

By the time the saddle bronc event started, Jack had filed a report with the sheriff's office and found a garage to retrieve Tamara's pickup and make any necessary repairs.

Clay was scheduled to ride High Lonesome, a sorrel horse with a blazed face. Not the top horse in the string, but a good horse to ride nonetheless.

Tamara had her horse saddled and warmed him up while she waited for the saddle bronc riding. Once it began, she rode up to the fence to watch. Clay would be the seventh to go. She was sitting on Charger watching the action in the arena when she felt a tug on her pants leg. Looking down, she was pleased to see Emmett standing there.

"Your young man is a fine rider," he stated.

"He's one of the best!" Tamara agreed.

"Does he have a good horse in the saddle broncs?"

"He's drawn High Lonesome. He should at least place on him," she said.

"I was just on my way back to my seat and saw you sitting here," Emmett said with a wave as he turned away.

Tamara watched him as he began walking away when a sudden thought came to her. "Hey, Emmett, you want to get something to eat with us after the rodeo?" she called after him.

Emmett turned and smiled at her. "It'll be past my bedtime, but I guess I can stand one late night."

Tamara laughed. "We'll meet you by the bucking chutes after the bull riding."

"I'll be there," he promised.

The first three saddle bronc riders made qualified rides. Kenny Cordell scored a seventy-four on Two-fortwo, Lon Buckner scored a seventy-two on Laptop, and Gerald Anthony scored a seventy-nine with a great ride on Okiedokie. The fourth rider failed to mark his horse out and the fifth rider bucked off a tough horse named Glory Days. Clay stood astride the chute as the gate opened on the sixth rider. A blown stirrup six seconds into the ride caused Randy Tate to grab leather, which means he grabbed the saddle to prevent being thrown, and was disqualifed.

Clay eased down into the saddle and placed his feet in the stirrups, setting them over the points of High Lonesome's shoulders. He gripped the braided rope rein in his right hand, running the tail of the rope between his pinky finger and ring finger. Holding his left hand in the air, he nodded his head.

High Lonesome reared high in the chute before spinning on his hind feet and lunging upward. When the horse's front feet hit the ground, Clay had his spurs in his shoulders, raking his sides as the animal lunged forward and twisted his body to the left.

The man sitting in the stands watched Clay's ride with the same vehemence he'd felt during the bareback riding. When the whistle blew, the man grimaced, knowing Clay had made another qualified ride. He waited impatiently for the announcer to call out the score. It was an eighty-one, which put him in first place for the time being. He felt certain it would be good enough to hold in the placings through the next two performances. That meant Clay would probably place in both of the events he'd ridden in, and that was exactly what he was being paid to prevent. Standing suddenly, he threw down the program he'd been holding, pushed his way roughly through the crowd, and walked to his car. Before he was out the gate, he dialed a number on his cellular phone. It was time to take the next step, he thought as he heard the phone on the other end ring.

Chapter Nine

Clay sat on the arena fence and watched Tamara run the barrels. Charger was in top form and brought Tamara through the cloverleaf pattern in 16.1 seconds. The closest time to hers after all the barrel racers had run was 16.6.

Clay walked beside her while she cooled Charger down. "How are you feeling?" he asked, concerned about her. They'd had, after all, a pretty strenuous day.

"I'm fine," she answered too quickly.

He raised his eyebrows and looked at her closely. Seeing his look, she smiled. "Okay, I'm not fine, but I am better."

Returning her smile, he put his arm around her shoulders. "It wasn't exactly the romantic ending I was hoping for today. But you have to admit it'll be a heck of a story to tell our grandchildren."

"Our grandchildren?" Tamara laughed. "Aren't we going to have children first?"

"Nah, I thought we'd go straight to grandchildren. Save ourselves all the problems of raising kids."

Tamara's laughter was a balm to Clay's soul. Cutting her eyes sideways at him, she spoke in a soft voice. "I don't know about that. I kind of like the idea of having children."

Clay smiled warmly at her. "Do you realize we're already talking about having children and we've only been together a week. Do you think maybe we're moving too fast?"

Momentarily stunned, Tamara could only look at him, a thousand thoughts running through her mind. Was she moving too fast? Had she said the wrong thing? She felt her cheeks grow warm with embarrassment.

Noticing her discomfort, Clay stopped and took her hands in his. "Hey! I was kidding. I was only trying to lighten things up. I don't know anyone I've ever felt as comfortable talking to. And if we can talk about having kids at this point in our relationship, we shouldn't have any problem talking about important things, like who sleeps on the left side of the bed, or who turns out the light at night."

Relief flooded through her as Tamara pressed her face into his chest and laughed with delight, hugging him hard. "You can turn off the light!"

Holding her tightly against him, he smiled into the blond locks of her hair.

Bold Tornado was a black Brangus; half Brahma, half Angus, known for coming out of the chute and spinning to the left. Clay had drawn him in the bull riding and knew that he could place in the money with a qualified ride.

By the time Bold Tornado was in the chute, half the bull riders had already bucked out. Only two cowboys had made a qualified ride. Dennis Atwater had ridden Suffering to a score of seventy-one and Antone Garcia had ridden Full Fright for a score of seventy-nine.

Clay was strapped to Bold Tornado's back as the gate man moved into place. Clay nodded his head and leaned forward as two thousands pounds of flesh surged from the chute. Two twisting bucks away from the chute gate, Bold Tornado planted his front feet and went into the left spin Clay had been anticipating. Digging into the tough hide of the craggy bull with his left spur, Clay jerked upward with his right spur, each time adding points to his score.

Clay was six seconds into the ride when he felt himself slipping backward off his rope. Feeling himself slipping, he planted his right spur in Bold Tornado's side trying to pull himself back. Knowing he had the rider on his back out of balance, Bold Tornado ducked back to his right in a quick move that pushed Clay further back off the rope and down on his left side one second before the buzzer sounded.

Hanging on for all he was worth, heart pounding with fear, Clay heard the welcome sound when it came. Hanging on the bull's side, he opened his hand to release the rope and felt himself slip further down toward those dangerous hooves that could wreak havoc if he fell beneath them.

The bullfighters moved in quickly, one to distract Bold Tornado and one to help free Clay. Bold Tornado, seeing a target move in front of him, shifted his weight and turned away from Clay at the same

time the other bullfighter grabbed the tail of the bull
rope and jerked.

Clay felt himself being propelled away from the
angry bull as his hand came free. Landing on his
shoulders and back, unhurt, he rolled quickly to his
feet in time to see the black bull move away from
him toward the open gate. Retrieving his rope, he
thanked each of the bullfighters before walking
around behind the chutes where Jack was waiting.
Clay knew the last seconds of his ride had cost him
points and wasn't surprised by the seventy-four the
judges gave him.

"I didn't think you were going to make it to the
whistle," Jack said as Clay rolled up his rope and
put it in his gear bag.

"I didn't think that last second would ever end,"
Clay responded.

"I know what you mean. I'm just grateful for those
two bullfighters. They really saved your bacon."

Clay chuckled. "They sure did. I thought there for
a little bit that Bold Tornado was going to grind my
bacon into sausage."

They watched the remaining bull rides together
from behind the chutes. There were only three more
qualified rides made, and at the end Clay was sitting
fourth. There wasn't much chance it would hold
through the next performances.

Tamara and Emmett were waiting for Jack and
Clay when they came out from behind the chutes.
Tamara introduced Jack to Emmett. "This is the man
that saved our lives," she said in way of explanation.

"Yeah, and almost killed us several times on the way here," Clay interjected with a grin.

"But I got you here on time, didn't I?" Emmett said.

"You sure did," Tamara agreed, patting his shoulder. "Emmett's going to have supper with us. But I've got to take care of Charger first."

"Great," Clay said, "but I'm driving."

Emmett laughed. "That's fine by me."

After making sure Charger was stabled for the night, they drove to a steak house of Emmett's choosing.

"This is the best place in town!" he explained, leading them inside.

"Hey, Emmett," a large man in a red apron greeted him as they walked in.

"Butch, how ya doin' tonight?" Emmett responded.

"Can't complain. Looks like you brought company with you."

"These are some new friends of mine," Emmett explained, gesturing toward the three behind him.

"Well, follow me," Butch said, picking up four menus. "I'll give you the best seat in the house."

Seating them at a round table in the back of the restaurant, Butch motioned to a waitress, who promptly brought them water.

"What do you recommend, Emmett?" Jack asked, looking up and down the menu.

"You can't go wrong with any of the steaks, but if you're really hungry, go for the large sirloin with all the fixin's."

After the waitress took their orders, Emmett excused himself to go to the rest room. While he was gone, Butch came by their table to check on them. "You folks doin' all right?" he asked.

"Yes, sir!" Clay nodded. As Butch started to turn away, Clay called to him. "Excuse me, Butch?"

Turning back, he gave Clay a questioning look.

"Do you know Emmett very well?"

"I've known him for almost fifteen years," he said. "I reckon I know him pretty well."

"We just met him today. He helped us out of a bad fix." He went on to explain quickly what had taken place.

"That doesn't sound like Emmett," Butch said. "He's not what you call the trusting sort."

Clay laughed. "He made me ride in the back of the pickup until we got back to our truck and he could see I was telling the truth."

Butch chortled. "Now *that* sounds like Emmett. I know you probably won't believe it, but that old man's probably one of the wealthiest men in southern Colorado."

Both Clay's and Tamara's jaws dropped in surprise. "You're joking!" Clay said in astonishment, remembering the beat-up pickup truck Emmett drove.

"Nope," Butch said. "He owns a large ranch northwest of here, and probably owns half of the city of Colorado Springs. When all these high-tech companies started moving in here, they had to have land to build on. Guess who owned most of that land?" Without waiting for a reply he answered his own question. "That's right—ol' Emmett. And don't think he's one of those that hoards his money. He's one of the most charitable men alive. If someone's down on their luck, Emmett's the first there with a helping hand or a handout."

Butch smiled and started to turn, then turned back. "One more thing. If Emmett considers you a friend, you're lucky. He's real choosy about who he gets close to."

Clay and Tamara exchanged surprised glances. Jack, noticing their looks, spoke up. "Looks like you two got real lucky indeed."

Clay glanced toward the rest rooms once again and noticed Emmett emerging. On his way back to their table, he stopped and talked to a couple he apparently knew. Watching the old man, he couldn't help but be reminded of the saying never judge a book by its cover.

During the meal, Jack and Emmett reminisced about rodeo in the old days. It turned out they had common acquaintances. As the meal drew to an end, Emmett leaned back in his chair. "I want to thank you two for today," he said, looking at Clay and Tamara.

Clay stopped chewing on the piece of apple pie he was eating. "You want to thank us?" he asked incredulously.

Chuckling, Emmett answered, "I've spent every day, since my wife died a year ago, getting up early and just going through the motions. I take care of my cattle and things on the ranch, and I've got several hired hands to do most of the work. But there hasn't been any excitement. Today, getting you two to the rodeo on time was an exhilarating experience."

He paused as a thought came to him. "It would have been more exciting if the police had been chasing us, but I guess you can't have everything."

Clay noticed the sparkle that came into the old man's eyes as he talked about the experience.

Emmett looked around the table at the smiling faces. "But I want you to know, Clay, watching you ride tonight was the greatest thrill I've had in a long time. You're good," he said. "I've seen few better."

Clay felt a lump in his throat and almost couldn't talk. "Thanks, Emmett," he finally managed to say, "and thanks for the rescue." With a sly grin, he looked at the old man and said, "I think you took five years off my life with your driving. I saw the tires on that pickup of yours. It's a wonder we didn't blow every one of them before we got to town."

Emmett howled with laughter. "I guess I should explain about the pickup," he said. "The pickup I normally drive is in quite a bit better shape than the one I'm driving tonight, but I broke a drive line on it today and had to drive the ranch truck. It's not in very good shape since it seldom gets used. I guess I really should keep it in better shape for emergencies such as this." Looking at his watch, he exclaimed, "Goodness! It's getting late and I still have to drive home. If ya'll are ready, I reckon I better get going."

When the check came, Emmett placed some money on the table, then stood smiling as he pushed his chair back into place at the table. "Supper's on me," he said and started walking out.

Jack, Clay, and Tamara sat dumbfounded as Emmett headed for the door. Jumping to his feet, Clay hurried after Emmett. Jack and Tamara looked at each other, then stood quickly and followed.

"Emmett, we were going to buy you supper for helping us out," Clay said when he finally caught up to the older man.

"Heh heh, I know that." Emmett chuckled. "That's why I paid with the fifty you gave me."

"I'll say one thing about you, Emmett, you are one surprise after another. I'll remember this day for a long time to come."

Jack and Tamara joined them outside. "Emmett, sure was nice of you to buy supper," Jack said.

"It was my pleasure," Emmett said, winking at Clay.

Tamara walked up and put her arms around his neck, hugging him tightly. "Thank you for everything."

Emmett was blushing when Tamara stepped back. "I reckon we better be getting on back to my pickup," he stammered.

Clay drove back to the rodeo grounds where they'd left Emmett's ranch truck.

"If ya'll get back into Colorado Springs, you give me a call. You can stay out at the ranch with me," Emmett offered, getting into his truck

"We'll do that," Clay said feeling at a loss for words and hating to say good-bye to this man who had come into their lives so suddenly.

"When you make it to the finals, I'll come out to Vegas and we'll have a great time," Emmett stated.

"I couldn't think of anything better," Clay said earnestly. "If you ever get down around Roswell, you look us up. We'll get the law chasing us and have a good ol' time."

Emmett threw back his head and guffawed. "I'll be there," he said and shut the door.

They watched as he drove off. "He's an amazing fellow," Jack said.

"Sure is," Clay said, and Tamara smiled.

It was late afternoon the next day before Tamara's pickup was repaired. Traces of sugar were found in the fuel tanks, so they had to be pulled off, drained, and reinstalled.

Driving down the interstate, Clay leaned over the steering wheel, going over in his mind the events of yesterday and what they implied. Jack leaned back against the seat, his eyes closed. "You asleep?" Clay asked quietly.

"Nope," Jack answered without opening his eyes.

"I've been trying to figure out why someone would do what they did. It's as if someone wanted to keep us away from the rodeo last night."

"I've been wondering the same thing," Jack said, now sitting upright.

"I can only come up with one conclusion," Clay stated.

"What's that?"

"Someone's trying to insure they make it to the finals by sabotaging other competitors."

Jack mused over the suggestion for a moment. "That could be, but we know most of the top riders, and I can't think of one of them that would pull a stunt like that."

"I can't believe any of them would either, but something's going on. Look at Cory Laird, Steve Cannon, and Billy Dodd. Each of them have had similar problems. And I think Harvey Daniels scoring me low in Springfield ties into this someway."

Jack turned and rummaged in a tote bag in the back seat. "I've got the programs from Springfield and Colorado Springs. Let's see who was at both. Maybe that'll give us a clue."

They matched the riders at both rodeos, coming up with the names of twelve cowboys who were at both of them, none of whom were high enough in the standings to benefit from either the low scores Clay had recieved or the incident in Colorado Spings. They were no closer to discovering who was behind the so-called accidents.

Clay stared at the back of Tamara's trailer ahead of him. "It doesn't make any sense. Do you realize how many cowboys would have to be eliminated to insure that one person made it to the finals?"

"Not to mention the cost. It would take several people traveling around the country to cover all the rodeos," Jack commented.

The three-hour drive to Raton, New Mexico, put them there with an hour to spare before the events started. After the rodeo that night, they would drive to Santa Fe, another four-hour drive.

Clay couldn't help looking suspiciously at everybody he met or saw. When he was alone with Tamara and Jack, he mentioned this to them. "I hate this," he exclaimed. "I look at everyone as if they might be the one that slashed our tires."

"I know what you mean," Tamara agreed. "I keep thinking about being out there alone in the pickup, scared to death. And every time I look at someone, I wonder if they were the one that caused it."

Jack listened to them vent their frustrations before saying anything. "I know you two had a bad experience, but you can't dwell on it. If you do, it will drive you crazy. We have to be careful and try not to give them a chance to do anything else, but if you let 'em get to you, they've already beaten you."

"You're right." Clay sighed. "We can't be looking over our shoulders all the time expecting trouble, or we'll be nothing but nervous wrecks."

"I'm already a nervous wreck," Tamara stated, "but I agree with both of you. I'm not going to let these jerks get to me."

"Good," Jack said. "Now let's get ready to rodeo!"

Clay rode a rank horse named Diablo in the barebacks. The dark bay horse bucked straight for two jumps, then ducked back to the left, pivoted on his hind feet, and jumped straight into the air. Clay never missed a beat, but spurred in time with each buck and scored an eighty-two to take the lead.

Black Demon, a large black, was Clay's draw in the saddle bronc riding. Coming out of the chute, the rangy horse rubbed Clay's leg against the chute post. Clay couldn't get his spur back into the horse's shoulder before his front feet touched the ground, and the judge, who missed seeing it, disqualified him for missing his horse out. Clay protested the call, but to no avail.

The bull Hard Rock was Clay's draw in the bull riding. The Holstein-looking bull had more tricks than a magician, and threw his head up and back in an attempt to break Clay's concentration. The large bovine bucked first left, then turned back to the right, twisting his body almost sideways before reversing his move. Clay stayed with him for the full eight seconds and scored a seventy-nine to put him in third place. With one more night's performance to go, Clay wouldn't know how he'd wound up until he either got a check or saw the standings in the *Pro Rodeo News*.

Tamara, despite her adventures in Colorado City, ran a 16.3 and was sitting second after her barrel run.

They grabbed a quick bite to eat after the rodeo and hit the road, heading for Santa Fe. Clay followed Tamara as they pulled out of the cafe. Jack would sleep until they reached Las Vegas, then he would drive and let Clay ride with Tamara to keep her awake.

Dottie Hightower had made motel reservations for Jack and Clay since she already had a house full of relatives who had come in for the rodeo. Tamara would be the only one to stay with the Hightowers. Pulling into Santa Fe in the early-morning hours, Clay and Tamara drove to the rodeo grounds to stable Charger. Will Hightower had made arrangements for a stall to be watched by the security guard he had hired to watch his stock.

Jack went straight to the motel and had their clothes unloaded and in the room by the time they arrived. "I woke Will and Dottie already, so you can go on over," he said, smiling at Tamara.

"I'll bet that broke your heart," Tamara remarked with a grin.

"Oh, it did! I can't tell you the number of times that ornery cuss has woke me up in the morning after I've been up driving all night."

"See if you can keep him away from here until at least ten o'clock so I can get some sleep," Clay said, kissing her good-bye.

"That should be as easy as stopping a charging bull," she said as she shut the pickup door.

Chapter Ten

They managed to sleep until eleven o'clock before Will banged on their door to wake them up. "I hear ya'll had a little trouble in Colorado Springs," he said when Clay greeted him.

"Just a little," Clay answered, climbing back under the covers.

"Tamara was telling us about it earlier. Sounds like you two had quite an adventure."

Jack sat on the bed and started pulling on his jeans. "I'm hungry enough to eat a horse."

"Well, if you'd get out of bed and quit lazing around all day, we can go over to the cafe and see if they'll cook you one."

"I'm going to take a shower first," Clay stated. "I've been smelling something foul ever since we left Raton, but I'm not sure it's me," he said, giving Jack a meaningful look.

"Don't look at me," Jack said indignantly. "I took a shower two days ago and I didn't even need one."

Clay rolled his eyes and pulled the covers over his head. "I'll be there in a little bit. Is Tamara up yet?"

"She's already up and waiting at the cafe," Will

commented. "She wouldn't let me wake you two up until now."

"Good girl!" Jack shouted. He pulled on his boots and stood up, buttoning his shirt and tucking it in. "Let's go. You're buying, aren't you?"

Will gave him a crooked grin. "Come on, old man. We'll fight over the bill *after* we've had something to eat."

Clay waited for them to leave then slowly got out of bed and took a shower. Twenty minutes later he was dressed and ready to eat.

Their room was on the back side of the motel, away from the street. Clay had to walk around the motel to get to the restaurant. Closing the door to the room, he turned and started walking to the end of the building. He sensed running feet behind him but before he could turn to see who it was, something crashed into the side of his head. Bright lights exploded in his eyes, followed by intense pain. Blinking to clear his head, he tried to turn and meet his attacker but another blow sent him reeling. He heard a voice followed by laughter, then someone kicked him viciously in the ribs as he rolled over. He opened his eyes for a brief moment and saw three men standing over him. Another kick to the ribs sent him writhing in agony. He heard someone scream as the point of a boot crashed into his head and blackness enveloped him. He never knew it was his scream he'd heard. Lying unconcious on the cold pavement, he didn't feel the final assault on his body as one of his attackers stood over him. Raising his boot high, the man brought his heel down hard on the back of

Clay's right hand. A groan escaped the inert figure on the ground as bones were crushed and ligaments torn. With a laugh, the attacker looked at his handy work. "Let's see him ride now."

"Let's get out of here before somebody sees us," another one of the attackers said nervously, pulling the man away by the shirtsleeve.

They ran to a car parked two doors down from Clay's room. Starting the engine, they backed out of the parking spot and pulled up beside the bruised and bleeding form lying on the ground. "Let's see you walk over me now, Mr. Bigshot," the driver of the car shouted and mashed the pedal to the floor, the tires squealing on the concrete drive, sending up a cloud of smoke.

Clay fought to regain consciousness. His mind was a total fog and he couldn't fight through the haze. He desperately tried to open his eyes but they felt like lead weights had been attached to them. He turned his head to the side and groaned as pain flooded through him. Finally able to open his eyes a little, he peered through the slits. Through his blurred vision, he thought he was in a cave; his befuddled mind tried to comprehend where he was. He could hear voices but couldn't make out the words. The pain was suddenly intense. His head throbbed, his sides ached, and the pain in his right hand was agony. He tried to lift it, but the merest movement made his mind scream, and he sank back into unconsciousness.

* * *

"The MRI results show there's no damage to his brain. He started to wake up while we were running the test. He has a concussion, but I don't think it's too serious; we won't know for sure until tomorrow anyway. We can't give him any pain medicine until we know he's out of the woods. We're going to operate on his hand in the morning to repair the damage. He's had some bad bruising to his ribs and two of them have hairline cracks, but none are broken. Right now, sleep will be the best thing for him. He's taken a terrible beating." The speaker was an emergency room doctor at the hospital. Tamara, worried when Clay hadn't shown up to eat, had gone to check on him and found him lying in the parking lot. Fearing he was dead, she'd run back to the restaurant screaming for Jack and Will. Rushing to the parking lot, they saw him sprawled in a pool of blood. Kneeling beside him, Will felt for a pulse and breathed a sigh of relief. "He's alive! Dottie, call an ambulance." Twenty minutes later they were at the hospital. It was a grim foursome that now faced the doctor as he gave his prognosis.

"I'm staying here with him!" Tamara said adamantly.

Dottie put her arm around the girl. "He's in good hands, dear, and there's nothing you can do for him. Besides, you've got a rodeo to go to."

"I'll stay with him," Jack said. "Ya'll take Tamara with you."

Tamara started to protest but Jack cut her off. "Now you know he'd want you to go ride. Besides, you haven't taken care of Charger today and he needs to be exercised."

She knew he was right, but she was still reluctant to leave. "All right," she finally relented, "but I'll be back as soon as the barrel racing is over."

"We'll be here waiting for you," Jack smiled. "He's going to be fine." He said it as much for his own reassurance as he did for hers.

They wheeled Clay into a private room. Jack sat in the only chair in the room, an uncomfortable excuse for a recliner covered with hard plastic. Every time Clay moved or made a noise, Jack was on his feet checking on him. Nurses came in constantly during the night to check on Clay's condition and to take his vital signs. They took him in for surgery at five o'clock the next morning. It took them two hours to repair the damage to his hand. Jack walked the floor until Clay was brought out of the operating room. Reassured by the doctor that everything went as well as could be expected, he followed the gurney back into the room.

Clay seemed to be resting peacefully, so Jack returned to his chair. Exhausted, he fell asleep in an upright position, and that's where Tamara found him when she came in. Shaking him gently, she whispered his name. "Jack . . . Jack." He came awake with a start, looking to where Clay lay.

"Why don't you get something to eat? I'll stay with him."

Wiping the sleep from his eyes and stretching his aching arms, Jack nodded. "I am a little hungry."

"How did the surgery go?" she asked.

"They said it went fine. He won't be using his hand for a while, but with a little luck, he should regain full use of it, with the help of some therapy."

Tamara nodded and brushed Clay's forehead. "He'll be back riding before you know it," she said, forcing a smile for Jack's sake.

"I doubt we'll be able to stop him," Jack said softly.

"Why don't you go back to the hotel and get some sleep?"

Jack looked doubtful. Tamara could understand his reluctance. "If he wakes up, I'll call you."

"I probably won't be able to sleep, but I think I will go lie down for a little while. That durned chair made my back ache something fierce."

Tamara saw him to the door, then took his place in the chair. She held Clay's left hand and talked to him about the rodeo that night, telling him about the rides in the bareback and saddle broncs. She giggled nervously when she told him about her barrel race. "I hit two barrels," she said. "I couldn't keep my mind on what I was doing. I honestly believe Charger thought I'd lost my mind."

Taking a deep breath and fighting to hold back tears, she squeezed his hand. "What have you done to me, Clay Tory? A week ago I was footloose and fancy-free, and now here I am going to pieces. I had planned to fall for a lawyer, or a doctor, or anyone but a cowboy. Of course, that was part of the plan in the battle with my father, but you changed all that, didn't you?"

Filled with pain killers, Clay slept all day and through the night. Jack, Will, and Dottie came early in the morning. Looking disheveled, Tamara hugged each as they came in.

"How's he doin'?" Will asked.

"He slept through the night," Tamara answered.

Dottie looked at her sympathetically. "Did you sleep at all?"

"A little," she said with a tired smile.

Taking her by the arm, Dottie spoke with authority, "Come on, dear. You need something to eat. We'll let the men stay with him for a few minutes."

Rather than argue, Tamara let Dottie lead her from the room. They walked to the hospital cafeteria where Dottie bought coffee and some cinnamon rolls.

Will sat in the chair in Clay's room while Jack perched beside him. They were talking in hushed tones reserved for funerals and hospital rooms and didn't hear the request that came from the patient until he hoarsely repeated, "I'm thirsty."

Jack nearly fell off the bed and Will sprang out of the chair to hover over Clay. It was like two mother hens worrying over their brood. "Hey, Clay. How ya feelin'?" Jack asked.

"I'm thirsty," Clay croaked again.

Will looked helplessly at Jack. "Can he have water?"

"How in the blazes should I know?" Jack retorted. "Press the button for the nurse and we'll ask."

After checking Clay's pulse and taking his temperature, the nurse assured them it would be fine to give the patient a drink.

"What happened?" Clay asked after sipping some water, grimacing as he lay back on the pillow.

"We were kind of hoping you could tell us," Jack said.

Speaking slowly, Clay said, "The last thing I remember is riding Hard Rock. Did he do this to me?"

Jack shook his head. "No. Hard Rock didn't do this. You're in the hospital in Santa Fe. We found you in the parking lot of the motel. Someone gave you a beating."

Clay closed his eyes. "I remember a voice, someone laughing. I can't remember who it was."

Jack and Will exchanged glances. "You need to rest," Jack said and Clay tried to nod, only to grimace again at the effort.

Tamara came hurrying into the room. Rushing to Clay's side, she clutched his good hand. "Hey cowboy, how ya doin'?"

Attempting a smile and failing miserably, Clay mumbled, "I've had better days."

Tamara smiled through her tears. "You gave me quite a scare."

"Sorry," he croaked.

"I'll forgive you only if you hurry and get well."

"That's one thing I promise you I'll do," he responded sleepily.

They were all hovering over the bed when the doctor came in. Will and Dottie stepped out, but Jack and Tamara refused to leave until they'd heard the prognosis. After checking all his vitals and muttering several "uh-huhs" and "umms," the doctor wrote more in Clay's chart, then turned to the anxiously waiting couple. "All his vitals are normal. His pupils look good and his reflexes seem to be in good shape. I think he needs to rest today. If he's well enough tomorrow, I'll release him."

Jack and Tamara stayed with Clay all during the day. Dottie wanted to throw all her company out of the house, and move Jack in, but he insisted on staying at the motel, saying it was closer to the hospital.

Once more, Tamara spent the night in the hospital room. Clay woke up for brief periods of time, mostly asking for something to drink. Tamara was always there to give him an ice chip or a small sip of water before he drifted back to sleep. She spent a restless night and finally fell into a deep sleep shortly before dawn. She woke with a start to see daylight streaming in through the drawn curtains.

"Hey, sleepyhead," a voice called, bringing her wide awake. Lifting her head and looking around the room, she saw no one else. Turning, she looked over at Clay's bed. He had managed to raise the head of his bed and was smiling weakly at her.

Springing from the chair she rushed to his side. "How ya feelin'?" she asked, kissing his forehead.

"Much better now." He grinned. "What happened to me?"

Tamara moved back and looked at him, hesitating to answer. "Uh, we don't know. We found you in the parking lot of the motel. Don't you remember us telling you this yesterday?"

Clay blinked his eyes. "I vaguely remember Jack saying something about that. I thought maybe I'd dreamed it."

"No, you didn't dream it," Tamara assured him.

"Was I run over by a car?" he asked.

"Maybe we ought to wait for Jack to get here," Tamara said.

Clay looked at her suspiciously. "Tamara, what happened?" he asked adamantly.

Tears began to form in her eyes once again, and she wiped them away with the sleeve of her shirt. "I didn't think I had any tears left," she said, laughing nervously.

Clay repeated his question in a softer tone. "Tamara, what happened?"

Shaking her head, she tried to form the words. "Clay, sweetheart, somebody beat you up. They hit you in the head with something, then apparently kicked you and broke your hand. You've got some cracked ribs and a concussion."

Clay struggled to comprehend what she was saying. "Somebody did this to me?" he asked.

Tamara nodded as the tears rolled unchecked down her cheek.

"Why would someone do this?" he asked, holding up his broken hand.

"I . . . I don't know," she stammered.

"I just don't understand it," Clay said. "I didn't do anything to anybody."

Tamara held his good hand to her cheek, not knowing what to say.

That was the way Jack found them when he walked into the room. "Hey, it's about time you woke up."

Clay's response was less than enthusiastic. "I wish I hadn't."

Jack was taken back. "What's this?" he asked gruffly.

"Tamara just told me what happened," Clay said gloomily.

"And?" Jack asked.

"Somebody intentionally did this to me!" Clay cried out. "It doesn't make sense."

Jack walked around to the opposite side of the bed. "Clay, listen to me. There's a lot of things in life that don't make sense. I can't tell you why someone did this to you. But you got to face it and go on. You can't let it get you down. Your body will heal, but if you let this get to you, your mind won't."

Clay looked away from Jack, closing his eyes. "They broke my hand."

"I know," Jack said softly, "but we'll have you back riding in no time."

Clay turned toward him slowly. "I don't know if I can do it."

"Give it some time, Clay. You'll feel different after you've had some time to recuperate."

The mood was somber when the doctor came into the room later that morning. "How's our patient this morning?" he asked cheerfully, then noticed the long faces and went quietly about his examination.

After checking Clay thoroughly, he closed his clipboard and announced, "I think you're ready to leave."

If he expected a jubilant reply, he was disappointed. Clay merely nodded. Looking from one person to the other, the doctor saw the despair on each face. "I don't know what's going on here," he said, speaking to each of them, "but I do know the healing process takes place in the mind as much as in the body. Now you can all mope around, feeling sorry for Clay here, but it's not going to do him a bit of good." Walking to the head of the bed, he looked Clay directly in the eye. "I would have taken you for a fighter. Tamara and Jack have been telling me what a great bronc and bull rider you are. I would say it takes a lot of guts to climb on the back of one of those animals." He paused, looking Clay up and down. "I don't see anything here that won't heal. Now if you want to stay in bed feeling sorry for yourself, that's fine, but you're going to have to do it somewhere else. And if you think you got it tough, come down to the children's wing with me and I'll show you some real bum deals. There's kids down there that won't live to see winter, and they didn't do anything to deserve it either." He put his pen in his pocket and turned away. "I'll have the release forms ready for you to sign at the front desk. I'll send a nurse in to help you get dressed."

Clay waited until the door closed behind the doctor. "Jack, get my clothes. I'm not going to let some nurse come in here and dress me."

Jack was glad his back was turned so he could hide the smile on his face.

Chapter Eleven

Clay was dressed and ready to go when the nurse came in, followed by a man in a rumpled suit and ugly tie. "Clay, this is Detective Romano. He has a few questions he needs to ask you," the nurse said, nodding in Clay's direction.

Clay sat on the bed and looked questioningly at the detective. Holding out his hand, Romano approached Clay. "Just a few quick questions and I'll be out of here," the detective said.

Clay held up his broken hand and the detective dropped his, looking around awkwardly.

"Ask away," Clay said. "I don't know much."

Romano took a pad out of his shirt pocket and flipped through several pages. Studying the notes he'd made, he began, "According to the doctor, you received a concussion, several cracked ribs, a broken hand, and several cuts and abrasions, apparently the result of an attack by one or more assailants." Looking at Clay, he asked, "Do you have any idea who might have done this to you?"

Clay shook his head. "No idea at all."

The detective studied him briefly, then continued with his questioning. "Has anyone threatened you lately?"

"Nope."

"Have you had an altercations with anyone in the past few weeks?"

"Nope."

"Do you owe anyone money? Have any gambling debts?"

"No," Clay responded, surprised by the line of questioning.

"Hmm." Ramano sighed. "We checked with all the guests who were registered at the motel. No one saw anything. We have no witnesses and no motive. I understand they didn't take anything?" he said, the last more as a question.

"No; my wallet was still in my pocket and there was no money missing."

Taking a card from his pocket, Romano handed it to Clay. "If you think of anything that might help, give me a call."

Clay looked at the card with disinterest and put it in his shirt pocket.

Romano nodded, then turned and exited the room. The nurse stepped into the hallway and came back with a wheelchair. "Your chariot awaits you, Mr. Tory."

"What's that?" Clay asked.

"It's your ride out of here. Now don't give me any lip, or I'll pick you up and put you in here myself."

Clay grinned. Looking at the size of her, he knew she could do what she threatened. He eased himself down into the chair and let her wheel him to the front desk, where she handed him several forms to sign. She then wheeled him out to where Jack was waiting with the pickup.

Dottie had moved her company into a motel and insisted Jack and Clay stay at the house for a few days until Clay was fit to travel. Jack knew better than to argue with her, so he packed their bags and checked out of the motel.

Dottie had a bedroom fixed up for Clay, but Jack had to bunk with Carl Hightower, the only one of Dottie and Will's sons still at home.

It was the last night of the rodeo, so everyone was out of the house, leaving Tamara and Clay there alone. Dottie gave Tamara a phone number in case of an emergency and fixed sandwiches for them to eat. "I'll be home as soon as the rodeo is over," she promised as she walked out the door.

Tamara smiled. "We'll be fine. Don't worry about a thing.

Tamara called home and told her father what had happened and that she was going to stay with Clay until he went home. Concerned, he questioned her about the extent of Clay's injuries. She was surprised at the anger in his voice when he cursed the sorry no-good lowlives that had done such a thing. He told her to give his regards to Jack, Will, and Dottie, and cautioned her to be careful.

"I will, Dad. Give my love to Mother and tell her I'll be home soon." Hanging up the phone, she walked into Clay's bedroom. "Dad said to tell you hello."

"How's he doing?" Clay asked out of politeness.

"He's fine. He's really ticked off about what happened to you. I've never heard him get so upset." She looked thoughtful for a moment, then continued, "Except for the time I ran away from home for a week." Clay looked at her expectantly. "I was seventeen and headstrong. We got into one of our usual fights about who was in control of my life. I got mad and ran away. I stayed with my aunt Maggie in Austin for the entire week. Aunt Maggie is Daddy's sister. She wouldn't tell him I was there. I thought he was going to kill both of us when he found out."

"I'd say he had good reason," Clay responded.

Tamara puckered her lips in thought. "I guess he did. I couldn't sit down for a couple of days." She was rewarded with a smile, something she hadn't seen for a few days.

They watched an old movie on the television Dottie had put in Clay's room, until he fell asleep. Tamara sat on the bed beside him, watching him sleep, her heart heavy as she looked at his broken hand and bandaged head.

On the second day, Clay got out of bed and walked gingerly to the front porch. He sat in a rocking chair and enjoyed the warmth of the sun.

As he sat there basking in the sun's rays, Will came walking up from the barn. "Looks like you're feelin' a little better."

"It feels good to be out of bed," Clay responded. He then asked, "Who were the winners at the rodeo?"

Will hesitated, uncertain if talking about the rodeo was good therapy for Clay.

Sensing his reluctance, Clay hurried to assure him. "Don't worry, Will. I'm not going to go bonkers. I really want to know. I'm probably going to be out of competition for several weeks, and I want to know who I'm going to have to catch when I get back in the saddle." He smiled to emphasize his mood.

"All right," Will relented. "Lon Richards won the barebacks. Calvin Todd placed second, Gene Smith third, and Tim Hicks fourth. Billy Ettinger won the saddle bronc riding." He stopped when he saw Clay wince.

"I was closing in on him," Clay said.

"And you will again!" Will stated.

"Who won the bull riding?"

"Gill Timbers."

"Gill Timbers!" Clay exclaimed. "Gill hasn't covered a good bull since I've known him."

"He covered Lancer," Will said.

"Lancer!" Clay cried again. "That's one tough bull. How on earth did Gill cover him?"

"I don't know, but he did, and did a good job of it too."

"Did Charles Prater place?" Clay asked.

"Fourth," Will said.

Clay groaned. "I had just moved ahead of him."

"Oh, I think you'll keep your lead. He drew Gladiator. He was hanging on the bull's side when the whistle blew and he hung up. Gladiator stepped on him and pulled the muscles in his arm. He'll be out of commission about the same amount of time as you."

"That doesn't make me feel any better," Clay responded.

"I know it doesn't," Will said. "But it's still early

in the season. You'll have plenty of time to get back on top."

Clay nodded. "I guess if I'd gotten hurt riding, it wouldn't be so hard to take. But to have this happen seems so senseless. I think it's not understanding why that makes it so hard to take."

"Sure it's hard to take, but bad things happen to good people all the time. It's the ones who pick themselves up and keep on going who come out on top."

Clay rolled his eyes. "You're beginning to sound like Jack. I don't know if I can handle two of you old geezers preaching at me."

Will gasped, then noticed the smile on the young man's face. "If someone hadn't already beaten you, I'd take a club to you right now."

"Threatening an injured man?" Clay asked innocently

Will chortled. "You've been around Jack Lomas too long."

By the third day Clay felt well enough to make the trip back to Roswell. Jack was impatient to get back to the ranch. He'd called Terry and Julie the night before and was told everything was fine, but that didn't stop him from worrying.

Tamara would travel with them to Roswell, spend the night at the ranch, then leave for San Angelo the next day.

They had to stop several times on the way home so Clay could get out and stretch his muscles to work the stiffness out. By the time they got to Roswell, Clay was stiff, sore, and worn out. Jack and Tamara helped him into the house and sat him in Jack's large recliner. Julie smothered him with concern, bringing him pillows and a cool glass of iced tea. She had fixed his favorite meal of beef tips and noodles. She took to Tamara right off and between the two of them, they made sure Clay wanted for nothing.

Jack, feigning disgust over all the attention Clay was receiving, turned to Terry. "Let's go look at the hay pasture. I can't take this anymore. It's going to be hard enough gettin' him back to work, but with all this attention he's getting from these women, he won't be worth killing."

Terry fell in behind Jack, turning at the door to smile back at Clay. Clay gave him a wink, smiling as they went out the door.

Tamara left the next morning. Teary eyed, she kissed Clay good-bye and promised to come back soon. She had a rodeo in Abilene that weekend, but didn't mention it to Clay, understanding how hard it would be for him knowing she was going and he couldn't.

After Tamara left, Jack loaded Clay in the pickup and took him into town to see the doctor. The hospital in Santa Fe had sent him Clay's file, complete with X rays and recommendations. After reviewing the files and examining Clay, Doctor Johnson, Jack's physician for years, concurred with the doctor in Santa Fe. "As soon as the cast comes off, we'll start you on physical therapy. Providing there's no major nerve damage, you should regain at least eighty percent use of your hand."

"Eighty percent?" Clay almost shouted.

"That's worst case," the doctor reassured him. "We'll know more when the cast comes off and we start therapy."

"How long do you think it'll be before I can use my hand again, Doc?" Clay asked.

The doctor cast a glance at Jack, who nodded. "A lot depends on how your therapy goes and how much you adhere to the program. If everything goes well, your hand should be healed somewhere between eight and twelve weeks."

Clay felt his spirits sag. "That's two to three months, Doc. If I miss that many rodeos, I'll never make it to the finals."

Doctor Johnson knew how hard Clay had worked to stay in the top fifteen and how much he wanted to make it to the finals. "I'm sorry, Clay. If there were some way I could speed up the healing process, I'd do it. But these things take time."

Clay was feeling miserable when they left the doctor's office. Jack remained silent, knowing the turmoil Clay was going through. Stopping at the bank to conduct some business, he left Clay sitting in the pickup. "I'll only be a few minutes. You sure you don't want to come in?"

Clay shook his head and stared darkly out the window, his depression evident.

The ride home began in total silence, with Clay continuing to just stare out the window. Jack glanced over at him several times trying to think of something to say that would bring him out of his mood. "You know, it doesn't have to be two to three months before you ride again. If you really want to ride, we can have you back in the saddle, so to speak, in three weeks."

Clay turned a skeptical eye to him. "How can we do that?" he asked dryly.

"You have more than one hand. Why can't you ride with your left hand?"

Clay looked down into his lap. "I don't think I can. My balance is in my right hand. I don't know if I can switch."

"Well we'll just have to find out," Jack said, suddenly enthusiastic. "We'll start as soon as we get home."

Clay gave him a startled look. "And how are we going to do that?"

"We'll begin exercising your left hand to build up strength. You've already been lifting weights, so it should be in pretty good shape. We just have to build up your wrist and grip."

Clay opened and closed his left hand, testing its strength. Maybe he could ride left-handed, after all. "As long as I don't have to move hay bales," he said, smiling.

Jack chuckled. "There goes my best idea."

Back at the ranch, Jack started Clay on exercises to build the strength in his hand. Rigging up a weight on a rope and pulley system, Jack started him out doing various exercises, starting with five pounds, doing ten repetitions. By the end of the week Clay was up to seven pounds and could feel the muscles building in his arm and wrist. Using the spring grips Jack had bought, he worked on building up his grip. He followed Jack's instructions to the letter, never arguing or complaining. Determination was etched into his face as he worked to regain his dream.

Cliff Allen was sitting in his office when he heard Tamara come in the house. Calling to her to come in, he waited for her to enter. "How'd you do?" She'd just gotten in from the Abilene rodeo.

"I'm in first right now with a sixteen-one. You're sure up late!" she said, sitting in one of the overstuffed chairs across the desk from her father.

"Yeah, I've been going over some of the ranch accounts."

"Problems?" she asked, raising her eyebrows.

"No, no," he said with a wave of his hand. "Just checking some things."

"I guess that's why there's no problems. You always keep a close eye on things, don't you?"

"Everything I can." He smiled. "I've been trying to figure out why Clay got beat up. Combine that with the other times when things were done to try to keep cowboys from getting to rodeos, and it sounds like someone is trying to play with the standings."

Tamara contemplated what he'd said. "Why would someone do that?"

"That's the big question. It could be one cowboy trying to insure he makes it to the finals, but I don't think so. It would take more than one person to pull off all these stunts and he'd have to be well financed. I think it's someone who's got a lot of money riding on the final standings."

"Does that bring anyone to mind?" Tamara asked.

"Oh, I know several men who would be capable of doing that sort of thing, but I don't think any of them are involved. It's just not their style."

"What can we do about it?"

"You leave that to me," Cliff said softly. "I'll make a few calls and see if I can come up with something."

"I'm going to Roswell in the morning to see how Clay's doing. You want to come along?" Tamara asked.

"I'd love to, but there's just no way I can get away. How long will you be gone?"

"I'm going to spend three days, then I'll be home."

"Tell Clay and Jack hello for me," Cliff said, kissing his daughter on the cheek.

"Good night, Daddy," Tamara said as she left his office.

"Good night, dear," Cliff responded, already punching buttons on his electronic phone directory. Finding the number he was looking for, he picked up the phone and started dialing, despite the late hour.

Chapter Twelve

Tamara drove up to the Lazy L Ranch in the early afternoon. Knocking on the screen door, she saw Julie come out of the kitchen, wiping her hands on the apron around her waist. "Hi, Julie. Is Clay here?"

Julie sighed, her agitation evident. "He's down in the barn with Jack and Terry. Been there every day for the last three days."

"What are they doing?"

"Beats me. I've asked, but they just grin like teenagers on a double date and tell me they're working. Ha, like I believe that!"

Tamara gave her a mischievous look. "I think I'll go down and see what's going on in there."

"Be careful they don't shoot you."

Tamara giggled. "I'll throw my hat in first to see what happens."

Walking down to the barn, she could hear strange sounds coming from within. As she neared the door, she could distinguish the sounds of men grunting as if lifting heavy objects. After the grunts there came a banging sound, as if something were hitting metal.

The barn had a large sliding door in the middle with a smaller door to the side. Trying the small door first, she found it locked from the inside. She started to knock but changed her mind and walked to the big door. Pushing against the end of the door, she felt it slide open enough to let her peer through the small crack. Looking inside, she was surprised to see Clay seated on a fifty-five gallon metal drum. The drum was suspended four feet in the air by a cable on either end. Each cable was run to a large circular car spring that was attached to the steel poles supporting the barn. Jack and Terry stood on either end of the barrel, pulling on short ropes that were tied to the barrel's bottom. A left-handed bareback rigging was cinched down on the barrel and Clay had his left hand in the rigging. While Jack and Terry alternated pulling on their ropes, the barrel would shoot upward, then fall back, bouncing against the car springs. The action was similar to that of a bucking horse. There were old bed mattresses spread around on the concrete floor to cushion Clay's fall.

Tamara stood mesmerized by the sight before her. Despite the effort being exerted by Terry and Jack, Clay managed to keep his seat, spurring the iron horse beneath him. Pushing the door open wider, she stepped into the barn. Jack was the first to see her, letting go of his rope and staring at her as she walked across the concrete floor. Clay and Terry noticed Jack had quit pulling, and followed his gaze.

"Tamara!" Clay exclaimed, jumping to the ground. "I didn't expect you for another couple of hours."

"Apparently," she said sardonically. "Is this on the doctor's list of therapy excercises?"

Clay gave her a sheepish look. "Probably not!"

Turning to Jack, she gave him a scathing look. "Is this your idea?"

"Now, Tamara—" he began, but she cut him off.

"Y'all are crazy, the three of you! His hand is still in a cast and the cut on his head hasn't even healed yet, and here you have him on a bucking barrel. Do you realize what would happen if he hit his head, or fell on his broken hand? And you," she said, turning to Clay, "don't you have better sense than to crawl on this contraption in the shape you're in?"

Terry was standing off to the side, a guilty grin on his face.

Clay looked at Jack, then over at Terry. Trying to keep a straight face, he turned to Tamara, who was standing with her hands on her hips and a stern look on her face. Jack and Terry made a hasty retreat, leaving Clay to face her alone. "Now, Tamara, there's no use getting upset. As you can see, we took precautions," he said, motioning to the mattresses on the floor. "And my head is fine. I haven't had a headache in over a week now. My cast comes off day after tomorrow, so that means it's almost healed."

She gave him a doubtful look. "Your head doesn't look healed to me."

"It is! I can even wear my hat now! There's really no reason for you to be upset. If I wait to get the use of my right hand back, I'll miss two to three months of rodeos. I can't afford to lose that much time. Jack and Terry are helping me learn to ride with my left hand." He paused to catch his breath. "And it's working. I've been exercising my hand, and with the bucking barrel, I'm getting my balance back."

Seeing the excitement in his eyes, she knew there was no way she could stop him. "Well, if you're sure your head is healed and you're not going to hurt your right hand, I won't say any more."

Clay pulled her to him, giving her a hug. "I'm sure," he assured her. "And next week after the cast comes off, I'm going to start practicing on our stock." He and Jack owned four bucking horses and four bulls that Clay used to practice on.

Tamara sighed and rolled her eyes. "I should have known better than to get involved with a rough stock rider. They don't have any sense when it comes to taking care of themselves. But then, most men I've known have that problem."

He grabbed her around the waist and started walking toward the house. "Don't say anything to Julie. She thinks we're working."

Tamara watched all the next day as Clay worked out on the bucking barrel. Impressed with the way he rode, she felt her fears melt away. But she still had reservations about his riding actual horses. She went with him to the doctor to have his cast removed. Afterward they went to the rehab center to start his therapy. Tamara and Jack paid close attention to the exercises he was to perform on his own, both promising to make sure he did them. Jack stopped by Wal-Mart on the way home. He came out with a large bag, refusing to tell them what was in it.

Clay worked with his right hand all the way back to the ranch. He had lost most of the mobility in it, but the doctor had warned him about that. "It sure feels good to have the cast off," he said when he noticed Tamara watching him.

"The doctor told you it would take time," she said.

"I know. I was just hoping it wouldn't be this bad."

Jack sensed Clay's disappointment and knew that if he dwelled on in for any length of time, he'd become depressed. "Hey, look in that bag in the backseat and see what I got."

Clay looked suspiciously at him. "What's in there?"

"Look and see."

Clay reached back and pulled the bag to him. Opening it, he looked inside, then pulled out the contents and gave Jack a puzzled look. "What's this for?" he asked, pulling out a roll of foam rubber.

"It's a safety precaution," Jack replied.

"What kind of safety precaution?"

"I saw a bull rider use it one time. He'd broken his arm and wanted to protect it so he could continue to ride, so he wrapped it in foam rubber to protect it. I figured we could wrap your hand when you ride."

Clay stared at the object for a moment then started to chuckle, and soon he was laughing outright. "I ought to look real good with this wrapped around my hand."

"I think you should wrap it around his head too!" Tamara exclaimed, looking rather perturbed. Jack gave her a barely perceptible nod of his head. She caught his meaning. "How soon do you plan on riding?" she asked.

Clay and Jack exchanged glances, then clearing his throat, Jack said, "We've got Lyle Jones coming out this afternoon. Clay wants to try a bareback today. Lyle's got a horse they use at the high school rodeos. We're going to start on an easy one."

Tamara's face paled. "Isn't that pushing it a little fast?"

Clay took a deep breath. Looking out the window for a moment he gathered his thoughts. He wanted to find just the right words. "Tamara, I have to know if I can ride left-handed. When the doctor told me it would be two to three months before my hand would be healed, I almost lost it. Then Jack suggested I try to ride left-handed and started me on a routine to build up my arm and strengthen my grip. It's given me hope, but I have to know."

Tamara bit her lower lip, trying to calm the storm inside her. She knew what riding meant to Clay. She knew if something happened to prevent her from riding, she would be devastated. "And what happens if you can't ride with your left hand?" She didn't want to ask, but she knew she had to.

Clay looked down at his hands, holding them palms up. "Then I build up my right hand and start back when it's healed," he replied softly.

"Whatever happens, I'll be there to help," she said, placing her hand in his good one.

Smiling, he squeezed her hand. "Thanks. That means a lot to me."

Jack smiled and began to hum a song.

*   *   *

Lyle Jones showed up just after lunch. Clay had eaten little, which caused Julie to be alarmed. No one had told her what he was going to do, knowing she would raise a ruckus. "Are you feeling poorly?" she asked when Clay pushed his half-eaten plate of food away.

"I'm fine," he assured her. "I'm just not very hungry."

"I'll save this for you in case you get hungry later," she said, taking his plate.

"I'd hate to be in your shoes when she finds out what you're doing," Terry whispered.

"I may sleep in the barn tonight," Clay stated.

Jack made a clucking sound with his tongue. "You boys just don't know how to handle women."

Three pairs of eyes bore into him, waiting for his words of wisdom.

"All you got to do is buck off and get hurt and she'll be so concerned, she'll forget all about being mad at you."

Terry laughed outright while Tamara rolled her eyes in disbelief. Clay looked once more toward the kitchen. "You may have a point."

The sound of a pickup coming down the drive brought all three of them to their feet. "Sounds like Lyle's here," Jack said, grabbing his hat from the hall tree. "I'll help him unload while ya'll help Julie clear the table."

Clay grabbed his hat and followed behind. "I think I'll help too."

Jack chuckled. "Coward."

Clay looked at him and grinned, glancing back over his shoulder.

Clay soon had his hand in the handle of the bareback rigging. His right hand was wrapped in foam rubber and bound with duct tape. He eased his spurs up over the horse's shoulders and leaned back, but he couldn't nod for the gate. He froze. It wasn't fear of the horse and it wasn't fear of getting bucked off. He'd been thrown many times before. It was fear of the unknown that suddenly gave him a case of rigor mortis.

Jack had his hand on the gate latch. "I'm going to open this gate at the count of five. One, two, three . . ." That was as far as he got. Clay nodded for the gate to open.

Jack released the latch and swung the gate wide. The horse hesitated momentarily, then turned and ran ten feet into the arena before burying his head between his legs and bucking the length of the arena.

Clay leaned back and spurred with each buck, keeping himself pulled up on his rigging and showing good form.

Terry and Lyle mounted on two of Jack's horses, waiting for Jack to motion to them, then moved in to help Clay down.

It was awkward dismounting with his hand wrapped the way it was, but Lyle was finally able to move in on his left and help him down.

Once on the ground, Clay took off his hat and wiped the sweat from his brow. Jack was standing by the open chute gate waiting for him as he walked back.

"So how did it feel?"

Clay shook his head and stared at the ground, refusing to meet Jack's questioning look.

Jack's spirits fell. He had thought Clay had made a good ride, but he knew it was more how Clay felt about it than how it looked. "Well, it was worth a try," he said, patting Clay on the shoulder.

Looking up, Clay nodded. "I guess it was," he agreed.

With a dejected look, Jack turned and started walking out of the arena, his shoulders slumped in defeat. Before he reached the gate, Clay called out to him. "Where ya goin'?"

"To the house," he answered without looking around.

"I thought I might try to ride Chester," Clay yelled. Chester was one of the horses Clay used regularly for practice.

Jack turned around slowly. "What did you say?"

"I said, I thought I might try to ride Chester!"

"Were you pulling my leg just now?"

"No!" Clay said sincerely. "You asked me how it was and I was honest. It was awful. That horse was terrible. I could have ridden him with my bad right hand."

"Clay Tory, I ought to ring your rotten neck!" Jack yelled.

Tamara and Julie had been sitting on the fence watching Clay. Both wore worried expressions during the ride, but their expressions changed to shock when they heard him say he wanted to ride Chester.

"He's going to get hurt," Julie said. "Can't you talk some sense into that thick skull of his?"

Tamara looked from Julie to Clay, ready to give her an affirmative reply, but the gleam she saw in Clay's eyes stopped her. Shaking her head, she smiled at Julie. "Nope. I couldn't stop him even if I wanted to. He's doing what he was born to do and if I managed to talk him out of it, he'd never forgive me."

Julie held the back of her hand to her mouth as the black horse named Chester was run into the chute and Clay's rigging was cinched to his back.

Sliding down into the chute, Clay once again worked his left hand into the rigging and placed his spurs over Chester's shoulders.

Jack was still perturbed about Clay's prank. "If you don't ride this sorry bag of bones, I'll have you moving hay from one side of the barn to the other for a month."

Clay leaned back and grinned at Jack. "Well, I don't cotton to the idea of doing your work, so why don't you open the gate and let's see if I can ride this sorry nag."

Jack opened the latch and pushed the gate open, smiling to himself as he did.

Chester was a seasoned bucking horse, having been on the rodeo circuit before Jack purchased him. Although he wasn't as tough as the stock Clay rode on the pro circuit, he still had plenty of try to him.

From Jack's point of view, he could see Clay was riding a little stiffer than he normally did. He could also tell he wasn't as confident in his skills, but he'd expected that. The main thing was that he was riding, and keeping in time with Chester, and there was no doubt he would make a qualified ride.

With a wave of his arm, Jack motioned Terry and Lyle to move in. As soon as he was on the ground, Clay walked straight to Tamara and Julie. "How did I look?" he asked, excitement still showing in his eyes.

"You looked wonderful," Tamara answered, smiling brightly.

"It looked like a crazy thing to do, if you ask me," Julie intoned, her eyes showing her concern.

Clay gave her one of his boyish smiles, which had always managed to dissolve her anger. "But I rode him, didn't I? And it felt great!"

Julie tried to hold her angry stare as Clay stood looking at her, but she couldn't stay mad at him. "Yes, you sure did ride him." She smiled.

Clay helped Tamara down off the fence and gave her a jubilant hug. "Just think, with a couple of weeks practice, I'll be back on the road."

His enthusiasm was contagious and Tamara felt his excitement course through her. "I'm so happy for you," she said and meant it.

Jack was grinning from ear to ear. "I was sure I was going to have someone to stack all that hay for me."

"That's what made me stay on," Clay answered with a grin.

"You need a little work, but I think with my expert training, you'll be ready to start back on the circuit in a week or two."

"I was just saying the same thing to Tamara," Clay said with a wide smile.

Lyle and Terry came up to congratulate Clay. "That was some pretty good ridin' for a lefty," Lyle said.

"Yeah and that foam rubber and duct tape looked real good too," Terry interjected. They all broke into laughter.

Chapter Thirteen

Jack woke everyone up at five o'clock the next morning. Tamara and Clay had stayed up late, looking at the latest standings in the *Pro Rodeo News*. Clay was sixth in the barebacks, seventh in the bulls, and still holding third in the saddle broncs. For her own part, Tamara was second in the barrel racing. They talked about the upcoming rodeos and determined which ones they would enter. It was almost midnight when they kissed good night at Tamara's bedroom door.

"Why you wakin' us up so early?" Clay asked as he stumbled into the kitchen wiping sleep from his eyes.

"We got to check the cattle today. I know the grass in the south pasture is about gone and both sections on the west side are getting real short. We've got to move some of the cattle to the two north sections and some to the east. If we get some rain in the next month or so, we might just make it with the hay we've got. We're going to start baling our hay pasture next week. We should get quite a few bales since Terry's been irrigating it. That was a good idea you had, Clay."

"I have one every now and again."

"Uh-huh, now if you can just figure out how to make it rain, we'll all be in good shape."

"We could put ants in Terry's britches and let him do a rain dance."

"If I thought it would work, I'd try it," Jack said with a wry smile.

"I might have something to say about that," Terry replied with a frown.

After a big breakfast of scrambled eggs, ham, homemade biscuits, and sausage gravy, they headed to the barn to saddle the horses and make a game plan. Tamara and Clay would move the cattle from the west pastures to the north pastures. Meanwhile, Terry and Jack would take the pickup and horse trailer to the south pastures and move the cattle to the east pastures. They would take Julie with them so she could drive the pickup and trailer back to the house, prepare a late lunch, then pick each of them up and bring them back to the house.

Clay and Tamara had to cut out two hundred pairs from the three hundred that were in the pasture. It took most of the morning to get that part of job done, since they had to make sure they had the calves paired up with their mothers. They began driving their herd through the dry, withered pastures, choking on the dust kicked up by the moving cattle. The hardest part was driving that many cattle through the narrow gates. It took both of them to push the reluctant cows through, and by the time the last one passed through the gate, the herd had gone in different directions. After three gates, Clay, Tamara, and the horses they rode were worn out and ready for a rest. They drove the herd to a windmill and let them drink their fill before allowing them to wander off to graze. After the cattle had drank, there was little water left in the holding tank. Clay watered the horses while Tamara wet her handkerchief under the fresh water spilling out of the windmill pipe. She wiped the New Mexico dust from her face. After watering the horses, Clay handed the reins to Tamara and held his head beneath the cool stream of water, letting it wash the grime and sweat from him.

"Julie ought to be here in about half an hour," Clay said, walking over to a juniper tree to sit in the shade.

"I think I've got blisters on top of my blisters," Tamara groaned, sitting down beside him.

Clay chuckled. "I know what you mean. I wish we had one of those Jacuzzis like they got at the motels. I could sure use one right now."

Tamara leaned back against the trunk of the tree and closed her eyes. "I've been wanting to ask you something, but I've been afraid to."

He turned to face her. "What is it?"

Opening her eyes, she looked into his. "Those men that beat you, do you have any idea who they were, or why they did it?"

He shook his head. "I have no idea. The only thing I can think of is that they wanted to keep me from rodeoing, but I don't know why."

Concern clouded Tamara's face. "What's to keep them from doing it again?"

"I've thought about that," Clay answered. "I can't

let these guys get to me. I just have to make sure I don't go anywhere alone like I did in Santa Fe."

"You didn't see anything?"

"All I can remember is a laugh, but I can't place it. It just comes to mind occasionally and I can almost put a face to it, but then my mind goes blank."

"What will you do if you find out who did it?"

"I'll cross that bridge when I get there," Clay said. "Until then I'm not going to dwell on it."

Scooting closer to him, she flexed the muscles in her arm. "They better hope I don't find out who they were. I'll kick their butts."

Clay laughed loudly and Tamara giggled. They were still laughing when they heard the sound of the pickup.

Jack let everybody sleep in late the next day, which meant he didn't start banging around in the kitchen until six-thirty. Despite the noise, Clay and Tamara slept until eight o'clock. Clay had an appointment with his physical therapist that morning. Jack stayed at the ranch and let Tamara drive Clay into Roswell at ten o'clock. They spent an hour going over the exercises Clay had to do every day. He promised he would do them. "I plan on regaining full use of my hand," he stated adamantly to the nurse helping him.

"Ninety percent of healing is in your mind." She smiled. "If you keep a positive attitude and work hard, you'll be back to playing the piano in no time."

Clay smiled at her wit. Thanking her for her help, he and Tamara left. Grabbing a quick sandwich before leaving town, they drove back to the ranch.

Jack and Terry were busy greasing the hay equipment when they returned. Clay leaned on the hay baler, looking down at Jack, who was underneath it with a grease gun. "I thought I'd ride Lumberjack and Tucson this afternoon."

Jack stopped pumping the handle on the grease gun. "You don't think that's overdoing it, do you?"

"I've got to get back on the circuit as soon as possible. The only way I'm going to do that is by practicing."

Jack crawled out from under the baler and stood up. Nodding, he said, "Let us get through with this equipment and we'll set things up."

Clay grinned with excitement. "I'll go ahead and get the horses in, and saddle Stormy and Chance."

"Whoa," Jack said. "Why do we need two horses saddled?"

Clay was already heading for the corral and stopped to yell back, "Tamara's going to help Terry. She can haze and Terry can be the pickup man."

Jack shook his head and chuckled, "I think you better watch out, Terry. I think he'd rather grab on to her. You could get replaced."

Terry looked from Clay to Jack. "That's the way it goes. You think you got something special, then the first pretty face that comes along, they push you aside like an old boot."

Jack chortled. "Try not to take it too hard. He's young and impetuous. Now let's get this baler greased before he starts bucking those horses without us."

* * *

Clay rode both horses that afternoon. Jack yelled instructions to him during each ride. Afterward they talked about ways to improve his performance. "You need to lean back a little more," Jack stated. "You're sitting up a little too straight. It's hard to make a change like you've had to do, and make everything work right. It's going to take a little time and practice to get it down right. Lyle called me today. Seems he bought a new bucking horse in Clovis yesterday. Wants to know if you'd be interested in trying him out."

"What's he like?" Clay asked.

"Lyle says he came from a pro stock contractor in Wyoming. Sounds like he might be a pretty tough horse. I think it might be a little soon to try one like that."

Clay thought about it for a moment before giving his answer. "No, I want to try him. I've got to find out if I can handle a rough horse. Ours are good for practice, but we both know they're not pro material. When can I try him?"

"I told him to bring him out tomorrow morning."

Clay nodded his head and smiled.

Clay was in the arena, ready and waiting when Lyle showed up the next morning. He helped him unload the sorrel horse from the trailer and run him into the chutes. "He looks good!" Clay commented. "But can he buck?"

"I sure hope so. I paid enough for him."

"What's his history?"

"He's an eight-year-old, came off a ranch in Wyoming when he was four. Nobody could ride him, so they sold him to an amateur rodeo contractor. No one could ride him there, so he was sold to a pro contractor for a hefty profit. He made it to the finals twice, then the contractor fell on hard times. They liquidated his stock and I bought him. That's the history."

"Sounds like he might be a good one. What's his name?" Clay asked as he picked up his rigging and climbed up on the platform.

"Red Dog."

Jack and Terry brought in the saddle horses. Julie and Tamara climbed to their perches on the fence. Tamara had planned on leaving early that morning, but had postponed her departure until after Clay rode.

Jack helped Clay cinch his rigging, then stood by to open the gate.

Clay climbed down on Red Dog's back and worked his left hand into the rigging handle. Though it still felt a little awkward using his left hand, Clay felt the familiar excitement wash over him as he eased his feet up over the horse's shoulders. Jack opened the latch on the gate and waited for Clay's nod. When it came, he threw open the gate and watched Red Dog explode out of the chute.

Clay felt the power in the big horse as the large beast flexed his legs and lunged skyward. It took all the strength he could muster to keep his grip and stay aboard.

Red Dog came back to earth stiff-legged and hard, jarring Clay's entire body. Clay gripped harder and moved his spurs back to Red Dog's shoulders and raked them back as the horse lunged forward again.

The sorrel horse had a number of tricks in his bag, including a series of left to right and back left quick bucks. Clay managed to stay with each of these, but when Red Dog suddenly reared, then pushed off hard with his back feet and twisted his body around in midair, Clay found himself jerked loose and heading to the ground.

Picking himself up, he watched the red horse run a complete circle around the arena, as if he were doing a victory lap.

"You made it six seconds," Jack said.

"Yeah, but I didn't make it the full eight."

"No you didn't, but that's one tough horse. He's as good as any you've ridden on the circuit and you've been thrown off some of them. I'd say you did real good."

Clay thought about what Jack said and had to admit it was true.

"You looked real good, Clay," Lyle said, leading his horse up.

"He's a good horse. You got yourself a winner there," Clay said.

"He did turn it on, didn't he?"

"Would you consider letting us keep him for about a week?" Jack asked.

"Sure," Lyle answered. "If you don't mind me bringing some prospective buyers out to watch him buck."

"I don't mind. Just let me know when they're coming so we can show them something."

"I've got Gary Holland coming tomorrow afternoon. Will that work?"

Jack rubbed his chin in thought. "I don't know if Clay'll be up to it by then. He's kinda down right now."

"Who says I won't be ready?" Clay asked defiantly.

Jack and Lyle laughed at his expected outburst.

"I'll call you tomorrow morning and let you know what time he'll be here."

Tamara stood beside Clay, listening to the exchange among the three men. "I thought you did real good," she said as they started toward the house.

"Thanks," he replied. "I thought I was going to stay with him, but he pulled a twist and jerked my hand out of the rigging."

"I'll bet that won't happen again," she said with a sigh, then added, "I guess I better get on the road or Dad will have the posse out looking for me."

"I wish you didn't have to leave."

"Me too."

"I won't see you again until the Weatherford rodeo, but I'll call you."

"You better," she said. "If you don't, I'll start looking for a doctor or lawyer to hang around with."

He pulled her to him, smiling as he looked into her eyes. "No you won't. You couldn't handle the boring life with someone like that. You've had a taste of life with Clay Tory and nothing less will ever be enough."

She was laughing with delight when he kissed her. "You've got an awful high opinion of yourself, Mr. Tory."

Light danced in his eyes as he held her. "Are you saying I'm wrong, Miss Allen?"

Kissing him full on the lips, she then stepped back. "I don't know. We'll have to see, won't we?" She smiled and opened the pickup door.

"Call me when you get home," he said.

"I will. You take care of yourself or I'll sic Julie on you."

Clay laughed. "You don't have to do that. She'll be bad enough as it is."

"I know it, and I gave her my permission to do whatever is necessary to keep you in line and healthy."

Clay groaned. "That's all I need. Two women ganging up on me."

"I think that's just what you need." Tamara smiled. "Maybe between the two of us we can straighten you out and keep you in line."

"Maybe," Clay responded with a grin. "At least it'll be fun finding out."

Tamara grinned and kissed him one more time. "I'll see you in Weatherford. You take care."

He watched her drive away. A feeling of loneliness crept over him as her pickup dwindled in the distance.

Chapter Fourteen

Tom Larrs leaned back and closed his eyes. He was sitting in his office on the top floor of the eighteen-story office building he'd bought four years earlier. The office space he occupied was larger than many of the homes he could see outside his picture window overlooking Los Angeles. He had just gotten off the phone with Hank Tallridge. Hank had been agitated to the point of yelling. They had both been following the PRCA standings and had noticed the sudden shift in leaders. That in itself hadn't bothered either of them, but the reports they'd received from Richard Pursley sure had.

Richard Pursley was the man Hank and Tom had hired to keep tabs on the day-to-day results. He had sent them his report three days prior. For the most part there was nothing surprising until they came to the paragraph listing injuries for each rider. There were a number of injuries that were very suspicious, including Clay Tory's. There were several minor ones, and one or two that would debilitate a competitor for a week or more. But what was most disconcerting was the people it was happening to. Most of the injuries occured to riders who were ranked in the top fifteen. Tom began checking the list against each of the lists held by the fifteen players, but could detect nothing that would point to one single player manipulating the odds. He was still trying to find the link when Hank's call came in. He had tried to assure him that it was just coincidence and there was no use getting alarmed, but Hank had the same intuition that Tom himself had. Someone was trying to hedge his bet, and this could be just the beginning of a run of misfortunes.

He had managed to calm Hank down by telling him he would look into it. He pushed the button on his intercom, and when his secretary answered, he asked her to get Collin Dobson on the phone. Collin was a private investigator he'd used on numerous occasions, mostly to check out people he was doing business with. Collin had always performed admirably and was discreet with the information he uncovered. Drumming his fingers on the desk, he waited for the phone to ring. When it did, he grabbed it after the first ring. "Collin?"

"Yes, Mr. Larrs?"

"How would you like to work for me for a few weeks?"

"Same arrangement?"

"Two hundred a day plus expenses," Tom agreed. "Plus a bonus if you uncover some vital information."

"What kind of information?"

"Why don't you meet me at the Towers Lounge at nine tonight and I'll fill you in on all the details."

"I'll be there!" The phone went dead in Tom's

hand. He placed it back in its cradle and leaned back
with a weary sigh. He prayed it was only a coincidence. If not, he had to find out who was behind it
and stop them as quickly and quietly as possible before it became public knowledge and the gaming
commission found out. Pushing the intercom button
again, he waited for his secretary to answer. "Ginger,
call Mrs. Larrs and tell her I'll be late tonight."

"Yes, sir, Mr. Larrs," came the crisp reply. He
leaned back in his chair once more, closing his eyes
and sighing again.

Clay tried Red Dog three times in the next two
days. He was thrown the first time after seven seconds. Jack pointed out some things Clay was doing
wrong, like overcompensating by leaning too far to
the right, and letting his left elbow move up during
the ride. He explained to him how to correct them,
and the next two times, Clay rode the horse the full
eight seconds. Both rides would have placed in any
rodeo, and he knew he was back in the game.

The next day, using the bucking barrel, Jack started
working Clay on saddle broncs. Using a buck rein
was a little harder, since Clay had to be able to let
out and take in slack using his left hand. After three
days he was almost as good with his left as he had
been with his right, and they started on the practice
horses. By the end of the week he was ready to step
up to tougher horses. Once again they called Lyle
Jones, who showed up with two horses. One was a
big black horse with a white star on his forehead,
called Samson for his size, weighing in at a little over

sixteen-hundred pounds. Samson was an old-timer of fifteen, having been a pro bucking horse for eight of those years. Lyle had bought him and a paint at a bucking horse sale in Oklahoma City three weeks before. The paint, named Tie Whiskey, was smaller than Samson, but according to Lyle, had just as good a reputation as the black horse.

Clay tried Samson first and rode him the required eight seconds. After resting for a few minutes, he saddled the black-and-white paint horse. He managed to ride for four seconds before being dumped unceremoniously by a quick jump to the left and another quick move to the right.

Jack walked out to where Clay lay, unhurt but his pride damaged. "You let him sucker you. You thought he was going to go left and then buck straight. You never saw his head move back to the right, did you?"

Clay shook his head. "I sure didn't."

"You're concentrating so much on using your left hand that you're forgetting the basic rules of bronc riding. Quit thinking about your hand and ride like you know how."

Tie Whiskey was run back into the chute and Clay remounted. This time he rode him a picture-perfect ride, a smile on his face as he slid to the ground.

"Good ride, kid!" Lyle exclaimed as he let him down.

"You were right," Clay said to Jack. "I didn't think about my hand, but just rode him. It was great!"

"Think you're ready for Weatherford?" Jack asked.

"I'm ready!" Clay responded. "I need to start practicin' for bulls."

Jack screwed up his face in distaste. "I was afraid you were going to say that. Why don't you wait a few weeks? See how you do in the barebacks and saddle broncs, then you can ease into the bulls."

Clay knew how Jack felt about him riding bulls—nothing would make him happier than to know Clay wasn't going to ride them again. But Clay just couldn't do that. He loved riding the great beasts, and he made more money riding them. "I'll make you a deal. I'll see how I do in Weatherford. If I can handle the barebacks and saddle broncs, I'll start training next week on bulls."

Jack gave a sigh of resignation. "I guess I'll have to settle for that, but I still can't see why anyone would want to climb on one of those animals."

Clay grinned. "Because the girls like bull riders!"

Jack gave him a disparaging look. "That's because they know they're stupid and can outsmart 'em."

"You're just jealous, Jack." Clay chuckled. "The reason the girls like bull riders is because we got skill and balance, as well as intestinal fortitude. Just because you never had the girls chasing after you, don't mean you got to get down on us."

"Hmmph," Jack exploded. "Intestinal fortitude, my fanny! It don't take guts to climb on a bull. Just lack of brains, and the more I hear you talk, the more convinced of that I become."

Clay laughed and put his arm around Jack's shoulder. "Why don't we clean up and go into Roswell. Since Julie and Terry are going in to see her mother and all we got to eat is leftovers, I'll buy you and Lyle lunch."

"I'll go for that," Lyle yelled.

"On one condition, though: You have to let me borrow your horses one more day," Clay said.

"What a man has to do to get a free lunch." Lyle grinned.

"That's the way it is with this younger generation," Jack said, walking over to Lyle. "They think a man can be bought for little or nothing. If I was you, I'd tell him to forget it."

Lyle looked at Jack and shook his head. "Nah, I don't want to haul these horses back today, anyway. Besides, this'll probably be the only free meal I'll get out of him, so I'm going to take advantage of it."

"Well you two old-timers better hurry up or I'm going to change my mind and go by myself."

Jack and Lyle looked at each other and grinned. "It was a sorry day when Ben talked me into taking that young whelp," Jack said dryly.

"I know what you mean," Lyle responded good-naturedly. "But we all have our crosses to bear."

Clay took them to the Cattleman's Cafe for lunch, enjoying the company of the two older men. Lyle left after eating, saying he had to get back to the ranch and get some work done. Getting in the pickup, Clay told Jack, "We need horse feed. Want to get some while we're in town?"

"We might as well. Save us from having to come back in tomorrow."

"How about dropping me downtown while you go get the feed? I need to do something."

"What's that?" Jack asked, his curiosity aroused.

"It's a surprise," Clay stated.

"Oh, what kind of surprise?"

"The kind that won't be a surprise if I tell you. Drop me by the First National Bank, and pick me up after you've bought the feed."

Jack pulled over to the curb and let him out. Clay didn't move until he saw Jack turn the corner on his way to the feed store, then he crossed the street and walked halfway down the block and entered a store. An hour later he emerged with a case in his hand. Looking down the street, he saw Jack parked half a block away. Walking to the pickup, he climbed in on the passenger side.

Jack had been leaning back against the seat dozing, but sat upright when Clay opened the door. "What's in the case?" he asked.

"Our new cell phone," Clay said, opening the case and proudly showing him his purchase.

Jack gave him a stunned look. "A cell phone? What do we need with one of those?"

"So we can make calls while we're on the road. I can enter rodeos. You can call Terry and find out about things on the ranch, and if we get stranded, we can call for help. These things are handy to have."

"How much did you pay for it?" Jack asked, eyeing the contraption suspiciously.

"I only had to pay eighty-two dollars for this particular model. It's the kind that you can use an external antenna with while you're in the truck and then carry it with you and use its own antenna. I get three hundred minutes a month for ninety dollars."

Jack rolled his eyes. "Are you sure we needed this?"

"Jack, this is the nineties. Everybody has a cell phone these days. Tamara even has one in her truck."

Jack's face broke into a smile. "Ah, it all becomes clear now."

Clay turned red. "That's not the reason I bought it. We need to be able to stay in touch."

"Don't you have to have a credit history to get one of those things?"

Smiling, Clay shook his head. "I used to date the manager of the store. She called Mark Chandler at the bank. He gave me a good reference and she gave me the phone."

"I bet Mark gave you a good reference. Last I remember, your bank account was nearing six figures."

"It's a little over that now, since I deposited my last winnings."

"Well I guess we're part of the electronic age now." Jack sighed. "I'm not sure I ever wanted to be, but at least you can talk to Tamara while we're traveling."

Clay blushed again, but said nothing.

The next few days were busy ones for both Jack and Clay. They were up early in the morning, Clay doing his exercises while Jack went over the ranch accounts and planned what needed to be done. They spent most of the morning riding out and checking the cattle. Afternoons were spent practicing both bareback and saddle bronc. In the evening, Clay did

his therapy routine on his right hand while Jack and
Terry discussed ranch details.

Jack called a day of rest for Clay on Thursday. "I
want you to take the day off and get rested up. We
leave for Weatherford in the morning."

"But we got things that need to be done before we
leave," Clay argued.

"Terry and I'll take care of 'em. You take it easy.
Call Tamara on your cell phone and find out where
we're going to meet."

"I've already called. We're meeting her in Abilene
at Kerry Tyler's house. She's bringing her two-horse
trailer so we can pull it with our truck. She's riding
the rest of the way with us."

"I still want you to rest. Go to town and visit your
mother or something."

"Yes, sir," Clay agreed reluctantly.

Clay hung around the house most of the morning,
until Julie, finally driven crazy by his constant wandering in and out of the kitchen, chased him out with
a broom. Finally, he took the pickup and drove into
town. He went by and saw his mother at work, catching her up on his life, but his mind kept wandering
during their conversation.

"Clay, you're nervous about the rodeo, aren't
you?" she asked after repeating herself for the third
time.

He gave her a blank look. "I guess I am. I've been
practicing for two weeks now and I've done pretty
good, but I still wonder if I'm good enough with my
left hand."

Lorraine Tory took her son's hand in hers. "Clay, it doesn't matter whether you're good enough or not. What matters is that you do the best you can. If you do that, you come out a winner either way."

Clay sat across the desk from her. Saying nothing as he thought about what she'd said, a smile came slowly to his face. "You're right; that's all I got to do. I can't do any more and worrying about it won't help. Thanks, Mom. You've been more help than you'll ever know."

"I hear that's what moms are for," she said, smiling at her son. "I know I wasn't a very good mother for a long time, but I want you to know I'm very proud of you and I plan on being there for you any time you need me."

Clay leaned across the desk and kissed her cheek. "I'll see you when I get back."

"Bring me a souvenir," she said, laughing.

"I'll do that," he stated, smiling as he left.

Jack and Clay left before daylight the next day. Julie insisted on cooking them breakfast before they left, though both Clay and Jack told her she didn't have to.

"I know you two; you won't eat another decent meal until you get back here. I'm cooking you breakfast and I won't take no for an answer."

Clay had driven Jack crazy the night before, checking and rechecking his clothes, his gear, the road maps, and cleaning out the camper, though Julie had already cleaned it earlier that day. Jack was sitting in the living room trying to read the paper while

Clay made several more trips out to the pickup. Finally, with an angry sigh he put down the paper. "Clay, settle down! You're acting like this is the first rodeo you've ever been to. Why don't you read a book or watch a movie on television?"

"I've just got to finish straightening out the camper and I'll be through," Clay said, hurrying out the door.

Jack shook his head, then picked up the paper and tried to read, only to have Clay come charging through the house again on his way to his bedroom.

The next day, Jack drove for the first part of the trip while Clay worked on his hand exercises. With each day, his right hand was becoming stronger and he was gaining more mobility. "If my hand keeps improving," he said, squeezing the power grips with all the effort he could muster, "I should be able to start riding with it in another month."

Jack applauded Clay's tenacity. But he knew it took more than determination to fix damaged nerves and bones. He prayed the young man wouldn't be disappointed.

Tamara was waiting for them in Abilene. She came running from the house, followed closely by Kerry Tyler, as Clay and Jack drove up. She gave Jack a bright smile and a hug hello before turning to kiss Clay. "I missed you so much! What took you so long getting here?"

"She's been about to drive me crazy. I swear she's looked at her watch every two minutes asking where you two were," Kerry said, giving Jack and Clay a hug.

"I let Jack drive part of the way and he wouldn't

get over sixty miles an hour," Clay groaned. "I finally had to quit my exercises and drive, or it would have been dark before we got here."

"Hmmph! I had to keep cautioning him to keep it under ninety. I just knew we were going to get stopped by the highway patrol and thrown in jail," Jack retorted.

"I'm just glad you're both here," Tamara stated. "Now we better get going; we've got another three hours to go."

Jack chuckled at her impatience. "You're right. If we hurry, we can get there by five o'clock."

They hooked up Tamara's trailer and loaded Charger in the back. Tamara rode up front with Clay, and Jack climbed in the back seat, stretching out and closing his eyes. "Keep it under eighty. We've got plenty of time and I want to get there alive and in one piece."

"Yes, sir," they chimed in unison.

Chapter Fifteen

Weatherford lay about forty miles west of Fort Worth. They passed the city limits a little after five o'clock, to an "I told you so" from the backseat.

Clay found the rodeo grounds and parked the pickup and trailer as close to the chutes as he could. Tamara saddled Charger and worked him in the arena while Clay and Jack looked over the stock. Clay had drawn Jawbreaker in the barebacks, a white-and-red paint horse. His draw in the saddle broncs was Tornado, a large brown horse with long shaggy hair. Clay had drawn him once before in Shreveport, Louisiana, and placed fifth on him.

Leaning on the fence looking out over the stock, Clay couldn't help but look at the bulls. They were standing quietly, some chewing their cud, acting unconcerned, as if they didn't have to perform later that evening. He was overwhelmed by his desire to ride any one of the beasts in the pen. Turning his back on the animals, he spotted Ronnie Ingram and Billy Ettinger leaning against the fence, who greeted Clay as he started toward them. "Hey, Clay. How ya doin'?" Billy asked.

Clay shook hands with them both, and noticed Billy's look at his injured hand as he did. "I'm fine!" he answered.

"I heard you got beaten pretty bad. Did they ever find out who did it?"

"Nope, but I sure hope to."

"How's the hand doin'?" Ronnie asked.

"It's comin' along," he said, flexing it.

"Are you riding tonight, or did you come to watch?" Billy asked, grinning as he did.

"I just came to watch!" Clay said sarcastically. "I couldn't stand being away from you."

"How are you going to ride with your hand in that condition?"

"He's going to glue himself on," Billy injected. "He's had a lot of experience doing that."

Clay pretended to be hurt. Using glue on a saddle was an old trick used by cowboys who tried to cheat by any means they could. "Only if I can borrow your glue, Billy."

"I used the last of it to win the saddle bronc riding in St. Louis last week."

"Yeah, I heard you won. Must not have been any competition there!"

Billy laughed. "Doesn't look like they hurt your sense of humor any."

Clay smiled. "I have to have a sense of humor. I live with Jack here," he said, motioning to Jack who was leaning against the fence nearby.

"I just wish I could put that sense of humor to some good use. Like getting some work out of him," Jack quipped.

Ronnie slapped Clay on the back. "It sounds like

you're outnumbered here. Why don't we mosey on over to the concession stand and get something to drink."

"That sounds like a good idea. Listening to all this drivel has given me a powerful thirst."

"Make sure you get a straw to drink it with," Billy quipped. "You're not old enough to start drinking from a cup yet."

Clay and Ronnie walked away smiling. Jack and Billy grinned at each other, then followed behind. As they walked around the edge of the arena, Billy spoke softly to Jack. "There's been four more so-called 'accidents' that have caused cowboys to miss rodeos."

"Anybody hurt?"

"C. J. Bell got roughed up a little, but other than that it's been mostly stolen batteries or slashed tires."

"Has the association done anything?" Jack asked, meaning the PRCA.

"They're looking into it, but so far there's nothing concrete for them to look into. They are publishing warnings, and giving tips on how to safeguard against possible attacks."

"Lot of good that'll do," Jack stated with anger.

"There's not much else they can do," Billy said in defense.

"They can hire security guards or detectives or whatever they need to do to stop these people."

"Jack, you know as well as I do they couldn't hire enough security to cover all the rodeos that are going on every weekend."

Jack gave a weary sigh. "I know, but it's frightening to think what could happen if these people aren't stopped."

Clay's nervousness increased as it drew closer to rodeo time. He was standing on the platform behind the chutes with his chaps and spurs on long before the grand entry began. Jack stayed close beside him, trying to keep him calm. He could never remember Clay getting this anxious before a ride. Even when Jack had first started going to rodeos with him, he had marveled at Clay's cool attitude.

Jawbreaker was run into chute number six. Clay and Jack cinched the bareback rigging down tight while the chute men strapped on the flank cinch.

They watched the first five bareback riders buck out. A seventy-six was the top score when Clay nodded for the gate and Jawbreaker exploded into the open.

Going straight down the arena, Jawbreaker bucked hard, neither ducking nor weaving. Clay marked him out perfectly, leaning back against his arm and spurring high. When the eight-second whistle blew, Clay was still spurring in classic style. He scored a seventy-eight, which held first place until the next-to-last bronc rider, when he got bumped to second by Lon Billing's score of eighty-one.

Billy Ettinger helped Clay climb back over the chutes. "Looks like that glue helped."

Grinning in response, Clay said, "Yeah, but getting the hair off the seat of my pants is almost impossible."

"It looks like you might win enough to buy you

a new pair anyway," Billy responded. "You really surprised me, junior!"

"How's that?"

"You ride almost as good left-handed as you do right-handed. Not that you're that good with either one."

"Thanks . . . I think."

"I can't wait to see how you do in the saddle broncs."

"I can only hope to beat you," Clay said with conviction.

"We've both drawn good horses. It ought to be interesting."

"You got Trojan, didn't you?" Clay asked.

"Yep, and you drew Tornado. I had him in Casper a couple of weeks ago and won a second. I figure that's the best you'll do tonight."

"Hmm, you might be right," Clay agreed. "Joe Tremmel is looking good lately. He might be hard to beat since he's drawn Gusher."

Billy laughed and stood up. "I got to go see my wife for a few minutes."

"How is Diane?" Clay asked. "I can't believe she hasn't left you for someone younger and better looking."

"She's fine. I don't know what I'd do without her. How are you and Tamara getting along?"

"Great," Clay responded. "As a matter of fact she's waiting for me now."

"Looks like we both better get going. I'll see you in a little while."

Tamara was waiting for him by the pickup. Jack

had gone in search of a snack and was then going to find a seat in the grandstands. "Looks like Clay Tory's back on the circuit," she said as he threw his gear bag in the camper.

"It still doesn't feel as natural as it used to, but it feels good to be back," he commented.

"Well I'm glad to have you back traveling with me. It wasn't the same without you. All those other guys I went with weren't nearly as much fun."

Clay gave her a sideways glance as they walked arm in arm. "Those other guys, huh?"

"Oh, just one or two. I wasn't sure you were going to make it back so I had to look at my options," she said with a smirk.

"Well it's a good thing for you I did come back," Clay said sincerely.

Tamara pulled away and looked at him. "And why is that?" she asked curiously.

"It saved you from wasting your time on someone who would just end up being a disappointment to you."

Laughing, Tamara moved in close beside him. "And you promise you won't ever be a disappointment?"

Looking into her eyes, he spoke earnestly, "I promise to do my best!"

Smiling, she spoke softly. "That's all I ask."

They sat with Jack through most of the steer wrestling, then Clay left to get his gear while Jack headed off to the bucking chutes.

As Clay opened the gate that lead into the area

behind the chutes, he stopped and looked at the buzz
of activity inside the confined area. He watched cowboys putting resin on their saddles, and those working their stirrup leathers on the ground to make
sure they were adjusted properly. Others were performing different types of stretching exercises before they rode. He stood there taking it all in, the
smell of horses like the welcome fragrance of honey-
suckle to his nostrils. He was glad to be here among
the elite group of men who pitted their riding skills
against the toughest animals alive, as well as each
other.

Throwing his saddle on the platform for Jack to
take, Clay strapped on his chaps and buckled on his
spurs, then went through his normal warm up routine of twenty leg stretches and twenty push-ups
away from the fence. Taking his glove from the gear
bag, he worked his hand into it, pulling it tight, then
wrapping the leather thong around his wrist and
tying it tight. Stepping up on the platform, he walked
over to chute number four. Jack was making the final
pull on the latigo and wrapping the end through the
D ring.

"Check that and make sure it's tight enough for
you," Jack said.

Clay forced his fingers between the horse and
cinch, satisfied with the job Jack had done. "It's perfect. Tornado's standing quiet tonight. He usually
pitches a fit in the chute."

"I think he knows who's drawn him and he's
given up already."

"I hope not," Clay responded. "I wouldn't want him to lay down as soon as the gate's open."

The saddle bronc competition started out tough from the beginning. Joel Greene, the first rider out, scored a seventy-six. Lyonel Thomas next scored a seventy-eight, and Billy Ettinger scored an eighty-two.

Clay took his seat on Tornado and called for the gate.

Tornado bolted from the chute, ran two lengths, then ducked his head, bunching himself and springing skyward. Clay pulled hard on the rein and raked the horse with his spurs. When Tornado touched down, he lunged forward in a high arc and landed stiff-legged, then bunched again, this time twisting himself to the right in midair.

To Clay, riding with his left hand felt strange and somewhat akward, since he was working a different side of his body than he was used to, and it required him to use his right arm to balance himself. His right hand throbbed from the tension, but he blocked it from his mind and enjoyed the exhilaration of the ride.

Tornado lifted his head slightly and jumped to the left, then lunged forward, using all the power in his back legs.

Clay stayed in the middle, using his spurs in time with each buck, giving to the rein when Tornado's front feet hit the ground and pulling hard when the horse lunged forward.

The eight-second whistle was music to Clay's ears. He grabbed the rein with both hands, gripping as tightly as he could with his right, and waited for the pick-up men to come along side.

Clay's score was an eighty-one, not good enough to take the lead, but more than good enough to make him grin as he climbed over the chutes to be greeted by Jack's smile and Billy's good-natured kidding. "Hey, Junior, I told you second was the best you'd do tonight."

"Just because you're kin to the judges and they can't tell the difference between a good ride and an old man's ride."

Billy laughed. "All kidding aside, that was a great ride for someone who had to switch hands."

"Thanks," Clay responded. "It still feels a little strange. I keep wanting to change hands in the middle of the ride."

"I don't blame you. I broke two fingers on my right hand once. I thought I was going to have to switch hands, but I managed to work it out."

"If it ever happens that you need to change," Jack imposed, "you come see me. I've got the best training program going for that sort of thing."

Clay laughed. "Especially if you like to move hay."

Billy looked from one to the other. "I think I better stay healthy."

"Good idea," Clay said, smiling at Jack.

Billy's and Clay's scores held through the remaining bronc rides, leaving them holding first and second, respectively.

Clay left Jack and Billy behind the chutes while he went to find Tamara before she ran barrels. She was standing outside the gate, mounted on Charger.

"Good bronc ride," she said as Clay came to stand beside her.

"I'm glad you liked it. I hope to have many repeat performances."

"And I hope to be there to see every one of them."

"It's a date then. As long as I can be there to see you run the barrels," Clay remarked. "There's something about watching you ride into the arena that makes my heart beat faster."

Tamara giggled nervously. "You got a deal, Mr. Tory. And it's almost my turn, so get ready to watch."

"My eyes will be glued to you at all times," he promised.

"Just make sure they're glued to all of me and not just one particular area."

Clay grinned slyly, but refrained from further comment.

When it was Tamara's turn, she thundered into the arena at a dead run, guiding Charger around each barrel with exact precision. Horse and rider worked together like a well-oiled machine. She crossed the electronic timer, stopping the clock at 16.3 seconds, the fastest time of the night.

Bringing Charger under control, Tamara wore a pleased smile. She patted the big horse's neck and talked to him in a soothing voice, trying to calm him down. Charger pranced around, knowing he had performed well.

"You looked real good out there," Clay said, catching hold of Charger's bridle.

"Thanks," Tamara responded, enjoying the compliment.

"Oh, not you," Clay teased. "I was talking to Charger. After all, he's the one that did all the work."

"Oh, is that right?" Tamara asked. "And just who do you think was cueing him to make him do all that work?"

Clay pondered the question for a moment. He and Tamara had only been together for a few weeks, but his feelings for her were so strong that he thought it was time to take their relationship to the next level. "I guess maybe you deserve some of the praise as well. Tell you what, I'll buy you both a carrot, how's that?"

"I'm sure Charger will like it but I've got to tell you, I'm not much of a carrot eater."

Holding his breath, he said, "The kind of carrot I was talking about dangling in front of you, you wouldn't want to eat!"

"And what kind would that be?" Tamara asked curiously.

"Oh, I was thinking about a ring."

Tamara sat on Charger's back totally stunned. Even Charger had stopped his dancing around as if he too were shocked. Tamara finally found her voice. "You aren't talking about an engagement ring, are you?"

"Well, I thought it might be a pre-engagement ring, if there is such a thing."

"A pre-engagement ring," Tamara said, letting the sound of it roll off her tongue. "I like the sound of that. And just think, when we get engaged for real, you can buy me another ring."

"Uh, maybe we ought to skip the pre-engagement and go straight to the engagement," Clay said, feeling his face grow warm.

Tamara appeared to consider his suggestion. "Oh, I don't think that would be appropriate. No, I think we better stay with the pre-engagement and then move to the engagement after we're sure we're compatible."

The shocked expression on Clay's face almost made her laugh out loud.

"I . . . I . . . don't you think we're compatible enough now?" Clay stuttered.

Tamara stepped off Charger's back. "Is that a marriage proposal, Mr. Tory?"

"Uh," Clay stammered. "I . . . uh . . . I think so. I didn't plan on it being quite like this, but I guess that's what it is."

Smiling brightly, Tamara leaned close to him and in her sexiest voice, whispered in his ear, "Clay, darling, I love you with all my heart and I would be delighted to marry you." Stepping back, she looked at his stricken face and almost burst out laughing. Bringing her emotions under control, she said, "But let's not be in a big hurry."

The relief on Clay's face was comical and almost caused Tamara to lose her barely contained composure. "Sure, Tamara. Whatever you want. I think a long engagement is a good idea."

Unable to maintain a straight face any longer, Tamara burst into laughter. "Relax, Clay. Surely you didn't think I was going to rush you into marriage."

"For a moment, I was sure I could hear the wedding bells already ringing." He grinned.

They both laughed, causing Charger to prance at the end of his reins.

Chapter Sixteen

Collin Dobson, the investigator hired by Tom Larrs, shifted in the seat of his rented 1998 Cadillac one more time. In his fifteen years as a private investigator, he couldn't remember another time when he'd logged as many miles for a client as he had since he'd started this investigation. Running down leads on each of the instances Tom had told him about had required him to travel to six different states in two weeks. Glancing at the notebook beside him, he let out a weary sigh. He still didn't have much to go on, but the pattern he was seeing definitely proved something was fishy. He was presently on the H. E. Bailey Turnpike between Oklahoma City and Lawton, heading to Witchita Falls to follow up on another lead he'd uncovered. So far he had eliminated twelve of the fifteen people on the list Tom had given him.

There were several things that bothered Collin about this case. One was the fact that only one cowboy had been seriously injured. The others suffered minor injuries compared to what had happened to Clay Tory. Another was that there was a distinct lack of witnesses, which in itself pointed to professionals, and that meant they were well financed. But what bothered him most was the fact that someone else seemed to be investigating these occurrences as well. The last four people he had talked to had already talked to someone else. He had the person's name, a Devin Price, but it wasn't someone he was familiar with. He'd gotten a description of a man about five foot eleven, clean shaven, and neat in appearance. He wore expensive suits and offered rewards for any information leading to the arrest of the responsible parties. Collin wrote this in his notebook with the intention of telling Tom Larrs about it tonight when he called.

He was looking forward to his interview in Witchita Falls. It would be the last one on his list. If he could find the person he was looking for early enough, he could catch a flight to Albuquerque, New Mexico, tonight and be in Santa Fe tomorrow afternoon. He had a strong suspicion Clay Tory was his best possible lead. After the tire-cutting incident in Colorado Springs and the assault in Santa Fe, it looked as if someone was especially targeting him. Knowing the police had no leads in the case didn't dissuade Collin at all. Many times in the past he'd been able to uncover vital information that the police had failed to find. Plugging a tape into the cassette player, he let his mind go to work on the people he needed to interview and the questions he wanted answers to.

At the same time Collin was entering the outskirts of Witchita Falls, Devin Price was in Santa Fe, talking with detective Romano of the Santa Fe Police Department. Romano was not eager to share information with this stranger in an expensive suit and a totally businesslike manner.

"What exactly is your interest in the Tory assault?" Romano asked, looking suspiciously at the man across from him.

"As I explained to you, my client is very interested in finding out who is responsible for these attacks. Clay Tory is not the only victim to date, though he has been the worst case reported."

"There have been other attacks?" Romano asked. "No one mentioned this during my investigation."

"At the time, there wasn't a definite link between what happened to Tory and the other contestants. Now we feel they are all related."

"And do you have any idea who is responsible?" Romano asked.

"That's why I'm here," Devin stated, impatience creeping into his voice. "As I told you twice before, I am trying to find out who is responsible. Have you uncovered anything else since the incident occurred?"

"Nothing of importance," Romano told him.

"May I see what you have?"

Romano looked warily at Price, not liking his tone of voice. After all, if Price was asking him for his help, he should try being a little nicer. "I'm not supposed to show this file to anyone," he said, patting a folder lying on his desk.

"If you'll show me what's in that file, I'll tell you what I know."

"Maybe you should tell me what you know and then I'll decide if it's worth showing you the file."

Devin Price sighed. "I know that there's big money involved. There's a good chance it's tied to a gambling syndicate, but as of yet I haven't been able to put names to the syndicate." He had, in fact, found three of the names through his various contacts, but he didn't want to reveal these facts to Romano.

"Is that all?" Romano asked, raising his eyebrows.

"That's all you get until I see the file."

Romano gave him another wary look. Picking up the folder, he held it for a moment, tapping the corner against the desk. "How do I know you have any more information?"

"The same way I know there's something worth seeing in that file," Price stated dryly.

Romano gave him a distrustful look, but finally relented and handed him the file.

Price opened the cover and scanned the contents quickly before handing the folder back to Romano. "You haven't got much, do you?"

"It don't matter what I got. You owe me for the privilege of looking at it."

Devin smiled thinly. "You're right, Detective. I do owe you information. There have been eighteen different possible assaults and vandalism associated with this case."

Romano waited, expecting more, and when Price remained silent, he slammed the file down on the desk. "This is bull! I trusted you."

"No you didn't," Price said with a sneer. "You just hoped I knew more than I did. But look at it this way, Romano, there's nothing more you have to do on this case. I doubt seriously if the people responsible live here, or will ever be back."

"What makes you say that?"

"The attack had to do with keeping someone from riding, unfortunately for a long period of time. Now that that's done, there's no reason for them to hang around. They're long gone, and it's my job to find them. Since you were kind enough to let me see the file, I'll send you a letter telling you how it all turns out." He smiled, turning on his heel and walking out, leaving Romano standing with his mouth open.

It was no wonder that when Collin Dobson showed up the next afternoon at Romano's office, he received less than a warm welcome. Only his shared anger at Devin Price helped him gain Romano's confidence.

For his own part, Devin Price spent his remaining time in Santa Fe talking to the motel attendants, the emergency room doctor, and the nurses who cared for Clay. The only real piece of evidence he had obtained was the opinion that the attack on Clay was done by amateurs and not professionals, which in itself was puzzling.

Collin Dobson came to the same conclusion as he lay on the bed in his motel room that night compiling the information he'd gathered on his journey. Calling his office, he talked to his secretary, giving her a list of people to call, along with questions to ask. "I'll call you tomorrow at this time for the answers."

*   *   *

Devin Price waited for the plane to take off before sliding his credit card through the seat phone dialing a number somewhere in Texas. After giving his report, he made recommendations and smiled as the voice on the other end agreed. "Yes, I do think Clay Tory is a key link to who's responsible. Someone had him taken out of action. If he can identify who did it, they can lead us to the person behind it all. Yes, sir, I'll make the necessary arrangements. I'll call you when I have more."

At the Dallas/Fort Worth airport, Price quickly found his luggage and walked to a limousine waiting for him at the curb.

"Where to, Mr. Price?" the driver asked.

"To the office, Raymond."

"Yes, sir."

Though the hour was late when he arrived at his office, Price made two phone calls, giving instructions to two of his field men. "I want reports daily," he said to each of them. Finishing several of his own reports, he left the plush office he occupied in downtown Dallas. He rode the elevator to the parking garage where the limo and driver were waiting. "Let's go home, Raymond."

"Yes, sir. You did remember Timothy's birthday, didn't you, sir?"

"Yes, I did. Thank you for asking. Is the party still at eight?"

"Yes, sir."

"Good," he said, looking at his watch. "I have time to shower and shave before the house is overrun with screaming eight-year-olds."

Raymond smiled into the rearview mirror. "Sounds like fun, sir."

Devin Price smiled back. "It is, Raymond. It is!"

Weatherford was the only rodeo Clay and Tamara made over the weekend. They had wanted to make more, but Jack had balked, insisting Clay take it easy and not overdo it.

"Let's see how you do with one rodeo this weekend. If you do all right, then we'll try more next weekend."

By the time they got back to Abilene, Clay was glad Jack had won the battle. He was tired and sore, both from the rides he'd made and from the traveling. They left Tamara in Abilene the next morning and drove back to Roswell. As they crossed the Texas/New Mexico border, dark clouds crowded the skies overhead. By the time they reached Hobbs, it was starting to sprinkle, and thirty minutes later they were in the midst of a deluge. Jack smiled and sang to the beat of the windshield wipers as they drove the last few miles to the ranch, watching the thirsty range soak up the water.

July is considered Cowboy Christmas, because there are so many rodeos during the month. It's easy for a cowboy to make three to four rodeos a week if he can get drawn in right. Everyone trying to make it to the finals was looking forward to July's arrival, Clay included. He and Tamara had already planned the rodeos they wanted to make and Jack had given his stamp of approval.

Clay was presently sitting at the kitchen table looking at the *Pro Rodeo Sports News* when Jack walked in. "We've got two weeks before the first rodeo in July," he said, looking up at Jack.

"And . . ." Jack promted.

"I was just thinking; the doctor says my hand is doing real good. I think I'm ready to start riding again with my right hand."

Jack gave him a skeptical look. "It's only been five weeks since your surgery. Don't you think you're pushing it?"

"You've seen me exercising it. My grip is strong and there's no pain. I really think I'm ready to try."

Jack thought about what Clay had said, then answered. "We'll go see Doctor Johnson the day after tomorrow. If he gives you the go-ahead, then we'll start practicing."

Clay nodded, though he didn't like the idea of having to get Doctor Johnson's approval. The old sawbones wasn't prone to hurry things, but he also knew it was useless to argue with Jack.

Clay spent the next two days performing all the exercises he could think of to strengthen his hand, including using a punching bag he'd set up in the barn. By the time they saw the doctor, Clay was so nervous, it was hard for him to perform the simple tests the doctor required without his hand shaking.

"Clay, what's wrong with you?" the doctor asked after trying for the third time to test Clay's grip.

"I guess I'm just nervous, Doc."

"About what? You're hand is coming along better than I ever expected."

Clay sighed. "I know. I've been working hard on my exercises and even invented some of my own."

"Then what are you fidgety about?"

Clay looked at the doctor, then turned his eyes to the floor. "Well, Doc, it's like this. July is the biggest rodeo month of the season, and if I'm going to make it to the finals, I've got to make a lot of shows and place in as many as possible. I've been doing all right with my left hand, but I'm not doing as well as I did with my right."

"And you want to start riding right-handed again. Is that it?"

Clay looked at the doctor and nodded.

"Well," Doctor Johnson said, rubbing his chin thoughtfully, "I don't see any reason you can't start using your hand again. All the tests, except the ones today, have shown exceptional healing. I think we can attribute that to your diligence in sticking to the therapy. I can't see any reason for you not to start back riding with it, except that I think you're crazy in the first place for wanting to. But that's your choice," he said, grinning.

"Will you be sure and tell Jack that it's all right for me to ride with my hand? He'll never believe me."

The doctor chuckled. "I'm not sure he'll believe me either. Now relax and let's finish these tests."

Jack indeed accepted the news with skepticism. "Are you sure his hand is healed enough to put that kind of strain on it?" he asked when the doctor called him into his office.

The doctor smiled and winked at Clay. "Yes, Jack, his hand is as strong as it was before it was broken;

maybe even stronger. I will admit it's been almost miraculous how fast the healing process has taken place, but that credit goes to Clay."

Clay smiled. "Part of the credit goes to Jack. He's been my inspiration and personal trainer. Without him, I wouldn't know how to move hay or walk across a piece of pipe."

The doctor looked questioningly at Jack. "Never mind," Jack said with a smile. "The boy's been bucked off on his head one too many times."

Clay talked excitedly all the way to the ranch. "I'm going to call Lyle as soon as we get home and see if he's got any good horses I can try. I figure if I can practice on three or four head to get my rhythm back, I'll easily be ready by July."

"You should be. Of course, you may have to move one or two barns of hay before you're really in shape."

Clay groaned. "I think I'll just continue to ride left-handed."

Jack chuckled. "Okay, maybe we can skip the hay moving, but I do want you to continue working on the weights and the balance bars."

"Right, Coach," Clay said with a grin, still elated about the prospect of riding with his right hand again. Picking up the cell phone, he dialed Tamara's number. Jack listened as he told her the good news. They were soon making plans for the upcoming rodeo and where they would meet. They had two rodeos in Texas the next weekend, one in Texarkana and the other in Nacogdoches. Jack and Clay would leave Thursday and meet Tamara in Abilene again.

They would all spend the night at Kerry Tyler's house and leave early Friday.

Clay started practicing on the horses he and Jack owned. At first, he felt awkward after riding left-handed for the past month and a half. Though he had worked hard to get his hand back in condition, the pressure of the bareback rigging made his fingers ache. He had to work hard to use his left hand for balance, and his first ride was anything but top-notch. It took two more rides before Clay felt things coming together, and after the fourth ride, with Jack yelling instructions, he felt as comfortable as he did before his hand was broken.

Lyle Jones brought two broncs Wednesday morning for Clay to try out. One was a steel-gray stocky horse with wild eyes. "I got him last week from a contractor in Oklahoma. He hasn't been bucked out for about six months, but he's supposed to be a tough one."

The other horse was a large bay with a head that looked too long for his body. "What glue factory did you save this one from?" Clay asked, giving the horse a doubtful look.

"I'll have you know this is one of the finest saddle bronc horses to ever come out of a chute."

"Oh, really?" Clay asked. "What's his name?"

"Brown Bomber," Lyle stated with pride.

"Brown Bomber?" Clay gasped. "Not the Brown Bomber that was bucking horse of the year in 1992?"

"The very same one. He's lost some of his edge, but he can still turn it on pretty good."

"I can't believe you got Brown Bomber! How'd you manage that?"

"He probably stole him," Jack interjected.

"I was the high bidder on a closed bid sale," Lyle stated indignantly. "I bought this horse for ten thousand dollars."

Jack looked appalled. "You spent ten thousand on that?" he asked, pointing at Brown Bomber.

Lyle smiled. "Yep, and I've already got an offer of fifteen thousand for him."

Jack and Clay exchanged shocked looks. "He must be some kind of bucking horse," Clay breathed.

"Why don't you put your saddle on him and find out?" Lyle challenged.

"Run him in the chute," Clay said, picking up his bronc saddle.

Jack waited until Lyle and Terry were out of earshot. "You think you're ready to try a horse this tough?"

"I'm as ready as I'll ever be," Clay said, flexing his fingers. "I plan on riding some this weekend that I hope are almost as tough." He climbed up on the chute as the bay horse was run in. He set his saddle in place and put on his bronc halter, measuring his rein before climbing aboard. With his feet in the stirrups, he eased them up over the horse's shoulders, pulled his hat down, and nodded to Jack.

Brown Bomber might have lost some of his spark, but he left the chute as if he'd been shot from a cannon. Clay buried his spurs into the horse's neck and squeezed hard with his thighs. Brown Bomber planted his front feet and kicked high with his back ones, leaving Clay almost perpendicular with the ground. He leaned back and pulled hard on the rein, holding himself tight against the swells of the saddle. When the big horse's back feet came back to earth, he flexed his haunches and pushed off, lunging upward and forward in a flying leap.

Clay spurred the points of the horse's shoulders, raking his sides and ending with his knees bent backward as his spurs touched the cantle of the saddle. Each time Brown Bomber hit the ground Clay felt like his spine was going to snap, and each time the horse lunged forward again, Clay's neck whipped back. Gripping the rein hard, he held himself tight against the swells and kept in time with each buck, twist, and lunge that the horse tried.

Though his hand ached from the exertion, Clay's grip was strong as he pulled on the braided buck rein and held himself in the saddle. As Brown Bomber bucked beneath him, Clay felt elated, knowing he was riding as well as he ever had. He was back in business and ready to compete.

Jack pushed the button on the stopwatch he was holding and waved to Lyle and Terry. Moving in beside Clay, they assisted him off the bucking horse. Lyle grinned at him as he helped him to the ground. "Old Bomber's still got some buck left in him, don't he?"

Clay grinned back at him, holding his back as he walked. "He's a rough old codger. I think I may have to have my spine realigned before I try the other one."

"Let me know when you're ready and I'll run the

other horse in for you. You got your bareback rigging ready?"

"It's at the chutes, resined and ready to go."

"I think you looked as good on that horse as you've ever looked," Jack said. "How's the hand?"

"A little sore, but it feels good," Clay responded, flexing his fingers to emphasis his point.

He rested for a few minutes while everyone talked about the ride and the horse. "Well let's see if this other horse can buck. This isn't Grand Slam is it?" Clay asked, referring to one of the toughest bareback horses on the circuit.

"No. His name is Gray Ghost."

"That sounds like a good name. I hope he floats like one," Clay said, rubbing his aching back.

This was going to be the real test of Clay's hand. Wedging it in the handle of the rigging put a tremendous amount of strain on it, even on the practice horses.

Clay climbed onto the horse's back and, steeling himself, nodded for the gate.

Gray Ghost stood in the chute for a brief moment, then turned slowly and walked out. It looked as if he might have forgotten how to buck. Clay kept his spurs positioned and his hand in the air. Gray Ghost looked around and suddenly seemed to remember what was expected of him. Flexing his legs, he lunged forward, suddenly turning into a bucking dynamo. His first few bucks were in a straight line, then he shifted positions in midair and went into a spin, turning two complete circles while bucking.

Coming out of the spin, the gray horse bucked the length of the arena, kicking high in the air.

Clay kept in time with each buck, working his spurs over the shoulders of the horse with each buck.

When Jack motioned for Lyle and Terry to move in, Clay was still riding with almost perfect form.

"Las Vegas, look out, here comes Clay Tory!" Jack yelled as Clay walked up to him.

Clay grinned bashfully. "Did it look as good as it felt?"

"You put all my worries to rest. You're riding as good as you ever did."

"I can't wait to get to Texarkana!" Clay said excitedly.

Jack chortled. "I thought you were going to say you couldn't wait to see Tamara." He paused for a breath. "I wonder how she'll feel when she finds out you're more interested in riding a bronc than seeing her?"

Clay blushed a deep crimson and started stammering, "Ah, you know what I meant! I *am* looking forward to seeing her. It's just that I'm anxious to compete riding right-handed again. I'm glad I was able to switch and at least keep riding, but I've never felt like I was riding my best, and I think it reflected in my scores."

"I'm sure Tamara will understand when I tell her," Jack said with an innocent look on his face.

Clay looked panic stricken for a moment until Jack's face broke into a grin. "Of course, if you promise to buy me a steak at the Cattlemen's tonight, I might just forget what you said."

"You like your steak medium rare?" Clay asked, relief showing plainly on his face.

Jack laughed. "Let's get these horses put away. I've got to go to the bank this afternoon."

"And I've got to pick up something I ordered last week," Clay stated. "Why don't we invite Lyle and Mary to eat with us? We've had several meals at their house and Lyle's helped provide several horses for me to ride."

"You're feeling extravagant today, aren't you?"

"I reckon it's because I feel so good," Clay said.

Chapter Seventeen

Sunrise Thursday morning found Jack and Clay on the road. Jack had insisted it was not necessary to leave quite so early, but Clay was persistent. Jack finally relented, stating he didn't want to stand in the way of Clay's love life, even if it meant losing some badly needed sleep. His one stipulation was that they had to stop in Midland and look at an irrigation system. He and Clay had talked about buying one to prevent what had happened this year. Things were a lot better around the ranch since the rains had come. There had been two more light rains in the last few weeks and the grass was growing again in all the pastures, which made Terry happy since he wouldn't have to haul hay to the cattle anymore until fall. The change in Jack had been remarkable. Before the rains started, his face looked worn and haggard to the point that Clay, Terry, and Julie had begun to worry about his health. But as soon as the rains began, he looked calmer and more relaxed. It seemed as if overnight he returned to his old self. After a few days of Jack's offhand comments, Clay remarked to Terry, "I think I liked him better when he was worried!"

They stopped in Midland and ate lunch, then drove to Dryland Irrigation Systems. The salesman showed them several units and explained the benefits of each and what the delivered cost would be. They took brochures with them so they could discuss which one would best suit their needs, telling the salesman they would call him in a week or so when they'd made up their minds.

They drove into Abilene at two o'clock. Tamara was surprised when they arrived so early. "I didn't expect you here until late this evening," she said when she greeted them.

"Hah!" Jack gushed. "He woke me up at three o'clock this morning. You'd have thought we had to drive a thousand miles today. I missed at least three hours of beauty sleep."

"If I thought it would have helped in that area, I would have left you in bed till noon," Clay replied tartly.

Laughing, Tamara and Kerry led them into the house.

They left Abilene early the next morning with Clay pulling Tamara's trailer, hauling both her and Kerry's horses. It was a six-hour drive to Texarkana, not counting the several breaks they took along the way. After reaching town at four in the afternoon, they reserved a motel room for Tamara and Kerry, then found a place to board the horses for the night before driving to the rodeo grounds.

Though they got there early, the arena was still the usual beehive of activity as preparations were being made for the night's performance. Many of the contestants were already there, milling about, looking at the stock, discussing rodeo news and exchanging greetings

While Tamara and Kerry exercised their horses, Jack and Clay looked over the stock and talked with the other cowboys.

Clay had drawn Cold Beer in the barebacks, and Lousy Day in the saddle broncs. He was excited about Lousy Day, but was less than enthused about Cold Beer. "Last time I had him in Carlsbad, he didn't buck that well. I only got a sixty-two."

"That was a while back," Jack claimed, "and you know how these horses can change. If he wasn't doing that good, I doubt Charles Duncan would keep him in the string."

Clay looked out over the pen of bulls. "I wish I'd entered the bull riding."

"You didn't know at the time that your hand would be healed enough to ride bulls," Jack said, though he was secretly relieved that Clay wasn't entered in the event.

Clay didn't say more. He knew how Jack felt about him riding bulls, but he made a solomn promise to himself; next weekend he'd be entered in the bull riding.

Neither Jack nor Clay noticed the slim man in his late twenties, watching them closely as they talked with other contestants. He had already bought his spectator ticket to the performance that night and would be in Nacagdoches tomorrow night. His name was Tommy Maddox and his assignment was to watch Clay Tory.

*   *   *

By rodeo time, the stands were filled with spectators and excitement was in the air. Clay's stomach was tied in knots, caused by anticipation of the two rides he was about to make. He tried to appear outwardly calm as he leaned against the chute, his chaps and spurs already strapped on, his glove resined and on his hand. His rigging lay on the platform by chute number three, waiting for Cold Beer to be run in.

"Looks like Kid Clay is back to ride," Billy Ettinger said, coming up beside him.

"Dadgum!" Clay exclaimed. "I was hoping to enjoy this rodeo without having to put up with an old-timer like you."

"You're just disappointed because you know that since I'm here, you don't stand a chance of winning the saddle bronc riding." Billy grinned.

"Hmmph," Clay choked. "I figured you'd stay away knowing I was entered, but then I reckon you're too old to know what's in your best interest."

"I think you both are full of yourselves," Jack interjected. "The only reason you two ever win is because there's no real cowboys left to compete against you. Why, if I was still a young man, I'd show both of you what bronc riding is all about."

Clay and Billy exchanged glances and then burst into laughter. Jack gave them an angry scowl. "That's the problem with young people today, they don't have any respect for their elders."

Clay stopped laughing. "Why, Jack, we respect you! It's just the bull you throw around that we don't have any respect for."

"That's right, Jack," Billy said. "You old-timers have invented so many stories about your rides and told them so many times that you've started believing them yourselves."

"If I wasn't so old and beat up, I'd show you two young upstarts what bronc riding is all about. But since I can't, I reckon I'll have to put up with your impertinent attitudes and disrespect."

Clay and Billy grinned at him, knowing that if Jack was younger he surely could, in fact, show them how it was done.

Cold Beer was run into the chute beneath them. Billy and Jack helped Clay set his rigging while the chute men strapped on the flank strap.

The first rider, Gill Jackson, rode a horse named Unstable to a score of sixty-six. Unstable was a good draw, but Gill got his right foot over Unstable's neck on the third jump and couldn't get his rythm back. It was only his exceptional skill as a rider that kept him from being thrown.

The second rider, Jack Waldon, had drawn TNT, a horse Clay had never seen before. A strawberry roan with a long head and broad body, he looked more like a prospect for the glue factory than a bucking horse. Clay paid close attention as the gate swung open. TNT lunged from the chute in one quick movement. His bucking style was fast and hard. It seemed as if his feet barely touched the ground before he was in the air again, each leap covering fifteen feet of ground. This kind of bucking horse required the rider to increase his spurring speed to stay in time with the horse's leaps, and Jack did a good job of it.

His score at the end of the ride was a seventy-one, a good score on a good horse.

Clay was mounted when TNT was run from the arena. He was ready when the chute men moved to the gate.

Cold Beer left the chute, running two lengths before he ducked his head and started to buck.

Jack had been right in his estimation of the horse; he had definitely improved. Bucking straight down the arena, he twisted in the air and bucked hard.

Clay spurred in time, laying his back along the horse's spine. Each time the horse's back feet hit the arena dirt, it whipped Clay back and forth violently, all adding to the judge's score. Clay's chaps were flapping with each jump as he jerked his knees upward with each lunge.

Clay scored a seventy-one to tie for first, but Benny Roberts turned in a seventy-three on a horse named Black Lorraine, a big coal-black mare who ducked and darted each time her feet hit the ground. Benny, a top rider, stayed in time with the mare, almost making it look easy.

Clay watched Benny ride and knew before the announcer called out the score that Benny had outscored him. Turning to Jack he said, "It was closer than I thought it would be."

"I hate to say I told you so, but I told you so!" Jack quipped in response to Cold Beer's performance.

"Yeah, yeah, I know, you're always right!" Clay replied cynically.

Jack chuckled. "I'm glad to know you're finally learning that."

Clay grinned at him and shook his head. "I just hope one day I can be as smart as you, Jack."

"Keep working, youngster, and you might just make it."

After riding Lousy Day, Clay was sitting in comfortable first overall with a score of seventy-eight. The closest score to him was Billy Ettinger's seventy-four.

"With a little luck, your score might hold," Billy remarked as they walked away from the arena toward Clay's pickup.

"It might," Clay responded. "I'll be glad to pick up a first place check for a change. I was getting real tired of watching you take all of them."

"I have to let you have one every now and then or else you might get discouraged and quit. Then who would I have to carry my gear bag for me?"

Tamara was waiting for them by the pickup. She had knocked over a barrel in the barrel racing, adding a five-second penalty to her time. Kerry was sitting second with a 16.3 second run.

"Ya'll got any plans for tonight?" Billy asked.

"Nothing special. Why?"

"Diane and I were going to get something to eat before we head to Little Rock. Why don't ya'll join us?"

They all agreed. "Let us get the horses boarded and we'll meet you back here in half an hour," Clay said.

Tommy Maddox, standing within hearing distance, grimaced. He had known Clay would be at the Texarkana rodeo. He also knew he would be in Nacogdoches tomorrow, but he didn't know where he was

spending the night. His orders were to keep watch
on Clay Tory the entire time until he returned to
New Mexico. Now he would have to follow them to
a restaurant and wait until they were through eating.
He had enjoyed the night's performance, but it had
been a long day and he was ready to get some sleep.
The sooner he found out where they were staying,
the sooner he could get his own room and get some
badly needed rest. He had a feeling that following
Clay Tory was not going to be a simple task.

It was after eleven o'clock when the group finally
broke up and left the restaurant. No one noticed the
rental car that followed them at a distance. It stayed
behind them all the way to the Holiday Inn. Tommy
watched as Kerry went into room 126 while Jack
climbed into the camper. He waited in the car until
he saw Clay kiss Tamara good night and join Jack in
the camper before he got out and hurried into the
hotel lobby. He was standing at the check-in desk
when the call he was waiting for came in. He listened
as the desk clerk answered.

"You're all set; eight o'clock wake up call, room
one-twenty-six," the clerk said into the phone.
"Thank you, Miss Allen, good night." After he hung
up, the clerk took the ten-dollar bill extending from
Tommy's hand. "I hope you make up with your girlfriend," he called as the man walked out.

Tommy drove down the street to the Hampton Inn
and got a room, leaving his own wake up call for
seven in the morning. He had told the desk clerk at
the Holiday Inn that he'd had a fight with his girlfriend and he didn't want to bother her that late at

night, but had wanted to see her as soon as she awoke. That was the reason he gave for needing to know what time her wake up call was for. Now he'd know what time to be back at the Holiday Inn in the morning. It was amazing how people were always willing to help when it came to a man's love life. He threw his suitcase on the extra bed in the room, undressed, and climbed into bed. He was asleep almost as soon as the light went out.

The next morning, Tamara and Kerry took their showers and dressed before waking Jack and Clay. While the men used their room to shower and shave, the girls took the pickup and fed their horses, and by the time they returned, Jack and Clay were washed, ready, and complaining about their empty stomachs.

It was only a three-hour drive to Nacogdoches, and as they had plenty of time to get there, they ate a leisurely breakfast before checking out of the hotel and retrieving the horses.

Tommy, refreshed after his night's rest, watched them pull away from the motel. He already knew where they were headed, so he stayed well behind them.

After hooking up the trailer to the pickup, they loaded the horses and drove back to Interstate 30 heading west. They still didn't notice the light-gray rental car that stayed behind them as they turned off on Highway 59 and headed south toward Marshall. Since they had time, Tamara talked them into stopping in Longview so she could go to the mall there.

Clay groaned when she mentioned it, but quickly relented when her elbow dug into his ribs.

Jack and Clay stayed with the pickup and horse trailer while Tamara and Kerry went in. "They could have done this in Texarkana," Clay stated dryly.

Jack was leaning back with his hat pulled over his eyes. "They could have, but then that wouldn't have been practical, and if there's one thing I've learned about women, it's that they're never practical. I think that's part of what they call feminine mystique."

"I suppose now you're going to try to convince me you're an expert on women."

Jack chuckled. "That, my young friend, is something no man can boast of. There is no such thing as an expert on women."

Tommy sat in the mall parking lot where he could keep an eye on the pickup and horse trailer. His yawns were coming more frequently as he fought drowsiness. Fortunately the girls only shopped for a little over a half an hour before he spotted them coming out and sat upright.

Tamara was all smiles as she bounced into the pickup. "I bought you something," she said as Clay slid in beside her.

"What is it?" he asked in anticipation.

"I'm not telling you until after the rodeo tonight."

"Why not?" Clay asked with a disappointed look on his face.

"Because I want to give it to you at the right time. I thought you and I would go out to eat alone tonight and I'd give it to you then."

"Sounds great to me," Clay exclaimed with a

smile. "But we only have one truck and Jack and Kerry are with us. What about them?"

Tamara gave him a knowing smile. "Don't worry, I'll take care of that."

Clay grinned like a little boy, making Tamara laugh with delight.

They arrived in Nacagdoches at three o'clock in the afternoon. Boarding the horses at the arena, Clay talked Jack into getting a room for the night at the Holiday Inn. While Clay, Tamara, and Kerry went for a swim in the hotel pool, Jack took a nap, giving Clay a warning before he left. "Don't wear yourself out chasing those girls in the pool."

Clay gave him a smile and a wink as he closed the door behind him on his way out.

Tommy Maddox checked into the Holiday Inn, getting the room above Clay and Jack's. He sat on the balcony and watched the three splash around in the pool, envying Clay and wishing he could join them.

At five o'clock they left for the rodeo grounds. The rodeo was in an indoor arena, which pleased everybody since it looked like there was a good possibility of rain.

"I might just sell the ranch and move to east Texas," Jack commented to no one in particular. "It rains more here."

As they started in to look over the stock, Clay stopped and stared at someone in the parking lot. Jack followed his gaze, seeing three cowboys standing by a car. "What is it?" he asked.

"Nothing," Clay answered, turning and walking into the arena.

Jack cast one more glance at the three before following Clay inside.

Floyd Davis didn't see Clay or Jack, intent as he was in talking to the two men with him, and didn't look in their direction as they walked into the arena.

Clay couldn't say why he felt uneasy seeing Floyd. The last time he could remember running into him was in Springfield, and as far as he knew that was the last time their paths had crossed. But why had he felt such anger when he saw him, and why did his palms suddenly become sweaty? he wondered as he wiped them on the legs of his jeans. Forcing Floyd from his mind, he walked with Jack to the holding pens. He found Shady Lady, his draw in the barebacks, and Cannon Ball, his draw in the saddle broncs.

"That's two pretty good horses you've drawn," Jack said.

"I'm happy. I just wish I was riding ol' Tombstone over there," Clay said pointing at a silver Brahma bull standing by the hay rack.

"Well, I'm glad you're not," Jack stated. "That's the one thing I've enjoyed since you got hurt. I haven't come close to having one heart attack."

Clay chuckled. "I know you don't like me riding bulls, but I just can't give them up. It's like part of me is missing if I don't ride 'em. I love barebacks and saddle broncs, but I live for the bull riding."

Jack nodded, knowing the feeling. It was the same one he once had when riding saddle broncs. "I understand. I know I give you a hard time about riding them, but I won't try to stop you, even if it does take

years off my life every time you climb on one of
those monsters.''

Clay merely nodded, understanding the older man's
reservations and thankful that he cared enough to be
concerned.

Chapter Eighteen

The bareback riding proved to have plenty of competition as the first six contestants all made qualified rides. Cullen Dwyer currently led with a score of seventy-four.

Shady Lady was a chestnut sorrel with a crooked white streak running from the point between her eyes to the tip of her nose. She was a seasoned pro, but hated the chute and fought the entire time they were trying to put the rigging and flank strap on. When Clay tried to climb on her back, she reared and pawed at the gate in front. Helping hands pulled Clay out of harm's way. He eased back down while another cowboy grabbed two handfuls of mane and held the horse's head to the side.

Clay held his breath as he eased his spurs along the boards and over Shady Lady's shoulders. He nodded as soon as he had them in place, and the gate swung open.

Shady Lady turned it on full steam with a series of twists and lunges that left the crowd breathless and marveling at Clay's riding skills. The sorrel mare fairly shook the ground when she landed, adding to the crowd's excitement.

It was no surprise to anyone when the announcer called out the judges' score of eighty-four. The applause and cheers echoed agreement and Clay smiled at the spectators as he passed by, waving to several in way of thanks.

Jack's smile couldn't have been any broader as he stood behind the chutes, his chest swelling with pride. Giving Clay a hand up as he climbed over the rail he said, "I don't believe I've ever seen a better ride. We're going to have to get us one of those video cameras so we can watch your rides."

"And who are we going to get to run it?" Clay asked. "I can't run a camera and ride, and I know there's no way you could ever use one."

"You're right about that!" Jack agreed. "I guess we'll have to get Tamara to run it."

"That'd work!" Clay said. "I'll get one as soon as we get home. I'd like to be able to see my rides too. It might give me some ideas on how to improve."

"And you could tape my riding instructions and watch them every night before going to bed."

"Oh no," Clay groaned. "That would give me nightmares."

"I think I may be on to something," Jack declared, ignoring Clay's remark. "We could tape my instructions and sell them, you know, like they do on TV. They've always got instructional tapes on fishing and golf. Why not one on bareback and saddle bronc riding by the great Jack Lomas, world champion saddle bronc rider?"

"Who we going to sell it to, the geriatric crowd?"

Jack gave Clay a hurt look. "You mean you don't

think all these cowboys would buy my instruction tape?"

Clay's face split in a wide grin. "They might, but just think, if they all knew what I know, they'd be as good as I am."

Jack threw back his head and laughed. "I guess you're right. I better stick with personal instruction and forget about trying to sell it to all your competitors."

"Good idea," Clay agreed.

They found Tamara and Kerry and walked around during the calf roping and steer wrestling events, talking to different contestants. None of them noticed Tommy behind them. He stayed close enough to hear what they were saying, though he avoided looking directly at them in case they looked his way.

After the fourth steer wrestler, Clay left the group to go get his saddle, halter, and gear bag from the camper. Tommy followed.

By the time the last steer wrestler threw his steer, Clay was on the platform with his chaps and spurs on, and his saddle and halter ready.

Cannon Ball was a snow-white horse with a long flowing mane and tail. Had he not been a natural bucker, he probably would have been used as a show horse. Clay had drawn him twice before; the first time he'd been thrown and the second time he'd place third. He was looking forward to trying him again.

Seven horses and seven cowboys pitted their skills against each other before it was Clay's turn. Out of the seven, the horses won four of the rounds. The leading score was a seventy-nine.

Clay was in the saddle and ready when the arena director called for him. He nodded his head and gave Cannon Ball the rein.

Cannon Ball had earned his name by leaving the chute as if shot from a cannon, and this time was no exception. As the chute gate cracked open, the white horse turned and was out before it could be pulled completely open. Clay barely missed scraping his leg on the rough wood.

It was a crowd-pleasing ride from the beginning as Cannon Ball abruptly turned left out of the chute, scattering cowboys in every direction. Never once did the horse lift his head as he hit the ground, bunching himself and springing upward. This move was repeated time and again, only varying in direction. He would turn left then spring right, and the next time turn right and spring left.

Clay used his spurs on each jump, though Cannon Ball was hard to get in time with and it kept Clay working just to maintain his seat.

If there had been one more second in the ride, Clay would have received a no-score as he came unglued just after the eight-second buzzer sounded. Cannon Ball had gone right, but instead of springing left as he had been doing, he sprang in the same direction, throwing Clay to the side. The next jump catapulted him from the saddle and left him sitting in the air with nothing but gravity between him and the arena dirt. Hitting hard on his side, Clay rolled in the soft dirt. His right hand was beneath him when he hit. Pain shot through his hand and arm, and he rolled quickly to relieve the pressure. Coming to his feet, he flexed his fingers and moved his wrist, relief flooding through him as the pain subsided and he discovered his hand had suffered no further injury.

The judges gave Clay a score of seventy-seven, which put him in second place. Overall he placed third, since there had been a score of eighty-one turned in the night before.

"Not a bad night's work," Jack said as Clay beat the dust off his clothes behind the chute. "A first in the barebacks and a third in the saddle broncs."

Clay was in high spirits as he got his saddle and pulled off his chaps and spurs. "This weekend should move me back up in the standings. Now all I got to do is hit it hard in July and I should be in good shape."

Jack was about to comment when Billy Monk called out to Clay, "You got an extra tie-down for a spur?"

"I think I got some out in the camper," Clay remarked. "Who needs it?"

"Sammy Jones. He just broke his and he needs one before the bull riding."

"Let's go out to the camper and I'll see if I got one," Clay said. Picking up his saddle and gear bag, he waited for the two cowboys to join him. "Jack, will you tell Tamara I'll be right back?"

Jack nodded and left to find her.

Tommy was standing by the gate that lead to the area behind the chutes. He appeared to be watching the action in the arena as the three cowboys walked past him. When he was sure they had passed, he turned and followed behind. He was close enough to hear what they said. As they walked between parked cars and trucks, he took alternate routes so he wouldn't be spotted. There were other cowboys and cowgirls in the parking lot. Some stood in groups talking, while others worked on their equipment or wrapped various parts of their anatomy with bandages.

Clay was leading the way to the camper with Billy and Sammy following close behind as they weaved their way through the cars. They were almost to the pickup when someone laughed off to their left, causing Clay to stop suddenly in his tracks. Billy, close behind, almost collided with him and was trying to regain his balance when Clay suddenly dropped his saddle and gear bag.

"What the . . .?" Sammy exclaimed, but Clay was already walking away, working his way through the parked vehicles.

"Hey, Clay, where ya goin'?" Billy called, but Clay didn't answer

Both Sammy and Billy exchanged questioning glances, then hurried after him.

As Clay rounded a van, he saw three men leaning against a car. The light in the parking lot was dim, but he still recognized the man in the middle. When Clay saw Floyd Davis standing there, a sneer on his face, the haze that had been clouding his mind lifted. Suddenly, Clay saw Floyd standing over him in the parking lot. He saw his boot coming toward him and he remembered the laugh. The same laugh he'd just heard. He was now within three feet of the men standing there, and when Floyd glanced up at him, Clay saw the fear of recognition come into his eyes.

Billy and Sammy rounded the van in time to see Floyd try to break and run, but Clay's boot shot out and tripped him. The two men with Floyd stood rooted, too stunned to react. By the time they thought to do something, Billy and Sammy were standing beside them, their burly presence dissuading them from interfering.

Floyd lay on the gravel, looking up at Clay. "What'd you do that for?" he asked pathetically.

"Get up!" Clay spat and watched as Floyd got slowly to his feet, never taking his eyes from the man before him.

"What's the problem, Clay?" he asked, backing away.

"It was you in Santa Fe! I didn't know that until just a moment ago when I heard you laugh, but I know it now. It's all clear. I remember seeing you standing over me, kicking me and laughing about it."

"You're mistaken," Floyd whined. "I was in Santa Fe, but I was nowhere around the motel where you got beaten."

"Yes you were!" Clay shouted. "It was you and I know it. Now you're going to tell me why."

"I swear it wasn't me! You're mistaken." Floyd's eyes were darting side to side, seeking an escape route, but by now a crowd had gathered, forming a circle around the two. There was no place for him to run. He looked at Clay and knew there would be no backing down. Suddenly he charged, swinging a wild right to Clay's head.

Clay had been waiting, knowing he was dealing with a trapped rat and like all cornered rats, this one was going to try something. Clay waited until Floyd started his swing before he moved. Ducking under the fist, Clay did a quick sidestep and let Floyd's momentum carry him by.

Floyd's face registered surprise as he stumbled into the spectators gathered to watch. As they pushed him back toward Clay, he turned and brought up his fists, expecting Clay to be close, but Clay was standing in the same spot, his hands at his sides, a contemptuous smile on his face.

Floyd stood without moving, waiting for Clay as he approached, his hands still at his sides. He looked as if he were out for a leisurely stroll. When Clay came within two feet of him, Floyd panicked and swung another wild right at his head. This time Clay blocked the swing with his left arm, and stepping in close and bringing his arm down, trapped Floyd's arm beneath his own. Before Floyd could react, Clay buried his right fist in his midsection and listened to the air whoosh from his lungs.

Floyd was gagging and fighting for air when Clay stepped back and swung a right uppercut to his face, smashing his lips and nose. Floyd's head snapped back and he hit the ground on his back, blood pouring from his nose and cut lips.

Clay commanded, "Get up!"

Floyd held up his hands. "No more."

In two steps Clay was on him, grabbing him by

the collar of his shirt and dragging him to his feet.
"I said get up!" All the pent-up anger from the
weeks of pain and recuperation came boiling to the
surface. "Why did you do it?" he asked, his knuckles
white around Floyd's bunched shirt collar.

"It wasn't me!" Floyd cried.

Clay released him, then stepped in with a left jab
that cut open the skin above Floyd's right eye. "Why
did you do it?" he demanded again. Floyd shook his
head, and Clay hit him again. "If I have to beat you
half to death, I will. Now why did you do it?"

Tommy Maddox stood on the outer fringe of the
crowd. He had followed Billy and Sammy and had
arrived in time to hear the exchange between Clay
and Floyd. He watched as Clay sent another left jab
to Floyd's head, and heard the dull thud as it
connected.

"Why'd you do it, Floyd?" Clay asked again.

Floyd's head throbbed from the blows. His nose
and mouth were pouring blood and he had to spit
to keep from choking on it. Up to this point he had
refused to confess anything, but as another blow
landed above his eye, he lost control. This time when
Clay asked him why he'd done it, he shouted, "Because I was paid to!" and charged in swinging, all
reason gone, like a mad bull.

Stunned by the confession, Clay was caught off
guard by the sudden rush. Floyd swung a wild right
that landed on his temple, causing stars to explode
in his brain. The blow spun Clay part-way around
and before he could regain his balance, two more
blows landed on his head, knocking him to the

ground. Experience had already taught him how Floyd fought, and the memory of those boots in his side made Clay roll when he hit the dirt.

Floyd watched wild-eyed as Clay fell. Sensing victory, he quickly aimed a kick at Clay's midsection, expecting to feel his boot sink into flesh, but instead he kicked at nothing but air and was caught off balance. In the next instant he was on his back as Clay moved quickly, kicking Floyd's other leg out from under him. Landing hard on his back, Floyd once more felt the air knocked from him.

Clay rolled and came to his feet, then stood waiting for Floyd to catch his breath. He asked, "Who paid you?"

Floyd pushed himself up on one elbow. "I don't know who they were. I was given the money by a man I'd never seen before and told to stop you from being at the rodeo that night."

As Clay heard the words Floyd spoke, deadly anger coursed through him. "You were supposed to keep me from the rodeo that night?"

"Yes!" Floyd replied, gulping breath into his lungs. Then he realized the implications of what he'd said and looked quickly at Clay, fear showing plainly on his face.

Clay grabbed him by the hair and dragged him to his feet, and as he came up, Clay swung a left to Floyd's jaw that sent him staggering into the crowd. By this time everyone had heard Floyd's confession and whatever sympathy he'd had before was now gone as the crowd pushed him back into the circle.

Staggering, Floyd was spun around and pushed

back toward Clay. A quick left to the jaw, followed
by a smashing right to the mouth, sent him sprawl-
ing into the crowd again, only to be pushed back
toward Clay once more.

Floyd stood before Clay, swaying on his feet, his
eyes swollen almost shut, and blood pouring into
them. His lips were cut and bleeding and his right
cheekbone was swelling. He tried to bring his hands
up to defend himself, but lacked the strength to lift
them.

Clay looked with disgust at the beaten man before
him. "You're nothing but scum, Davis. You were too
much of a coward to face me in a fair fight, so you
attacked me from behind, and you even brought two
other cowards to help do your dirty work. If I ever
see you again, I won't stop. I'll beat you until your
mother bleeds." Clay then hit him once more with a
right jab and watched as Floyd's eyes glazed over
and he sank to his knees, then fell to his side in the
gravel. Without looking at him again, Clay turned
and searched the crowd for the men who had been
with Floyd, but there was no use looking. As soon
as the fight had started, they had slipped through
the crowd, gotten into Floyd's car, and were heading
north on Highway 59.

Tamara stood holding Charger just outside the circle of people. She'd heard the shouts from the crowd
and had ridden over to see what was happening,
getting there in time to hear Floyd's confession. Her
first instinct had been to charge through the crowd
and place herself between the two combatants, but
common sense had prevailed. She knew the anger

Clay felt at being beaten and mangled, and she knew that if she stopped him before he felt vindicated, he would never forgive her. So she sat on Charger and watched as Clay sent one blow after another into Floyd's face and body until he was knocked to the ground, where he now lay motionless.

Clay was in a daze, the kind that comes when the body releases large amounts of adrenaline and then slows down. It fogs the mind and makes reasoning difficult. He walked through the crowd and saw Tamara standing there. He wanted to go to her. He wanted to tell her it was all right. When he reached her, she smiled and took his hand, holding it gently as she lead him away from the crowd of people without speaking a word.

Jack watched them walking away, a puzzled look on his face. He'd been behind the chutes waiting for Clay to return and knew nothing about the fight that had taken place until somebody had run in yelling, "Fight! Fight!" By the time he'd gotten outside, it was all over and the crowd was breaking up. He didn't even know Clay was involved until Billy Monk told him what had happened. His first thought was to find Clay and make sure he was all right, but then he remembered seeing him walk away with Tamara. As bad as he wanted to find him, he knew he couldn't. Not right now anyway.

Chapter Nineteen

The rodeo was still going on when they left. Tamara had decided against an intimate dinner and suggested they all go eat together. Little was said about Floyd or the fight. Clay was in a somber mood and said nothing during the meal. It wasn't until later that evening, alone in the motel room with Jack, that the subject was broached. Both of Clay's hands were aching and he kept them wrapped in ice.

"Floyd said someone paid him to keep me from the rodeo in Santa Fe. I have a feeling he went a little further than he was supposed to. But that still doesn't answer the question of why someone is trying to prevent me or anyone else from rodeoing. It still doesn't make any sense."

"No it doesn't," Jack agreed. "Floyd said a man he didn't know paid him to stop you. It sounds like somebody is taking pains to make sure they're not linked to this, and if that's the case, then you can bet big money is involved. The problem is, I don't know what we can do about it at this point."

"Tamara told me her father is doing some checking on his own. She said he knew some people that might be able to find out what's going on."

Jack thought about what Clay said. "Cliff Allen has ties to a lot of business people. He may be able to come up with something. Remind me to call him when we get home. Maybe we can work together to find this mysterious man who paid Floyd."

Tommy Maddox had watched Clay destroy Floyd Davis with what he considered cold brutality. Not that he blamed Clay at all. If he'd been in his place, he was sure he'd want to do the same thing.

After the crowd wandered away, leaving Floyd bleeding in the gravel parking lot, he had helped take the injured man to his rental car and sat him in the passenger seat. Floyd was groggy and disoriented, which made it easy for Tommy. Providing a wad of tissues, he pressed them against Floyd's bleeding nose and told him to hold them there. At the Holiday Inn, he was thankful to see the vacant spot by Clay and Jack's room. They weren't back yet.

Taking Floyd by the arm, he helped him up the stairs and into his own room. After laying him down on the extra bed, Tommy got some ice and wrapped it in a washcloth, then exchanged it for the blood-soaked tissues Floyd still held. So far, Floyd had not spoken, nor had he questioned Tommy about what he was doing. Tommy doubted if he was even capable of thinking clearly at this point.

Leaving the injured man on the bed, Tommy stepped outside on the balcony and pulled the cell phone from his shirt pocket and dialed a number. The phone on the other end was answered after two rings by a woman with a very formal, no-nonsense voice.

Tommy made his request and waited for her reply.

"One moment, please," the crisp voice answered.

I'll bet she's a sourpuss old spinster, Tommy thought as he waited for his party on the other end to pick up.

"Tommy, how are you?" a man asked in a pleasant voice, which was always the way Devin Price responded.

"I'm fine. I've got something you might be interested in." He went on to tell him about Floyd Davis.

The man's voice changed instantly. Tommy could hear the excitement creeping into his questions. As quickly as one was answered, another was fired at him, until Devin had all the information.

"I want you to move him out of that motel as quickly as possible, before Clay Tory gets back. Don't bother checking out, just get him out of there. Drive to Lufkin and check into another motel, then call my secretary and tell her where you are. She'll get ahold of me. I'll be there as soon as I can, tonight if possible. Do you have sleeping drops?"

"Yes, sir!" Tommy answered.

"Good. As soon as you get a room in Lufkin, use enough on Mr. Davis to keep him out until morning. I don't want him leaving until I get there."

"Yes, sir," Tommy answered again, already in the room putting his few belongings in his travel bag.

"You've done real well, Tommy. There will be a bonus in your next pay envelope. Just make sure Mr.

Davis is able to answer a few questions when we get there."

"I will, sir," Tommy didn't miss the *we* in his last statement, and wondered who else was coming, but he didn't have time to dwell on it; he had to get Floyd out of there. Taking his bag to the car, he threw it in the backseat and bounded back up the steps. Floyd was asleep, and Tommy had to shake him hard to bring him awake enough to get him to his feet. Taking his arm and draping it over his shoulder, Tommy held Floyd around the waist and half dragged him down the stairs and back into the car. Racing back up the steps, Tommy glanced quickly around the room to make sure he hadn't forgotten anything before tossing the key on the bed and closing the door behind him. Going down the stairs two at a time, he jumped the small hedges, opened the door of the car, and slid behind the wheel, then turning the key in the ignition, backed out. Looking behind him, he saw Clay's pickup pull in at the far end of the parking lot. Without looking back again he put the car in drive and pulled out onto Highway 59 and headed south. Glancing over at Floyd, he was relieved to see his nose had stopped bleeding and he was out cold.

After driving the short distance to Lufkin, Tommy found a motel on the south side of town. It was a small inn with few occupants. Tommy turned up his nose as he opened the door of the room and stepped inside. The carpet was a dark-green shag, the kind that went out of style in the late seventies. There were several holes where cigarettes had been dropped or a chair leg had worn through, but the room was on the back side away from traffic, and there were two beds. He managed to get Floyd out of the car and into the bed furthest away from the door. As distasteful as it was, Tommy undressed him down to his underwear, noticing several more cuts and bruises around his chest and stomach. After getting Floyd under the covers, Tommy retrieved a small case from the trunk of the car. Removing a small bottle from inside the case, he opened the top and poured a good amount of the liquid on a washcloth, then held it to Floyd's nose for the count of fifteen while holding the palm of his other hand over his mouth. Floyd groaned and tried to move his head away, but Tommy held the cloth securely until Floyd took several deep breaths. Satisfied that he had administered enough to keep him asleep for several hours, Tommy took an alarm clock from his garment bag and set it for four o'clock. He didn't know what time his boss would be there, but he wasn't about to let him catch him asleep.

Clay woke in a better mood, throwing a pillow at Jack to wake him.

"Watch it, Junior," Jack mumbled, taking the pillow, curling it under his arm, then turning his back to Clay.

"I think I'll call the girls and see if they want to take a dip in the pool before breakfast," Clay said, reaching for the phone.

"That's a good idea. What time is it anyway?"

"It's seven-thirty."

"Wake me when you get through with your swim."

"I'll bring you some pool water."

"You do and I'll loosen the cinch on your bronc saddle the next time you ride."

Clay laughed. "You play dirty, don't you?"

"Only when it comes to my sleep. Now get out of here and let me get some."

Tamara and Kerry were still sleeping when Clay called, but they agreed to meet him at the pool. Both were glad to see him in a better mood. The swelling had gone down in both hands and though they were sore, there didn't appear to be any serious damage.

After breakfast they loaded their clothes in the camper, checked out of the motel, and started home. They ate lunch in Fort Worth and debated spending some time at the Fort Worth Stock Yards, but decided they'd better get back. Jack had finally used the cell phone to call Terry at the ranch and find out if the hay meadow was ready for cutting. He told him there were several head of calves that needed doctoring and it was almost time to turn the bulls back in with the cows.

Clay had listened to the conversation and made a nasty face when Jack talked about the hay. "Hey, girls, ya'll want to come out to New Mexico and help with the haying?"

"Gee, I would, Clay." Kerry smiled sweetly, "But I've got to go in for brain surgery that week and I just can't miss it."

"I'd come," Tamara said, "but I think that's the

week I have to have a root canal, and there's no way
I can miss that."

Clay sighed as his shoulders slumped. "Boy ya'll
get to have all the fun."

Jack had been listening to the banter among the
three of them. "I don't know what all the fuss is
about. Before you came along, I cut it, baled it, and
hauled it in by myself."

"Sure you did." Clay smirked. "And you used to
walk to school barefooted in the snow, uphill both
ways."

"Now how did you know that?" Jack asked, mim-
icking surprise. "Besides, moving hay is one of the
best ways to stay in shape. Builds muscles and character at the same time."

"I agree about the muscles, but I doubt very seriously if hauling hay can build any character."

"Well now, that's where you're wrong. Where do
you think I got all my charm from?"

Laughter resounded in the close quarters of the
pickup truck.

Arriving in Abilene early in the evening, Tamara
and Kerry tried to convince Clay and Jack to spend
the night there and leave early in the morning, but
they both insisted they needed to get back to the
ranch, and left shortly after arriving.

Jack and Clay arrived at the ranch after midnight,
tired and road sore, but glad to be home.

"Don't wake me till at least nine o'clock," Clay
pleaded.

"I doubt I'll be awake before then," Jack said wearily, limping into the house.

True to his word, Jack didn't get out of bed until after nine. Julie was in the kitchen when he walked in.

"I heard ya'll come in last night. I figured you'd want some breakfast. Is Clay going to get up soon?"

"I'll get him up," Jack said, walking back down the hall to Clay's door. Knocking, he opened the door and looked in. The bed was made and there was no sign of Clay. Just as he turned back toward the kitchen, Clay came through the front door. "Where you been?"

"I was down checking on the stock and looking at the hay field."

"I thought you weren't going to get out of bed before nine o'clock."

"I woke up around seven-thirty and couldn't go back to sleep. I guess I was too excited to finally be home."

Julie called them from the kitchen and they hurried in to give her their breakfast requests. It was obvious from the smile on her face that she was glad to have them back as well.

Terry came in while they were eating their breakfast, having been out checking on the windmills. "We've got two that need to be reworked pretty soon, and about forty head of calves that have colds, pink-eye, or both. There's two cows in the caprock pasture that have some hoof-rot. I gave both of them a shot of antibiotics the day before yesterday, but they need another one. The hay field is ready to cut.

I got a new part for the broken baler, but I haven't had time to get it put on yet and I haven't been able to find any extra hands to help with the hay hauling. That fence in the north section is about to fall down and needs new wire too." He stopped, looking expectantly at Jack and Clay.

"So what have you been doing while we were out working?" Clay asked, only to be met with an angry look from Terry. "Hey, I was only kidding," he said with a smile, relieved when he saw Terry relax and smile.

"I know there's a lot to be done right now," Jack interjected. "But we're here to help now. I'll call Mark Romine and get him to come out and rework the wells. Clay, you get on the phone to some of those fellas that come out here to practice and tell them if they want to use our stock anymore, they better get out here and help us get this hay in. We'll start Wednesday. First thing in the morning, we'll doctor the calves and if we have time, we'll stop by and doctor the cows. Tuesday morning, you two load up the barbed wire and posts that are down in the shed and go fix the fence. I'll put the part on the baler so it'll be ready. If I get that done, I'll start cutting the hay so it'll be ready by Wednesday. How does that sound?" he asked, looking from Terry to Clay.

They looked at each other, surprised at how simple things worked out. "That sounds good to me," Terry said.

"Me too!" Clay chimed in.

"We'll be leaving Friday morning for Clarendon,

Texas, so we got to have everything done by Thursday afternoon.''

Things went pretty much as Jack had planned. The windmills were fixed in short order. The calves were roped and doctored, the same with the cows. The fence was repaired and back in good shape, and Clay had five helpers on the day they baled hay. By the end of the day they had five hundred eighty-two bales in the barn. All in all, not a bad three days of work. Clay had even found time to practice on the horses and bulls in between hauling hay and doctoring calves.

Jack and Clay spent Thursday in town taking care of business, paying bills, and ordering feed. Clay had Jack drop him downtown, saying he had to pick up something.

"What have you got to pick up?" Jack asked.

"Something I ordered for Tamara. It was supposed to be in last week, but it didn't come in. It should be in by now."

"What is it?" Jack asked, his curiosity aroused.

"I'm not telling you." Clay grinned. "It's a surprise and I don't want you letting the cat out of the bag. By the way, I plan on having a romantic dinner with her this weekend, so you'll have to make arrangements to go out with the Hightowers."

"I don't see why I can't go along with you," Jack said with a sincere look on his face.

"Because it's a romantic evening. I realize you probably never had one of those, but I plan to have several and they don't include a third party."

"I know what a romantic evening is. I had one,

once. When Mary and I were dating, I took her to a horse auction and stopped at the Blue Moon lounge on the way back. We danced all night."

"I apologize, Jack. You're are a real romantic, but I think I'll handle this one by myself."

"Okay, but if you change your mind, just let me know and I'll be glad to tag along and help."

Laughing, Clay got out of the pickup and walked down the street, wondering how he'd ever gotten along without Jack Lomas in his life.

Chapter Twenty

Floyd Davis looked out the window of the bus as it traveled through the rolling hills of east Texas, on Highway 259 heading into Oklahoma. His life had changed drastically in the last three days. He didn't know where he would go from here, except maybe home for a little while. Not that home was any great shakes, but it was the only place left for him to go. He thought back on the events that had transpired and wondered how it had come to this.

Tommy Maddox had awakened at four o'clock and checked on his ward. Floyd was still sleeping soundly, his breathing deep and even. After taking a shower and shaving, he had put on the only suit he'd brought with him. He had wanted to slip out for a quick bite to eat, but had decided against it. He kept his cell phone close to him just in case someone called him on that number.

At five-thirty a knock came on the door. Tommy jumped at the sound and glanced over at Floyd, noticing his eyelids flicker, but he remained asleep. Opening the door, he wasn't surprised to see Devin Price standing there, dressed as impeccably as ever. But he was surprised to see two other men with him. He didn't recognize either of them.

"Hello, Tommy," Price said, stepping quickly into the room. The two men followed him in. "Tommy, this is FBI Agent Kirkson." He nodded toward the man closest to him. He looked like he could have been a linebacker for the Dallas Cowboys and Tommy could see the suit he wore was tailored to accommodate his broad shoulders. The other man was introduced as Derek Block, a professional sketch artist. He was a small man in his mid-thirties. He wore horn-rimmed glasses and carried a large artist's sketch tablet and a box that Tommy assumed were his charcoals and paints.

"How is he?" Devin asked, looking at Floyd.

"He took a pretty bad beating, one he definitely deserved."

"Did you use sleeping drops on him?"

"I last gave him some around midnight. He should be about ready to wake up."

Devin opened his briefcase and pulled out a small vial. Breaking the top off of it, he held the vial under Floyd's nose. Struggling against the pungent odor, Floyd tossed his head from side to side, but Devin kept the vial under his nose until he opened his eyes and looked up, bewildered by his surroundings.

"Hello, Mr. Davis. How are you feeling?" Devin asked him in his smooth conversational tone.

"Who are you?" Floyd asked, looking at the four men in the room, his eyes wary as he tried to clear his head.

"My name is Devin Price, and this is Agent Kirkson, Mr. Block, and my associate Tommy Maddox, who brought you here."

"Where am I?"

"You are in Lufkin, Texas."

"What am I doing here?"

"A good question! I have been hired by a party or parties that are very interested in finding the person or persons responsible for attempting to prevent cowboys from attending rodeos in order to manipulate the standings." He paused to let Floyd absorb what he'd said. "We are certain this is being carried out by an illegal gambling syndicate. We already have several names of people involved with this syndicate, but what we're really after is the name or names of those responsible for trying to influence the standings."

"I . . . I don't know who's responsible. I don't know anybody that's trying to influence the standings," Floyd cried.

"I've already introduced you to Agent Kirkson, who's with the FBI out of Dallas. What has transpired is a federal offense, and you, Mr. Davis, are guilty of conspiracy to commit fraud."

"But I didn't do anything," Floyd whined.

"You took money to stop Clay Tory from riding, and according to my sources, you paid one of the judges at a rodeo to give Mr. Tory a low score on his rides. In my estimation, Mr. Davis, that's doing something. Now Mr. Kirkson is going to ask you some questions and you are going to give him honest answers. If you lie about anything, he is going to take you to Dallas and lock you in a federal jail where you will stay until all this is straightened out. Do you understand?"

Floyd looked at Kirkson and nodded weakly.

Kirkson questioned Floyd for over an hour. By the time he was through, Floyd was ready to admit to crimes he hadn't even committed. He told him about the man in the sunglasses who paid him to bribe the judge. He admitted he was only supposed to stop Clay from making it to the rodeo in Santa Fe, but he'd taken it upon himself to attack Clay and beat him. He even gave details of how he'd planned and executed the assault. Though Devin felt anger burn within, he kept his normal calm demeanor and remained silent, taking notes as Floyd talked.

Kirkson finished his interrogation and nodded to Devin. Clearing his throat, Devin looked at Floyd who was beginning to perspire in the confines of the room, though the window air conditioner was running full blast.

"Would you like a drink of water?" he asked Floyd, his voice filled with concern. Tommy knew it was all part of the interrogation process and knowing Devin as he did, he was sure he was as disgusted by Floyd's story as he himself was.

"Yes, please," Floyd croaked.

Devin nodded to Tommy, who filled a glass from the pitcher of ice water he'd gotten earlier. Floyd gulped down the water and handed the glass back to Tommy, who filled it once more. Taking the glass, Floyd sipped slower, looking expectantly at the four men in the room. So far Derek Block hadn't spoken a word, but just sat listening and watching. Devin Price looked at him, then back to Floyd.

"Now Mr. Davis, you are going to spend some

time with Mr. Block here, who is a professional sketch artist. You are going to describe the man who paid you and Mr. Block is going to sketch him. Now, in case you are thinking of making up an image, let me explain the rules to you. We have enough evidence at this point to convict you of several crimes, but it's not you we're after. It's the man who paid you and ultimately the person who paid him. If you're not one hundred percent honest in your description and we find out—and we will—we will prosecute you to fullest extent of the law. Which means you will be spending the next several years as a guest in one of Uncle Sam's institutions. Do I make my meaning clear?"

Floyd nodded slowly, and Devin could see the fear in him. He knew that his point had been received and understood, but more important, he knew that Floyd was going to cooperate.

It took Derek Block two hours working with the information Floyd provided to draw the face of the man who had hired him. By the time Floyd said, "That's him. That's the man who paid me the money," everyone except Kirkson was perspiring. Tommy marveled at the man's composure. He himself had removed his coat and loosened his tie soon after Block had started. Block had his sleeves rolled up as he worked. Devin Price had removed his coat, though he didn't loosen his tie, but Kirkson remained as he was, his suit still in place and not a bead of perspiration showing on his brow.

Devin Price looked at the face outlined on the

page. "How soon will you be able to put this into the computer?" he asked, looking at Kirkson.

"I'll have it in tonight. With a little luck, we'll have a name within twenty-four hours."

"Good. Now, about our friend Mr. Davis," Devin said, looking at Floyd. "Do you want to explain what happens to him from here?"

Kirkson nodded and stood, walking slowly toward Floyd until he was towering over him. "You live in McAlester, Oklahoma, is that correct?"

Floyd nodded.

"Since your cohorts took your car, we will furnish you with a bus ticket to McAlester. You will remain in McAlester until this matter is resolved. If any of the information you have given us today turns out to be false, we will bring charges against you in federal court. If you leave McAlester before we have resolved this matter, we will find you. Do you understand everything I have told you?"

Floyd nodded again.

Kirkson turned to Devin. "Didn't you have something you wanted to add?"

"Yes I did," Devin answered, sitting on the edge of the bed across from Floyd. "The people I represent strongly suggest that you withdraw from professional rodeo immediately."

Floyd's swollen eyes widened in shock, a questioning look coming over his face.

Devin continued, "This suggestion is in your best interest. You see, if you fail to comply with their request, they will not only convince Clay Tory to press charges against you, they will also convince the directors of the PRCA to bring charges against you for bribing a rodeo judge. If you were convicted on either charge, and I'm sure you would be, you would be facing between two to seven years. I'm sure you will agree the alternative you're being offered is a much better deal. From what I hear, you weren't very good anyway. You have until we reach the bus station to give me your decision.''

Floyd gazed at him with a crestfallen look. He knew he was beaten and there was nothing left for him to do but accept their offer.

Sitting on the bus now, Floyd couldn't help but notice the looks the other passengers gave him, but he didn't care. His world was changed forever and right now all he wanted was to get home and crawl into bed and sleep for a long, long time. He would decide what he was going to do with his life after he woke up. He had agreed to drop his PRCA card, and Devin had made him promise he wouldn't show up at any pro shows for at least a year.

As Floyd traveled north toward Oklahoma, Collin Dobson was sitting in his office in Los Angeles. He had narrowed his list down to three possible suspects. Studying the latest profile he had on each of the three possibles, he divided the pages in half, and at the top of each page he made two headings; on the left side he wrote a big YES, on the right side he wrote a big NO. Reading each profile once again he wrote under the YES column anything that looked suspicious. In the NO column, he put down things that could eliminate them as suspects. After spending two hours poring over the information, he eliminated one name, leaving two. One was Charles Pratt from Miami, and the other was Stan Dickson from Phoenix. Both were in debt up to their ears and needed money in a bad way. Pratt came from a wealthy family and might be able to borrow, but according to the report, his family had cut him off. Stan Dickson had no wealthy family and nowhere else to turn.

Sitting back in his chair and staring at the two sheets, Dobson spoke out loud, "If I were a gambling man, I'd put my money on Dickson." He folded the two sheets of paper and put them in his coat pocket, then picked up the phone. "Make me flight reservations to Dallas for Thursday. I need the usual; rental car, motel reservations for Thursday night, and a list of motels in Cleburne, Texas. Oh, and Margaret, send a box of candy to Gail Johnson at the PRCA headquarters in Colorado Springs. Have the card signed, 'Thanks for the help. Peter.' Margaret didn't ask questions. She had worked as his personal secretary for fifteen years now and was used to his strange and sudden requests. Gail was the woman who had finally given Dobson's associate the name of the rodeo where Clay Tory would be entered this weekend. He planned to create the opportunity to talk to Mr. Tory.

Jack and Clay left before dawn Friday morning. They wouldn't be meeting Tamara in Abilene as usual. She was in Dallas on business for her father and would meet them in Cleburne later that evening. It was a nine hour drive, so Clay drove the first leg and Jack drove the final one in order to let Clay relax.

They would make the Cleburne rodeo Friday night

and the Denton rodeo Saturday night. Dottie had made them motel reservations already. They would spend Friday and Saturday nights in Denton and drive home on Sunday. Since the Hightowers were providing the stock for the Denton rodeo, Clay had already made plans for Jack to spend the evening with them. Dottie had been delighted when he had called, and requested she and Will occupy Jack for the evening while he and Tamara enjoyed some time together. She assured him she would make sure Jack was taken care of.

Jack had finally relented to Clay's constant request to start riding bulls again. Clay's joy was obvious by the rebel yell he let out on hearing the news.

They rolled into Cleburne with plenty of time before the rodeo started. They found the arena on the outskirts of the city, but instead of going in, they drove around town for a while, looking at the sights and enjoying their leisure time. Tamara wasn't meeting them until six o'clock, so they had plenty of time to relax before going to the arena. It was five-thirty when they pulled in and parked, heading first for the stock pens. Big Bertha was Clay's draw in the barebacks, Salem was the horse he got in the saddle broncs, and Landmine was the bull he'd drawn. Jack and Clay were looking the animals over when they saw Tamara pull in. Once she was parked, Clay hurried over, grabbing her as she stepped out of the pickup. He hugged her tightly, lifting her feet off the ground and whirling her in a circle before setting her down.

"I sure did miss you," he said, giving her a deep kiss.

Breathless, she pulled away and said, "If missing me makes you act like this, I'll have to find more ways to make you miss me!"

"Oh, you will, huh? Well, all you got to do is stay out of my sight for more than an hour and you'll have your wish."

Tamara laughed again and threw her arms around him. "I'd rather just stay with you and see what happens."

"Good idea." He chuckled.

While unloading Charger, Guy Terry walked by, and seeing Clay, he stopped. "Hey, Clay, Tamara. How's things going?"

"Couldn't be better," Clay responded as he stepped out of the trailer leading Charger. "How are things going with you?"

"Not bad now. Last week was kind of frustrating, though."

"What happened?" Tamara asked, taking the lead rope from Clay and tying her horse to the side of the trailer.

"I guess you could say I got hijacked."

"Hijacked?" Clay asked, a puzzled expression on his face.

"Yeah, I was on my way to the rodeo in Duncan, Oklahoma, and I stopped for breakfast in a little cafe outside Henrietta, and somebody slipped something in my coffee. When I woke up, I had been stripped down to my underwear and left lying in a corn field somewhere east of Tulsa."

"How terrible!" Tamara exclaimed.

"That's not the worst of it," Guy added. "When I walked up to a house to get help, they called the sheriff on me and had me arrested. I spent two days in jail before I could get my cousin to come get me out. It took me another two days to find my car. It was at a police impound in Shawnee. They'd found it abandoned on the highway. I missed the Duncan rodeo and I'd drawn Suicide. The last time I drew him was at the finals last year. I won the go-round on him."

Each of the ten performances at the national finals is considered a go-round. Money is paid to the top five contestants in each event in each go-round. Since the amount of prize money paid out in each go-round is larger at the finals, placing in several can make a big difference in the standings as each contestant's winnings goes toward his overall earnings to determine the world champion in each event.

Clay listened in stunned silence. Tamara took her brush and began grooming Charger. "Do you have any idea who did it?" she asked.

"Not really. I heard about Clay's run-in with Floyd Davis. I understand Floyd was the one who attacked Clay in Santa Fe. When I heard about it, I thought maybe Davis was behind it. He could have been in Henrietta Friday and back in Nacogdoches Saturday."

"Yeah, he could have been," Clay agreed, "but I wouldn't hang my hat on it. Floyd attacked me because he hated me. He said somebody paid him to do it, but that's not the main reason he came after me. I've heard of a lot of cowboys being kept away from rodeos. I think there's more than one person working to do this. I don't yet know the reason behind it, but Jack has talked to Tamara's father and they're going to see if they can get the association to hire some investigators to look into this matter."

Guy exhaled loudly. "I just hope they can put a stop to it soon. Ever since this has happened, I catch myself looking over my shoulder all the time to see if I'm being followed. I can't help but look at every stranger as if they're after me."

Clay and Tamara exchanged a knowing glance. "I know exactly what you mean," Clay said. "After we had that incident in Colorado Springs, I felt like anyone I didn't personally know was out to get me."

Guy smiled ruefully. "I hope no one walks up behind me and grabs me by the arm. I'm liable to swing first and ask later."

Clay grinned at him. "I'll be sure to remember that."

Tamara and Clay left Guy and went to find Jack. Neither of them noticed the two men watching.

Chapter Twenty-one

Tommy Maddox had once again been assigned to keep an eye on both Clay and Tamara. He had wondered why Devin wanted him to continue his vigil, but dared not ask. He was getting paid to follow orders and that's what he was going to do. He had a small black-and-white photocopy of the man Floyd Davis had described. His name turned out to be Crawford Lance and the FBI already had an extensive file on him. Devin had warned that under no circumstances was he to approach him if he showed up. He was told to just keep an eye out for him while watching Clay and Tamara.

Collin Dobson leaned against his rental car, occasionally glancing at the people talking. He waited until Clay and Tamara had walked away and were almost to the bucking chutes before casually walking toward them. When they approached Jack, Collin stopped and leaned against the arena fence, sipping a can of soda. When the three began walking away, he waited until they were halfway around the opposite side of the arena before starting after them.

Tommy Maddox sat in one of the vacant seats in the stands watching as Clay, Tamara, and Jack walked around, stopping to talk to other contestants who were there early. He didn't notice the man that was leaning against the post at the end of the stands, glancing their way occasionally, but there was nothing about him that would draw attention. He could have easily been one of the local businessmen putting on the rodeo, or a spectator who had arrived early.

By the time the rodeo started, Collin was quite frustrated with the fact that he hadn't been able to get Clay alone. All he wanted was fifteen minutes with him in order to ask some questions, but Clay had stayed close to both the girl and the old man. He watched as Clay and Tamara walked out to his pickup and removed a gear bag from the camper, then made their way back toward the chutes. The girl walked with him until they were almost to the arena, then turned and walked up to the stands. There was no chance to get Clay alone now.

Collin and Tommy both sat in the stands watching Clay ride Big Bertha. This was Collin's first time seeing Clay ride and though he knew little about the sport, he was amazed at the athletic ability of the young man. Realizing the strength and agility it took to ride a horse of that caliber, Collin gained a new respect for Clay as Big Bertha performed a twisting leap high into the air. Clay remained in the middle of the mare's back, and raked her with his spurs.

Clay felt no pain in his right hand as he was jerked hard with each of Big Bertha's jumps. The sorrel mare hit hard on her front feet, then pivoted her body to the right while still in the air. As soon as her back feet touched the ground, she lunged forward, kicking hard and repeating her move, this time twisting to the left. Clay kept his balance throughout the ride, using his upper body strength to hold himself in the center of the mare's back and the strength in his legs to pull himself forward and on top of his rigging as Big Bertha lunged forward.

The eight-second whistle rang out, and Clay grabbed a handful of mane as he waited for the pickup men to move in beside him. Collin applauded with the crowd, realizing without having to be told that he'd just witnessed a winning ride.

Clay moved into first place for the evening's performance. As he walked to the truck carrying his gear bag, he heard the sound of shoes crunching on the gravel behind him. Dropping the bag, he wheeled to face his pursuer.

Collin stopped quickly, holding up his hands, palms out in a show of surrender. "I mean no harm," Collin quickly explained.

"What do you want?" Clay asked defiantly.

Holding the lapel of his coat open so Clay could see he had no weapon, he reached inside and slowly pulled out a business card and handed it to him.

Clay hesitated, then reached out and took the card.

"I'm Collin Dobson, and I'm a private investigator. I've been hired to find out who's behind the problems you cowboys have been having."

"Who hired you?"

"I can't reveal that. My client wishes to remain anonymous. Do you mind if I ask you a few questions? I won't take much of your time."

"I don't know if I can be of any help," Clay said. "I don't know who's behind it."

"I'm sure you don't, but you might have information that could help me to find out who is."

"Like what?" Clay asked warily.

"I heard through the grapevine that you found out who attacked you in Santa Fe." He pulled out a notepad and flipped through the pages until he found what he was looking for. "I believe his name is Floyd Davis?"

Clay felt the bile rise in him at the mention of Floyd's name. Fighting to control his emotions, he answered, "That's his name, all right."

"Did he say why he attacked you?"

"He said somebody paid him to do it."

"Did he say who it was?" Collin asked, scribbling in his notebook.

"No, he just said a man paid him. He didn't know who it was."

"Did he say what the man looked like?"

"No, and I didn't ask him."

"Do you know where Mr. Davis is now?"

Clay's eyes narrowed and Collin could see the fury behind them. "No I don't, but I don't think he'll be anywhere close."

Collin merely nodded, understanding the hidden meaning there.

"That's all the questions I have. You have my card—if you think of anything else, I'd appreciate it if you give me a call. Call collect, anytime."

"If I think of anything, I will," Clay said, putting the card in his shirt pocket.

Collin nodded and walked away. Standing a few yards away, hidden by a pickup, Tommy Maddox watched the man walk off. He had heard most of the conversation and had gotten the man's name. He knew Devin would be interested in knowing that another private investigator was asking Clay questions.

Clay found Tamara and Jack sitting in the stands.

"Where have you been?" Jack asked. "I was going to come look for you, but I was afraid I might lose my seat."

"I was talking with a private investigator. Someone hired him to find out who's been causing all the problems."

Tamara and Jack both looked at Clay in surprise.

"Who hired him?" Jack asked.

"I don't know," Clay answered. "I asked him, but he wouldn't tell me. I figured it was somebody with the association."

"I don't think so," Tamara said reflectively. "I was talking with George Thomas, the chairman of the board, earlier this week and he told me that the association hasn't decided what to do yet. It will probably be another week before they make a decision."

"Well, I don't know who he works for, but if he can find out who's doing these things, more power to him," Clay said.

Tamara, Jack, and Clay watched the calf roping and steer wrestling. Both events held a high level of excitement. Luke Parrish and Bo Clancy were respectively in first and second place in the standings in steer wrestling. There were only a few dollars seperating the two, and both were entered in that night's

performance. Almost the same was true in the calf
roping, with Don Maynard and Gene White vying
for the first-place slot. The first calf ropers roped and
tied their calves in just over ten seconds with a 10.3
being the fastest. Don Maynard was up next and the
audience held it's breath as he backed his horse into
the roping box. Nodding for his calf, Don hit the
barrier just as it released. Swinging his loop twice
over his head, he threw with deadly accuracy and
caught the long-legged Brahma calf around the neck.
Before the calf reached the end of the rope, Don was
on the ground, running toward him. Flanking the
three hundred pound bovine in one easy motion, he
looped his pigging string on the calve's foreleg and
gathered up the two back legs. In the fluid motion
that bespoke hours of practice, he made three wraps
and a half hitch and threw his hands in the air to
stop the watch that marked his time. The audience
waited for the announcer to call out the time, then
went wild upon hearing that it was an astounding
8.9. There were two more calf ropers before Gene
White's name was called.

Tension was thick as all eyes watched Gene back
into the box. Except for the difference in the two
ropers it could have been a rerun of Don Maynard's
run. Gene White hit the barrier at precisely the right
time, two swings with the rope and he caught his
calf. With the same quick movements he was down
the rope, flanking the calf and tying it. If the crowd
had been tense after Don's run, it was even more so
now while waiting for the official time to determine
which of these two professionals would take first

place. Laughter erupted as the announcer called out Gene's time. "Ladies and gentlemen, it seems we have a tie. Gene White just turned in a time of eight-point-nine." Gene White smiled and tipped his hat as the crowd broke into applause.

The steer wrestling was almost as exciting. Luke Parrish threw his steer in 3.8 seconds. The closest time to his was a 4.3. Bo Clancy was the last steer wrestler to go and the only one with a chance of beating Luke. Bo rode into the box on the left side of the steer and his hazer rode into the right side. Nodding for the coriente steer, Bo and his hazer charged forward, catching up to the lanky, long-horned animal twenty feet in front of the chute. As he came alongside, Bo dropped onto the steer's back and let his horse carry him into the steer's horns. As his feet hit the ground, he dug in and pulled hard, bringing the six-hundred-pound steer around. When Bo pushed down on the left horn, the steer's nose came up allowing, Bo to catch it in the crook of his left arm. As the steer continued to come around, Bo twisted his neck. Using his body and strength as well as the steer's momentum, he threw the rangy animal to the ground. His time was a 4.1, not good enough to beat Luke, but good enough for second place.

"I always enjoy a good match," Jack said, "and I can't remember when I've seen a better one."

Clay and Tamara both agreed. "I guess I'd better get ready for the saddle bronc riding," Clay said, looking at the horses being herded into the chutes.

Before the calf roping got under way, Tommy Maddox was on the phone with Devin Price, telling him about the conversation he'd overheard between Clay and Collin Dobson.

"Yes, sir, that's his name. No, sir, I don't know where he's from, but he gave Clay Tory a card with his name and phone number on it. If I could get that card, we could find out where he's from."

Tommy listened as Devin gave him instructions. "Yes, sir, I'll stay away from him. Yes, sir, keep an eye on Miss Allen and Mr. Tory. Yes, sir, I understand." He hung up the phone and returned to the arena. Finding a seat well above the three, he kept one eye on them all during the calf roping. He then watched Clay ride Salem to a score of seventy-five, only to be moved into second place by Ian Grant, who scored a seventy-nine on Tumbleweed. When it was time for Tamara to ride, he watched from behind the arena fence, where he could see both her and Clay, who was sitting on the fence by the entrance gate cheering her on. Tommy then moved back to the grandstands to watch Clay during the bull riding.

Landmine, a small black-and-white bull, was tough to ride because of his size and quick moves. Clay managed to stay with him for six seconds before being thrown when the small bull twisted hard to the left and dipped his shoulder, pulling Clay forward and down. A quick move to the right moved Clay off his rope and sent him flying toward one the bullfighters. Instead of being mad, Clay picked up his bull rope and tipped his hat to the bull as he ran out of the arena. Normally Clay would have been angry with himself for being thrown. He'd ridden tougher bulls than Landmine before, but because of the injury to his hand, he hadn't ridden bulls in over a month, and was out of practice. He knew it was only a matter of time before he got his rythm back.

Tamara had Charger loaded by the time Clay retrieved his bull rope and they headed for Denton. It took them a little over two hours to get there and get Tamara's horse stabled.

With Charger bedded down for the night, Jack climbed into the pickup and said, "Get me to the hotel. I'm wore plumb out and need a soft bed."

Will Hightower woke to the banging on his door. Getting out of bed, he stumbled through the darkness hunting for the door knob. Grumbling under his breath, he opened the door to find Jack standing in the dim light.

"What do you want at this time of night?" he asked in an angry voice.

"I just wanted to let you know we made it in all right. I knew you'd be worried about us."

"Yeah, I was losing sleep worrying about you."

"We're in the room next door. How about waking me up around eight o'clock and we'll have breakfast."

"Jack Lomas, if you don't go to bed and let me get some sleep, I'm going to make you get up and go with him to feed in the morning!" Dottie yelled from the darkness.

"Sorry, Dottie," Jack whispered.

"Don't sorry me, just get out of here before I pull this pistol from under my pillow and shoot you. I'll claim you were a burglar."

Jack chuckled. "I'm going. I'll see you in the morning."

"It's already morning," Will stated, closing the door with a bang.

Jack smiled to himself as he opened the door to his room, wondering what time Will would wake him.

Clay, already in bed, noticed the sly smile Jack wore. "You look like the cat that ate the canary. What have you been up to?"

"Just paying Will Hightower back a little."

"Uh-huh, and what is he going to do to pay *you* back?"

"I figure he'll probably be knocking on our door around six o'clock in the morning."

Clay groaned. "I wish you two would leave me out of your ongoing battle. I need to get my rest."

"Don't worry, I'll answer the door when he knocks."

Clay sighed in frustration and pulled the covers over his head.

Jack only miscalculated by fifteen minutes. Will was pounding on their door at six-fifteen. Clay came awake with a start and Jack sat up in bed with a smile on his face as he looked at the clock on the nightstand. Bounding out of bed, he hurried to the door. "Good morning," he sang, and was delighted to see Will's face crumple in disappointment. "I'll be dressed in just a moment and we'll get some breakfast.

"Well hurry up! Dottie's hungry."

"I'll be right there," Jack exclaimed, closing the door and leaning wearily against it.

"Don't come back 'till nine o'clock!" Clay said sleepily as Jack pulled on his clothes.

"All right, but I should make you get up since you're leaving me with Will Hightower while you go out on a romantic evening with Tamara."

"Get out of here and let me get some sleep!" Clay shouted, drawing a laugh from Jack.

Tommy Maddox sat in his motel room looking out the window. He hadn't been able to get a room closer to Clay's, and had to settle for one three doors down. Tamara was in a room in between them. His vantage point didn't offer much of a view, but he could see both pickup trucks and part of the parking lot. If Clay and Tamara walked to the restaurant, he would be able to see them. His car was parked two doors down, and if they drove somewhere, he was ready to follow. Looking at his watch, he noticed that it was eight o'clock and he had seen no sign of either Clay or Tamara. He had seen Jack and the Hightowers walk across the parking lot to the restaurant, then return to the Hightowers' pickup and leave. Getting up to get a bottle of water, he almost missed the man placing a piece of paper under Tamara's windshield wiper. Returning to the window, Tommy was just in time to see the man look furtively around before hurrying off, but he got a good look at him. It was Crawford Lance. His heart pounding, Tommy rushed to the door and cracked it open to peer out. He spotted Crawford getting into a light-blue, late-model Chevrolet sedan that was parked several doors down. He watched as the car backed out and started toward the street. Thinking quickly, Tommy grabbed his cell phone from the table and rushed out to his car. Backing out of his parking spot, he was just in time to see the Chevrolet turn left and drive off at an unhurried pace. He was dialing Devin's phone number as he pulled into traffic and began following Crawford.

Pulling onto Interstate 35E, Crawford Lance glanced quickly in the backseat. His passenger seemed to be sleeping soundly. It had been easier than he'd hoped. The previous night he had noted Clay's and Tamara's room numbers, then checked into another hotel down the street, only to return to their motel early this morning. His plan had been simple. He would grab either Clay or Tamara and take them to Dallas. If he was lucky enough to get Clay, he would simply keep him drugged until after the rodeo and then let him go. If he got Tamara, he would leave a note for Clay, telling him not to make the rodeo tonight or he'd never see the girl again. As it turned out, it was Tamara who had emerged from her room first, alone. It had been simple to come up behind her and place the chloroformed rag over her nose. She struggled hard at first, but the drug soon overtook her and she sank into his arms. Her small, lithe frame was easy to carry to the car and place in the backseat. Looking around, he made sure nobody had seen him. There had been no one in the parking lot when he put the note on the windshield of her truck. Except for Tommy Maddox.

Tommy stayed well behind Crawford's car. Devin Price hadn't been in the office when he had called.

He left urgent instructions for him to call him on his cell phone as soon as possible. They had been on Interstate 35E for fifteen minutes when the phone beside him rang. He jumped and grabbed it. "Devin, is that you?"

"It's me, Tommy. What's going on?" Devin asked in a calm, reassuring voice.

Tommy quickly explained whom he was following and asked for further instructions.

There was a long silence as Devin considered the situation. "I want you to break off surveillance this instant. Crawford Lance is a dangerous man. I don't want anyone getting hurt."

Tommy was flabbergasted by the order. "Sir?"

"I want you to break off. Now," Devin repeated

Dejected, Tommy removed his foot from the accelerator and began slowing his speed. Keeping the other car in sight, he started looking for an exit and was turning his eyes when something in the other car made his heart lurch. He had seen blond hair rise above the backseat for an instant, then disappear. He knew right away who was in the car.

"Mr. Price, I think we have a problem."

"What is it?" Devin asked, his voice rising slightly.

"Miss Allen is in Lance's car, sir."

"What?" Devin shouted.

"I just saw her, sir. Apparently Crawford has kidnapped her."

"Tommy, you listen to me and listen carefully. Do not let that car out of your sight. Where are you now?"

"I'm about forty miles north of Dallas on Interstate Thirty-five E."

"Okay, I'm going to call in some help. You keep them under surveillance and we'll join you as soon as possible. I'll be back in touch with you shortly."

"Yes sir," Tommy replied, starting to perspire.

"You're a good man. I know you can handle this."

"Yes sir," Tommy replied as Devin hung up.

Crawford glanced around nervously once more. He had seen Tamara lift up for just an instant then lie back down. It had given him a brief start until he realized that in a few moments he would be at the motel, and he would be able to administer some sleeping pills that would keep her knocked out long enough for him to insure Clay Tory didn't ride. Taking the DFW Airport exit, he headed west on Interstate 635, merging easily with the Saturday morning traffic. Glancing occasionally in his rearview mirror, he saw nothing that would lead him to think he was being followed. Ten minutes later, he exited on Valley View Lane and headed south.

Tommy was in the center lane of traffic when he saw Crawford exit ahead of him. Slowing his pace, he let two cars pass on the right before falling in behind them. As he'd hoped, two of the four cars in front of him exited on Valley View Lane, putting him three cars behind Crawford and his kidnapped victim. He exited the interstate in time to see Crawford turn left and head south. Only one of the cars in front of him went the same way. The other two turned north. With only one car between them, and it being a two-lane road, Tommy waited for the count of fifteen before turning to follow. Crawford was a quarter mile ahead of him now and at times lost from view as he rounded a curve or topped a small rise. Tommy fought the urge to increase his speed and close the distance. He jumped again as the cell phone on the seat beside him rang.

"Yes?" he answered, his nervousness reflected in his voice.

"Tommy, where are you now?"

"I'm on Valley View Lane heading south about a mile from Interstate Six-thirty-five."

"We're ten minutes away. Have you still got him in sight?"

"Yes, sir. He's about a quarter of a mile in front of me."

"Good. We'll come in behind you. Give me a description of the car."

"It's a light-blue, late-model Chevrolet sedan. Texas license Tango, Charlie, Foxtrot, one, six, four."

"Very good, we're on our way. Keep him in sight. I'll call you right back."

Tommy wiped the sweat from his brow with the back of his sleeve and slowed as the car between him and Crawford turned off. He could still see the sedan in front of him, but the distance had grown and there were too many places along this road where he might turn off. Pressing the accelerator, he increased his speed as the car ahead once more disappeared around a curve in the road.

Chapter Twenty-two

Clay arose at eight-thirty, then showered, shaved, and dressed. Looking at the clock on the nightstand, he saw it was a quarter after nine and wondered if Tamara had gone to feed Charger without waking him. Stepping out into the bright sunlight, he saw her pickup still parked in the same spot as last night. He failed to notice the piece of paper on her windshield. Walking the short distance to her room, he knocked on the door and waited for the sleepy response he expected. When no answer came, he knocked again, wondering if she might be in the shower. When again he got no answer, he pressed his ear to the door but could hear nothing. Turning away he saw that the Hightowers' pickup was gone, which meant they and Jack had probably gone to the rodeo grounds already. Thinking Tamara might have gone to the restaurant without him, he walked across the parking lot and went inside. There was no sign of her anywhere. The cashier remembered Jack and the Hightowers, but couldn't remember seeing anyone that morning that fit Tamara's description.

Walking back toward the motel, Clay was starting to worry. It wasn't like Tamara to leave without telling him. He thought she might have gotten a ride with the Hightowers, but quickly dismissed the idea. He walked back to her room and knocked once more, this time with the force of concern. Still no sound came from within. Turning, he looked at her pickup and finally noticed the note. Thinking it was from her, he relaxed and even grinned as he pulled the paper from beneath the windshield wiper. His smile quickly vanished and panic swept over him as he read what it said, his mind not willing to believe it. He read the message three times before he could make himself believe it wasn't a hoax. He looked around the parking lot, as if by some chance he would see Tamara standing there laughing at him, but he knew in his heart she wouldn't be. He knew someone had taken her. He started toward her room then turned back to his pickup, but before he reached it, he heard Will's pickup approaching. Without thinking, he bolted toward the truck, shouting as he ran. Will had to slam on the brakes to avoid hitting him. Jack came out of the pickup, alarmed at Clay's behavior.

"Clay, what in the thunder's wrong with you?"

"Someone's taken Tamara!" Clay shouted in desperation. "We've got to find her."

"What? Who's taken her?"

"I don't know. I just got this note off her windshield."

"Let me see," Will said, taking the note from Clay's trembling hand.

He quickly read the note, his face clouding with anger as he read.

"What does it say?" Dottie asked, sliding out of the pickup.

"It's addressed to Clay. It says, 'We have Miss Allen. If you ride tonight, you will not see her again. If you don't ride, she will be returned unharmed. Don't go to the police if you want her back. Stay in your room by the phone, we'll call.' That's all it says," Will concluded. "There's nothing we can do. We don't have any idea where they've taken her. They could be miles away in any direction by now. All we can do is wait and hope," Will said.

"I swear, if they do anything to hurt her, I'll track them down and make them regret the day they were born," Clay said between clenched teeth.

Dottie put her arm around his shoulder, tears of concern in her eyes, "I don't think they'll harm her. They want to keep you away from the rodeo. As long as you give them what they want, she'll be fine." Clay nodded, a feeling of desperation sweeping over him as he let her lead him to his room.

Crawford Lance turned into the Four Seasons Hotel and pulled around back, parking close to the delivery entrance. Before checking in the morning before, he had found an alternate entrance into the hotel that wouldn't require him entering through the main lobby. Taking a room on the third floor, he had retraced his route and was satisfied he could use it without detection. Killing the engine, he looked around to make sure there was no one around before getting out of the car. He opened the back door and pulled Tamara's sleeping form from the backseat and stood her up, taking her arm and draping it over his shoulder. She mumbled incoherently as he helped carry her up the walk and through the door. Once inside, he maneuvered her down the hallway to a freight elevator. He leaned her against one of the inside walls and pushed the button for the third floor. This would be the hardest part. If he ran into anyone in the hallway, he would tell them his daughter had been celebrating her twenty-first birthday and had overdone it, but he knew that if he were seen he would be remembered and could be identified. He was no fool. He knew he was guilty of kidnapping and what the results would be if he were caught. Usually, he would have hired someone else to do this kind of work, but he hadn't the time to find someone he trusted. He didn't want a repeat of the Floyd Davis fiasco; not that Floyd hadn't achieved better results than he'd anticipated, but things like that have a tendency to draw attention and Floyd was an amateur.

Putting on his sunglasses and a baseball cap he had tucked in his back pocket, he waited for the elevator doors to open. Holding Tamara upright with one hand, he looked up and down the hallway, relieved to see no one in sight. Half dragging her, he made it to the room undetected and opened the door, sighing with relief as he laid her on the bed and closed the door behind them. He turned the thermostat down on the air conditioner and felt the cool air wash over him.

Picking up the phone, he dialed a number, glancing over at Tamara. Her breathing was deep and even. Satisfied, he turned his attention back to the phone. "Mr. Dickson," he said when it was answered on the other end.

Tommy rounded the corner just in time to see the sedan pull into the hotel parking lot. Slowing his speed, he continued to watch the entrance and proceeded down the street. Looking ahead, he found what he searched for. On the opposite side of the street half a block away was a small business with no cars parked in front. Slowing down, he turned into the drive and parked in one of the spaces in front, facing away from the hotel. Turning around in the seat, he could see both entrances to the hotel. He watched for several moments, knowing that Crawford could be checking to see if he was followed. The phone beside him rang and he picked it up.

"Yes!" he answered.

"Where are you?"

"I'm parked across from the Four Seasons Hotel. Crawford Lance went into the parking lot and drove around behind the hotel. I haven't seen a car leave since he arrived."

"Keep watching. He could be switching cars."

"Yes, sir."

"I'm going to stay on the line. If anyone leaves, you relay it to me. We're closing in from both ends now."

"Yes, sir."

Five minutes later, Devin's limousine pulled in and parked beside Tommy. The front door opened and Tommy got in. There were three other men in the backseat with Price.

"Tommy, this is Agent Adams, Agent Warren, and you already know Agent Kirkson," Devin said in way of introduction. "The highway patrol has this section cordoned off. No one has left the hotel since he went in?"

"No, sir," Tommy answered. "What are we going to do now?"

"We're not going to do anything that might bring harm to Miss Allen," Devin said with determined emphasis, looking at each of the men. The three agents glanced at each other before nodding their assent.

Devin continued, "We need to find out if Crawford Lance has taken a room here. I suggest that Kirkson and I go in and ask a few questions. We'll decide how to best handle it after we know where he is." Getting affirmation from all, he told Raymond to drive to the hotel entrance and wait.

Devin and Kirkson stayed in the hotel for almost an hour, while Tommy and the two agents kept watch. The silence in the limousine was unbearable as no one made any effort to talk.

Finally Devin came out of the hotel, walking quickly to the limousine.

"We think we've located him," Devin stated as he climbed inside the limo. "Fortunately the desk clerk on duty is the same one who was working yesterday. Seems our man checked in early yesterday morning under the name Louis Taylor. The clerk remembered him from the dark sunglasses he wore; seems that's one trademark our friend keeps. We have taken two adjoining rooms across from his. Kirkson is working on the phone taps right now. Fortunately the hotel keeps a log on all calls through the switchboard, so we already know that he made a call a few minutes ago to Phoenix. The agency's checking it.

"Agent Warren, you and Tommy go to the desk and check in. Try to act as if you're in town on business. The desk clerk has your names and will give you a key to one of the rooms. I have made arrangements to have some luggage delivered to your room, courtesy of the hotel. We have promised we will do our best to keep this quiet and not disturb the other guests. For this, the hotel is willing to give us their full cooperation.

"Agent Adams, you will wait thirty minutes then come to room three-eighteen and knock on the door. You will be greeted as a business acquaintance here for a meeting. If you see Crawford Lance, you will do nothing until we know he has Miss Allen in the room, and that she's safe. Everyone clear?"

Adams and Warren nodded. Tommy turned to Devin. "I was wondering, sir, if I should place a call to Clay Tory and let him know we are in control of the situation. There's no telling what he might do when he finds out she's been taken."

Devin considered the suggestion. "I don't see what good it would do to call him at this point. Let's wait until we really have control of the situation before placing that call."

"Yes, sir," Tommy agreed, looking at his watch. It was ten o'clock, an hour and a half since he'd left the motel in pursuit of Crawford Lance. It seemed like it had been a week.

* * *

Clay paced the floor in the confines of the small motel room, his anxiety growing with each passing second of the clock. "I can't stand this! I feel so helpless."

"We all do," Dottie lamented, "but there's nothing we can do. Why don't you and Jack go take care of Tamara's horse. Will and I'll stay here by the phone in case someone calls."

"That's a good idea," Jack said, getting up out of his chair. "Come on, Clay. I'm sure Charger is wondering where his breakfast is."

Clay allowed himself to be led from the room. On the way to the stables where Charger was boarded, he stared solemnly out the window. "This is my fault. They took her to keep me from riding. I'm the reason she's in danger."

"This isn't your fault," Jack exclaimed. "You didn't have any way of knowing these people would do something like this and you can't blame yourself. Tamara wouldn't blame you either. We'll get her back and we'll find out who's behind this, and when we do, they'll pay."

Clay turned back to stare out the window. They'll pay, all right, he thought.

Charger whinnied as Clay approached his stall. Stroking the soft neck of the big animal, Clay felt like burying his face in Charger's long mane and crying. Taking feed and hay from Tamara's trailer, he grained and watered the horse, then lead him into the open ring for some exercise. He was loping the horse in a circle when someone called his name.

Looking up, he saw Jack standing beside the man he'd met last night. Taking the lead rope from Charger's halter, he let the big horse run free in the large enclosure.

"I hope you don't mind the intrusion," Collin Dobson said. "The Hightowers told me I could find you here."

Clay remained silent, wondering what Dobson wanted. Dobson looked from Jack to Clay. When they said nothing, he cleared his throat. "I wanted to talk to Miss Allen, ask her a few questions. I went by her room at the motel, but she wasn't in, so I went to your room hoping she might be with you. That's when the Hightowers told me you were out here. Is Miss Allen with you?"

When he'd first seen Dobson, Clay thought he might be involved in her kidnapping in some way, but looking at him now he was sure he knew nothing about it. "What did you want to ask Tamara?" Clay asked.

"I just had some questions about your misadventure in Colorado Springs."

"You know about that?" Clay asked, suddenly wary.

"I told you, I've been investigating these instances, trying to find out who's behind them."

"And do you have any ideas?" Clay asked with such anger, it caught Dobson by surprise.

"I have some ideas, but that's all they are at the moment. I don't have anything concrete at this point."

Clay glared at him. "Mister, if you have any idea

at all who's behind this, you better hope you find them before I do."

Dobson was once more taken aback by the force of Clay's anger. He sensed something had occurred since talking with Clay the night before. "Has something happened?" he asked innocently.

Clay's eyes blazed. "They took Tamara to keep me from riding tonight. They're holding her somewhere until after the rodeo."

Dobson sucked in his breath. This was getting out of control. "I'm sorry. I didn't know. Is there anything I can do?"

"Not unless you know who's got her," Clay spat.

"I wish I did, but I don't have any idea who would have done something like this. I am sorry. If there's anything I can do, call the number on my card, they'll get in touch with me." He hesitated, seeing the pain and anger in the young man before him. "I don't think they'll harm her. The people behind this are professionals. They know what would happen if any harm came to Miss Allen. She'll be released as soon as they know you weren't at the rodeo."

Clay nodded but said nothing as Dobson turned and walked away. Standing in the ring watching the man leave, Clay almost smiled as Charger came up behind him and softly nuzzled his ear.

Chapter Twenty-three

Collin Dobson stopped at the first pay phone he came to. He used a cell phone on occasion, but didn't trust them enough to use them often.

"We have a problem," he stated bluntly as Tom Larrs came on the line, then went on to explain what had happened. "This is getting messy. I suggest you disband the syndicate and start covering your bases. This thing could blow wide open, and it's going to make a real big stink when it does."

"Do you have any idea who's behind this?" Tom asked.

Dobson gave him the two names that were on the top of his list and the reasons why he suspected both. "If I were a gambling man"—he smiled to himself— "I'd put my money on Stan Dickson."

"How much time do you think we have?"

"It's hard to say, but I'd plan on no more than a week. Like I told you earlier, someone else has been investigating this, and from what I can tell, they're real close."

Tom sighed. All he'd wanted was a good sporting event with high odds. Now he was facing possible criminal charges. "Call me if you hear anything."

"Do you have any contacts in Dallas who could alert us if they hear anything about the kidnapping?"

Tom thought for a moment. He did have one or two contacts in Dallas, and one of them owed him a favor. "Yeah, I know someone. I'll call him. Where can I get in touch with you?"

Dobson gave him the name of the motel where he was staying. "I'll be there for about two hours, then I'm on my way to Phoenix to have a talk with Mr. Dickson."

There was a moment's silence before Tom answered. "Let me invite Stan out here and we'll both talk to him. I want to hear what he's got to say."

"You're paying the bills. I'll be waiting for your call," he hung up the phone and got back in his car. "Fools and their money," he muttered angrily.

Crawford Lance lay on the bed listening to Tamara's even breathing. He had given her a mild sleeping drug to make sure she remained in a deep sleep. Looking at his watch, he saw that it was a little past noon. He picked up the phone and ordered room service; a club sandwich and a soda. The five men in the room across the hall listened to the conversation on a tape machine that was recording all calls in and out of room 317. So far this was the only call that had been made since they had installed the tap. They had a name of a business in Phoenix that matched the number called earlier, but nothing could be done until Tamara was released.

Tommy Maddox tried to remain calm and relaxed, but his impatience was starting to show. He wondered how Clay was holding up, and knew he was bound to be frantic with worry. Picking up one of the sandwiches sent up by the hotel, he tried to eat, but found it tasteless and set it aside. The minutes seemed to tick by excruciatingly slowly as he looked once more at his watch. It was twelve-thirty. He held the watch to his ear to make sure it was still running. Devin Price watched him from across the room, smiling at the gesture.

A knock on the door startled Tommy. He watched as Agent Warren let in a man with a large black case.

"Good, it's here!" Devin exclaimed.

Watching with interest as the case was laid on the table and opened, Tommy wondered what was inside. He soon found out—the case contained an elaborate video monitor and surveillance devices.

Soon they were all gathered around the table. A blueprint of the hotel was spread out before them. They had waited for the guests in the room next to Crawford to check out. Now they were going to occupy that room as well.

"If we drill here, we will be able to see the entire room without Mr. Lance knowing. We'll have to wait until he's in the bathroom before we drill. Adams, that's your job," Devin said, handing him a set of earphones attached to what looked like a suction cup. There was a small black box connected to the device that contained its power supply.

Tommy knew the plan. They would make sure Tamara was in the room and safe. That was priority one. Once that was done, they would watch for Crawford to take a bathroom break, open the outer door with the key they'd acquired from the hotel and take him down. Then they would get the people behind Crawford.

The room next to Crawford's, room 315, became the command post for the FBI as Adams glued himself to the wall separating them from Crawford Lance. Agent Warren stood by with a small drill, ready to penetrate the wall on the opposite end at ceiling height. Kirkson had the long tube camera ready to slide into the hole, having already hooked it up to the video monitor in the case.

The snap of fingers brought everyone's attention to Adams. He held up one finger, and Warren stepped up on the chair. When Adams signaled, he began drilling. The drill hardly made any noise as it penetrated the two layers of Sheetrock, then withdrew. The tiny camera was inserted and turned to give a view of the two beds in the room. All was in place when Adams held up his hand, signaling Crawford was coming out of the bathroom.

Tommy stood behind Kirkson, watching the monitor. They could see Crawford on one bed; apparently he suspected nothing, and lay reading a paperback. Tamara was sleeping on the other bed. Every once in a while Crawford would glance over at Tamara, but other than that he didn't move.

Tommy looked at his watch. It was now two o'clock. He hoped it would all be over soon, but looking at Crawford lying nonchalantly on the bed, he wasn't sure it would be.

* * *

Collin Dobson answered the phone in his motel room on the first ring. "Dobson here!" he said, then waited, knowing it would be Tom Larrs on the other end.

"You were right," Tom spoke quickly, "the girl was kidnapped. I had to call in some big favors, but I found out the FBI knows where she is. She's being held in the *Four Seasons Hotel* near the DFW airport off Valley View Lane. The FBI and Devin Price of Price Limited have them under surveillance. The man who grabbed her is named Crawford Lance."

Dobson stiffened at the mention of the name. "I've heard of Crawford Lance. He's a very nasty character. He's freelance, hence the name Lance, but the mob uses him on a regular basis to remove obstacles, if you get my drift."

"Sounds like a real nice fellow. Do you think the mob's connected with what's happening now?"

"I don't think so. It's not their style. If they were involved, there would be bodies, not just mishaps."

"So you still think Stan Dickson is the man behind this?"

"I don't have any reason to change my mind."

There was a prolonged silence, then Tom spoke, almost in desperation. "If the FBI get Lance and he tells them who he's working for, they'll follow the trail back to me."

Dobson thought about it for a moment. "I don't think Crawford Lance will talk. After all, his professional integrity is on the line. If he talks, it'll ruin him. But there is still the chance they can connect him in other ways."

"I'm calling Stan today and having him fly out here tomorrow. Can you get back here? I'd like to have you here when he comes."

"I've got one more thing to do, and I'll be out of here. I'll call you when I get in."

"Right!" Tom said, hanging up the phone.

Dobson returned the phone to its cradle and sighed. "When the rich play, the poor pay," he said to himself, thinking of Clay and Tamara.

The tension in the small motel room could have been cut with a knife. Jack and Will had tried to ease it a little by telling stories about the life they'd led while on the circuit, but gave up soon after starting. Dottie had finally managed to bring a small amount of relief when she started talking about some of the things she remembered from Tamara's younger years. Clay listened with rapt attention as she talked, his mind envisioning Tamara as a young girl. Jack and Will had brought lunch, but no one felt like eating, and the untouched food still sat on the table. The clock on the nightstand showed three o'clock.

A knock on the door brought everyone to their feet, but they stood rooted as if their boots were nailed to the floor. It took a second knock to shock them into mobility. Clay was closest and opened the door, disappointed to see Collin Dobson standing there.

"Hello, Clay. I'm sorry to bother you, but I've got some information I thought you might like to have." When Clay didn't respond, he went on, "I know where Tamara is."

"Where?" Clay cried, his pulse quickening.

"If I tell you, you have to promise me you won't go there."

Clay looked at him as if he were crazy. "Tell me where she is!" he demanded.

"Calm down, Clay," Jack said, placing his hand on the young man's shoulder. "Why can't we go there, Mr. Dobson?"

"She's being held at a hotel in Dallas. The FBI have her and her abductor under surveillance. You would only be in the way and could get both yourselves and the young lady hurt if you interfere. Rest assured, everything is being done that can be done. She's going to be fine."

"Who's got her?" Clay asked.

"A man named Crawford Lance. He's not a very nice man, but I'm sure he won't harm her."

"Is he the one behind all this?" Jack asked.

"No, he's just the muscle behind it. Someone else is funding it."

"Who?" Clay demanded adamantly.

"I don't know yet, but I'm working on it. If I find out, I'll let you know." Dobson knew he wouldn't, but he didn't think it would hurt to tell them he would. "I've got to go. I just wanted to stop by and tell you what I'd learned. She should be back safely, real soon." He nodded and turned toward his car.

"Mr. Dobson," Clay called. When Dobson turned back, Clay held out his hand. "Thank you for telling us. It helps knowing something's being done."

Dobson shook Clay's outstretched hand, wishing there was more he could do. "Good luck, son," he said with a smile and walked to his car. He felt better than he had in a long time.

Tommy was riveted to the small monitor in the case. He'd been staring at it for the past thirty minutes, watching Crawford Lance read and Tamara sleep. He was close to nodding off himself as he continued to hope for a quick ending to this situation. He was about to ask one of the other men to relieve him when Crawford looked at his watch and stood up.

"We've got action!" Tommy whispered urgently. Agent Adams was instantly beside him, a microphone held to his mouth as the other two agents positioned themselves in the hallway, ready to move on his signal.

Tommy and Adams watched as Crawford crossed the room to the small dresser. Opening a zippered case, he took out a bottle of pills and opened the top, taking one of the pills and walking into the bathroom. Adams was about to give the go-ahead when Crawford re-entered the room with a glass of water in his hand. Taking Tamara by the shoulders he lifted her to a sitting position. Tommy could see she was half awake but still groggy. Taking the pill, Crawford placed it in her mouth, forcing it back against her throat. He held the water to her lips and made her swallow several mouthfuls before setting the glass down and wiping the spilled water from her chin. Laying her gently back down on the bed, he looked at his watch one more time, then sat on the bed he had been occupying previously, and watched her.

Tommy watched the scene on the monitor, wondering what kind of pill it was Crawford had given Tamara, guessing it was a sleeping pill of some type.

Agent Adams announced quietly that it was a false alarm and the other agents joined them in the room. Everyone had taken a seat and Tommy was talking to Devin when Crawford stood up, put on his sunglasses and ball cap, then picked up the small case and walked out the door. When Tommy turned back to the monitor, Crawford was gone. Momentarily stunned, Tommy could only stare at the spot where he'd last seen the man.

"He's gone!" he finally managed to shout, bringing everyone in the room to their feet.

Devin glanced at the monitor, then starting giving orders. Adams placed the electronic hearing device to the wall while Warren and Kirkson entered the hallway. They took their positions and waited for Warren to give the signal. The only part of the room not in view from the monitor was the bathroom. Crawford had to be there, but as Agent Warren listened, he shook his head. "He's not in there," he whispered.

Devin had been watching the monitor over Tommy's shoulder, a frown creasing his brow. "Go in," he whispered into the microphone and Tommy watched the screen, seeing the door break open and the two agents entering, their weapons drawn. He watched as they looked into the bathroom then turned away.

Devin was immediately out in the hallway and into the other room before Tommy could react. When he finally walked in, Devin was checking Tamara's pulse as the FBI agents rushed out in an attempt to locate Crawford.

What followed was organized chaos as Devin called for the ambulance that had been waiting downstairs. Paramedics rushed in to care for Tamara. FBI agents swarmed the room to gather evidence and Devin talked to the hotel personnel. Feeling drained, Tommy Maddox followed the stretcher out to the ambulance.

"Which hospital are you taking her to?" he asked.

"Humana," the paramedic said.

Tommy nodded and walked down the street to his car. Sitting in the front seat, he called information. Once he had the number he wanted, he dialed the motel in Denton. When Dottie Hightower answered the phone, he explained in as few words as possible, without identifying himself, what had happened. He could hear the relief in her voice when he told her Tamara was fine and on her way to the hospital. Hanging up, his brow creased. It had been a long day and Crawford Lance had gotten away. By the time the FBI had gotten downstairs, his car was gone. Being this close to the airport, they guessed that was where he'd headed, but they had no way to cover all the flights out of the one of the largest airports in the world.

Tommy pulled up in front of the hotel as Devin Price came out. "You did a good job, Tommy. If it wasn't for your quick thinking, we wouldn't have gotten this close."

"But we missed him. We sat here all day waiting

to catch one man, and in the end he walked right out with us watching and we don't have anything to show for it."

"We've got plenty to show for it. Miss Allen is safe and I now have the name of the man Crawford called in Phoenix. I'm on my way there to meet with him."

Tommy raised his eyebrows in surprise. "I thought the FBI said they wouldn't investigate the phone number in Phoenix until after they'd caught Crawford."

"The FBI didn't get the name. I made a phone call to another of my field agents and had him track it down. Seems it belongs to an investor named Stan Dickson, a real high roller. Our man down there is keeping tabs on him until I get there. Hopefully we can have this mess cleared up shortly and we can all take a break. Until then, I need you to keep an eye on Miss Allen and Mr. Tory."

Tommy nodded. "Which one should I watch tonight?"

"I'll have someone else keep an eye on Miss Allen. Why don't you go back to Denton and see how Mr. Tory is doing. Have you called them yet?"

"I just did."

"Good. I'll let you know what I find in Phoenix," Devin said, getting into the limo.

Tommy sighed wearily as he climbed behind the steering wheel of his car. He was glad he was single; it wouldn't do to have a wife with a job like this.

Chapter Twenty-four

Clay sat on the edge of the bed, relief washing over him as he listened to Dottie tell him again that Tamara was safe and on her way to the hospital. Coming to his feet, he said, "I've got to go see her!"

"Whoa, hold your horses," Jack said, grabbing him by the arm. "It's almost five o'clock. There's no way you can get to the hospital in Dallas, see Tamara, and get back here in time for the rodeo."

Clay gave him an astonished look. "I don't care about the rodeo. I've got to make sure Tamara's all right. That's all that matters right now!"

Jack gave Will and Dottie a pleading look. Dottie nodded and turned to Clay. "Clay, honey, there's nothing you can do right now. The man told me Tamara would probably be asleep for several hours. It might be morning before she wakes up. If you miss the rodeo tonight, you've let whoever's done this terrible thing accomplish what they set out to do." She paused to catch her breath and let what she'd said sink in. "Now none of us in this room is going to try to tell you what to do. You have to do what you think is right, but if it was me, I'd go out there tonight and ride those animals like they were the men that had done this. Then I'd go to the hospital and tell Tamara how well I'd done. She'd be real proud to know they didn't win."

Clay stood silent, his mind churning in turmoil as the emotions within threatened to overwhelm him. He started toward the door, then changed his mind and turned back. "They didn't win."

Crawford Lance settled back in his seat aboard the Boing 737. He would be back in Atlanta in less than an hour. Thinking back, he was not pleased with what he'd done. He couldn't say why, but he knew things had not gone as planned. He had no way of knowing how close he'd come to being caught, but he felt it. He had warned Stan Dickson time and again not to move too fast; there were still several months left in which to ensure his lead, but Dickson had insisted on moving ahead. There was too much riding on the outcome and he had to be certain the results could be achieved.

Clay Tory had been the last obstacle in the way. His surprisingly quick return had thrown a wrench into the well-oiled plans, laid so carefully and executed without flaw.

The last thing Crawford wanted was to be directly involved in a kidnapping, but to get results, sometimes you have to take risks and he knew he'd taken a big one. He had demanded a larger sum for his services and Dickson had agreed. Three other contestants this weekend had failed to show up for performances also, all due to Crawford's network and careful planning. Dickson's team should be well out in front, giving him the assurance he needed.

As the wheels of the plane touched down, Crawford allowed himself to smile, something he rarely did. He would be staying home for a few weeks now. He had convinced Dickson to back off and let things cool down. They had plenty of time before the finals to regain the lead if it was lost.

Stepping out of the plane and into the enclosed ramp, Crawford didn't notice the men on either side of the door until they pressed against him. One pushed something hard into his spine while the other one spoke quietly.

"FBI! Let's not cause a scene. Keep walking." The gun was thrust harder against Crawford's spine for emphasis. He smiled again.

By the time Clay arrived at the rodeo grounds, news of Tamara's abduction had spread like a grassfire on a windswept prairie. Clay was stopped time after time by well-wishers and sympathy givers. Before leaving the motel, Cliff Allen had called to let them know the FBI had been in touch with him. Dottie had finally convinced him there was no need for him to come to Dallas, as she would personally see to Tamara's welfare. As a matter of fact, she was on her way to see her in a few minutes and would have Tamara call him as soon as she woke up. Before hanging up, Cliff had asked to speak to Clay. Nervously taking the phone, Clay expected the worried father to berate him for once more placing his daughter in danger, but instead Cliff Allen had asked how he was holding up and gave him encouragement.

Standing behind the chutes, waiting for his horse to be run in, Clay tried to keep his mind on the business ahead of him. Trojan was the horse he'd drawn in the barebacks and was the next one to be run into the chutes. Clay's rigging was placed on the horse's back and tightened down, while the flank strap was put in place by the chute help. There were two riders to go before Clay, and he watched with detached interest as they rode out; then it was his turn. Climbing into the chute, he worked the resined glove into the handle, but before he could take his seat, Jack leaned down close to his ear.

Whispering softly, he said, "Ride to win."

Clay knew what he meant as he slid up on his rigging and positioned his feet. He had mentally been berating himself for putting Tamara in harm's way. It was still hard to believe she was safe since he hadn't seen her or been able to talk to her. His concern for her well-being had left him in a depressed mood, and that wasn't conducive to riding broncs. Jack knew he had to have the right mental attitude, and by riding to win, Clay would beat the people who were behind Tamara's abduction. Gritting his teeth with solid determination, he nodded to the gate man and brought his feet in contact with Trojan's shoulders as the horse spun out of the chute and into the arena.

Trojan's feet had barely hit the ground before he jumped forward, clearing the ground by five feet. Clay lay along his back, his arm stretched tight as he raked the horse's shoulders in classic bareback fashion.

Trojan's bucking style was one of constant change. If he couldn't throw a rider with one trick, he'd use another one, and he was using them all as Clay fought to stay centered on his back, spurring in time to the horse's jumps. A wild leap into the air was followed by a series of short bucks followed by a spin, all failing to free the rider from his back, but adding to the judge's score as Clay made the eight-second whistle still spurring.

Clay barely heard the crowd as his score was announced. An eighty-three gave him a commanding lead in the bareback riding, but he didn't feel the excitement that normally came with a successful ride. He walked back to the chutes, his face expressionless as he climbed back to the platform to stand beside Jack.

"Good ride," several of the cowboys gushed as Clay untied the leather thong from his glove and took off his chaps.

"Thanks," he responded without feeling.

Jack noted his mood, but said nothing. There was nothing he could say.

The saddle bronc riding went much the same, with Clay placing second on a horse named Soulless. Jack watched him ride, his concern beginning to grow. Clay was riding as well as he ever had, but something was missing—his spirit. He could get by with his spiritlessness in the barebacks and saddle broncs, but the bulls were a different story, and Jack was worried. Clay had drawn a bull called Glory Days, a big black bull that was a cross between a Brahma and a Charlois. He was huge, but Jack had seen him buck on other occasions and knew he was also very quick and extremely nasty.

Jack waited until Glory Days was run into the chute, then pulled Clay to the side. "Listen to me," he said, making sure he had Clay's attention. "You've got to get your mind focused on what's going on here and get it off what's happened or you're going to get yourself hurt. If you can't put your entire mind into riding that bull over there—" he sighed and looked at the brute, "I want you to turn him out."

Clay took a step backward and started to protest, but the angry look on Jack's face made him stop. There were four bull riders to go before him and he knew he had only a few minutes to make a decision.

As Clay stood there looking at the bull in the chute, Jack pulled out something from his shirt pocket. Clay, struggling with his thoughts, was not paying attention until Jack nudged him and thrust something into his hands. It was the cell phone.

He stood staring at the contraption he was holding, not understanding until Jack said, "Go ahead, talk."

Holding the phone to his ear, he hesitated before weakly saying, "Hello."

"Hello, honey," Dottie's voice greeted him.

"Dottie?" Clay asked, surprised.

"Yes, Clay. I'm here in the room with Tamara. She's going to be fine. The doctor said she was given a sleeping pill but should wake up in a little while."

Clay held the phone to his ear, a thousand questions coming to his mind but none to his lips. "If . . . if she wakes up before I get there, tell her I love her, will you?"

"I think I'll let you tell her that yourself. Jack's been telling me you're not all there. Of course, anybody living with Jack can't be all there," she said teasingly. Clay smiled. "I've got everything under control here. You go ride that bull like you're supposed to and then get on down here. I know this young lady is going to want to see you when she wakes up."

"Thanks, Dottie, I'll be there in a little bit," he said, hanging up the phone and handing it back to Jack.

"Feel better?" Jack asked, putting the phone back in his pocket.

"Yeah, I feel better, but right now I'd better get my rope on that bull over there or they're going to turn him out without me."

Jack knew it was a different Clay who climbed into the chute. He still wasn't pleased to see him climb on the back of one of those things, but at least he felt better about it.

Clay eased himself down on Glory Days's broad back and adjusted his bull rope so the handle was centered. His mind filled with determination as Jack pulled the rope tight. "I'm going to ride the hair off you, you sorry excuse for a bucking bull," Clay said quietly, causing Jack to smile. Clay moved up until he was almost sitting on his hand, then dug his spurs into the bull's sides and nodded for the gate.

Glory Days came out of the chute spinning to the left, bucking hard into the air as he did. It was a constant motion of hooves, hide, spurs, and limbs as bull and man fought to conquer each other.

Clay kept his right hand stiff, holding his body back as the black bull dipped his right shoulder and kicked his hindquarters into the air. Only by sheer strength and determination did Clay manage to hold himself upright and stay seated.

Four twists to the left ended Glory Days's crazed spin as he straightened out and jumped toward the chutes, scattering cowboys in all directions. Clay dug in his spurs and pulled hard on the rope. The bull next tried a series of vertical leaps that left his front feet planted and his hind feet straight up in the air, but this too proved unsuccessful, as Clay remained tied on his back. In one last effort the black beast turned again into the chutes and scraped his right side along the rough boards in an attempt to throw the man from his back. The buzzer sounded as Clay's leg came in contact with the boards. Letting go of his rope, he jerked his hand free and grabbed the top board, swinging himself free. Helping hands reached down and pulled him safely to the top of the chute as Glory Days turned to seek his prey. The big bull stopped ten feet away and looked at the cowboy perched on the top rail. As if sensing he had lost this round, the beast shook his head, snorted once, then exited the arena through the gate that opened to let him out.

Tommy Maddox stood in the crowd, whistling and yelling for all he was worth. He had watched Clay ride in both the saddle broncs and barebacks but neither ride had come close to comparing with the ride he had just witnessed. Since he had been assigned to watching Clay and Tamara, he'd had the opportunity to watch several rodeos. The bull riding was the most exciting sport he'd ever watched. He'd seen some good bull riders make some great rides, but he'd never seen any ride like the one he'd just witnessed. He felt a great deal of satisfaction knowing he had been instrumental in that ride taking place, so it was no wonder he was beaming when the announcer excitedly called out an eighty-eight for Clay's score. Still beaming, he looked around the arena until he saw what he was looking for. A small local television station had been taping the rodeo, probably to show highlights during the nightly sports recap. Leaving his place in the stands, he walked over to the cameraman and was soon talking to the person in charge.

It was definitely a different Clay who climbed behind the chutes. His face was split in a broad grin, as he received slap after slap on the back accompanied by "Congratulations, Clay" and "Well done, cowboy."

"I may hate for you to ride those sorry critters, but you do put on a good show," Jack said to Clay.

"I wish Tamara could have been here to see it," Clay said, unbuckling his chaps.

"Me too," Jack responded. "I'll get your bull rope; then we can head that way."

"Thanks," Clay said, the smile still on his face.

Jack retrieved Clay's bull rope from the arena, then found Will and told him they were leaving. Knowing they were heading to Dallas after the rodeo, Jack and Clay had packed their bags and checked out of the motel. Jack promised to send Dottie on her way as soon as they got there. Ten minutes later, they were headed south.

Tommy Maddox followed behind, his mind replaying Clay's bull ride as he listened to the Garth Brooks tape he'd bought on his car stereo. "I never liked country music before," he said to himself and grinned.

It was after midnight before they were let into Tamara's hospital room. Dottie Hightower was still there, dozing in the large chair beside Tamara. Gently waking her, Clay first asked about Tamara.

"She's been sleeping peacefully. The doctor was in earlier and said she should be waking soon. Best I can figure, she's been sleeping for over sixteen hours. When she wakes up, she's going to be ready to go partying for a week. I just hope you're up to it."

Clay grinned. "I guess maybe I better get some vitamins. Will's waiting for you in Denton."

"Yeah, the old fella can't sleep until I tuck him in."

"Will you be all right driving back alone?"

Dottie smiled. "All I've been doing since I got here is sleeping. I'll be fine."

She started out but Clay grabbed her arm. Pulling her to him, he hugged her tightly, saying, "Thanks for everything. I couldn't have made it without you."

Dottie smiled and kissed him on the cheek. "You take care of my girl," she said, squeezing Jack's hand on the way out.

Clay brushed Tamara's forehead with his fingertips. She moaned and turned her head, but continued to sleep.

"Why don't you go to the camper and get some sleep?" Clay suggested to Jack. "I'll stay here with her until she wakes up."

"You come get me when she does," Jack said.

Clay nodded and sat in the chair previously occupied by Dottie. Taking off his hat and placing it on the stand, he leaned back and closed his eyes. In five minutes he was sleeping soundly.

He had been asleep for several hours when a sudden sound startled him awake. Opening his eyes, it took him a moment to remember where he was. Looking toward the bed, he was shocked to see that it was empty. Coming to his feet, he looked around in panic. His first thought was that Tamara had been taken again. He was about to scream for help when the door across the room opened and Tamara stepped out. Relief flooded through him and he stood there weak and shaking, staring at her.

"Clay?" she asked, seeing the ashen look on his face.

He crossed the room in three strides and had her in his arms before she could say anything more.

Tamara finally pushed him away gently, afraid he was going to suffocate her. "What happened? Why am I here?" she asked when she could finally breathe.

"You don't know?" he asked, leading her back to the bed.

"No! The last thing I remember was taking a shower in the motel in Denton, then I woke up here and saw you sleeping in the chair. I had to go to the bathroom."

"How do you feel?" he asked.

"I feel fine, like I've slept for hours."

Clay laughed. "You have," he said, then went on to tell her what had happened. They were still talking when the nurse came in and handed them a small package wrapped in brown paper.

"What is it?" Tamara asked as Clay unwrapped it.

"It looks like a videotape," he said, holding it up to read the title on the spine. "It's of the rodeo last night, but I wonder who sent it?"

Neither of them saw Tommy standing down the hallway, smiling.

Clay reached in the pocket of his jeans and pulled out a small box. "I was going to give this to you last night over a romantic dinner, but it seems you decided to take off with another man," he said with a smile, handing her the box.

Tamara's eyes were bright with excitement as she took the small box and opened it. Squealing with delight, she removed the ring from its case and held it up to the light. It was a thin gold band with a cluster of diamonds surrounding a larger diamond. "It's beautiful," she said, turning to watch the stone's fiery sparkle.

Clay reached over and took the ring, then as Tamara watched in amazement, he placed it on her finger.

With tears brimming in her eyes, Tamara smiled brightly as she looked at the ring and thought about what it represented. Turning to Clay with mischievous smile she asked, "Is this a pre-engagement ring?"

Clay laughed and shook his head. "Nope, this is the real thing. It's now official. We're engaged."

Tears of utter joy flowed freely down Tamara's cheeks. "I think this is the happiest day of my life."

Grinning, Clay said, "I can understand why. You've been kidnapped, drugged, and slept for sixteen hours. That should make anybody's day."

Tamara smiled and stuck out her tongue at him.

Chapter Twenty-five

Tom Larrs sat in a chair across from Stan Dickson in his office in Los Angeles. Collin Dobson sat on the sofa a few feet away.

Tom cleared his throat and addressed Stan. "I've asked you here today to clear up a few things that have been bothering me lately."

"What sort of things?" Stan asked amicably.

"Things like cowboys getting beaten up, or their girlfriends getting abducted, or others being drugged and left in fields, or tires being slashed and batteries stolen. I have a whole list of things that have happened and they all point back to one person: you!"

"Me?" Dickson shouted in protest. "What does any of this have to do with me?"

Tom sighed and rolled his eyes. "Do you know a man named Crawford Lance?"

Though he hid it quickly, both Tom and Collin saw the look of surprise that crossed his face.

"No, I don't know anyone by that name."

Collin, tired of the game being played, stood and walked over to stand in front of Stan Dickson. "You not only know him, you have been in contact with him no less than four times in the last two weeks.

He called you in your office yesterday and you spoke for exactly two minutes eighteen seconds. During that time, one Miss Tamara Allen was being held hostage in a hotel room in Dallas, Texas. The reason for her abduction was to prevent Mr. Clay Tory from competing in the rodeo at Denton. I have proof that you are the one who hired Mr. Lance to abduct Miss Allen. I am prepared to turn this information over to the authorities unless you come clean right now."

Tom Larrs had been watching Stan Dickson's face closely. Before Collin had started talking, he had worn an almost contemptuous look, but as Collin continued, Tom had seen that look change to one of fear, then to utter hopelessness. By the time Collin was through, Stan was confessing to everything.

"I'm broke; I've lost everything. The only way I could think of to bail myself out was to win the bet, but I had to make sure I won. I've got a backer who was willing to loan me half the money now for the entire amount when it was paid, but I had to show him I could manipulate the standings. I had to have my team out in front by next week. If I was able to accomplish that, I would have the money the week after."

Tom Larrs looked sadly at the man sitting in front of him. "Why didn't you come to us? We could have helped you. I know several investors, and I could have found someone to loan you money."

Stan shrugged his shoulders. "Pride, I guess. I wanted to do it on my own."

Tom gave a disgusted grunt and started to speak

when the intercom on his desk buzzed. "I told you I didn't want to be disturbed!" he shouted.

His secretary's voice came tentatively over the line. "I know, sir. I tried to tell that to the gentleman standing here, but he informed me if you didn't see him right away he would break the door down."

Tom started to his feet as the door to his office burst open and Devin Price walked in. "Good morning, Mr. Larrs, Mr. Dickson. And you must be Collin Dobson," he said, not offering to shake hands with any of them.

"Who are you and what are you doing in my office?" Tom stammered.

"My name is Devin Price and I'm here because I was hired to find out who was creating the problems on the rodeo circuit. My investigation has led me to this office."

"Who hired you, Mr. Price?"

"I did!" came a voice from the outer office and they all turned to see Hank Tallridge come through the door.

"Hank!" Tom exclaimed in surprise. "What's going on?"

"What's going on is that someone was trying to manipulate the standings and in doing so was jeopardizing the lives and well-being of several contestants." Walking over to Dickson, he stood within inches of him and asked, "How far would you have gone? Would you have killed some of those cowboys to make sure your team won? If you were willing to have a girl abducted and held hostage, what's to stop you from doing worse in the next one?"

"I didn't know Lance was going to kidnap the girl. He didn't tell me until after he'd already done it. I thought he was just doing the usual things like slashing their tires and stealing their batteries. I never wanted it to go that far."

Tom Larrs was still standing, staring at Hank in shock. Devin Price had taken a seat on the sofa and was joined by Collin Dobson.

"Hank, you hired a private investigator to look into this?"

Hank, still angry, turned to Tom. "Yes, I did. I told you I was concerned about the reports we'd been getting, but you didn't seem to be as concerned, so I hired Mr. Price to look into it and it's a good thing I did. His firm is the one that followed Crawford Lance to the hotel and called in the FBI when he took the girl."

A look of panic swept over Stan Dickson and he sat back in the chair he'd previously occupied. The room went silent as all eyes looked at Stan. Finally, Devin Price stood, all eyes turned toward him.

"I don't see why this whole thing can't be handled quietly. Other than Crawford Lance, no one outside this room really knows what took place or why. As long as he keeps quiet, that is, and I'm pretty sure he will, especially if you offer a little incentive. There's no way this can be linked back to any of you. Of course, Mr. Dickson, you will have to come up with a plausible excuse as to why Crawford Lance was calling you, but I'm sure with your experience, you can come up with something.

"Now the only thing that remains is reimbursing

the contestants for their troubles. I'm sure you gentlemen can come up with something acceptable, and my agency will be glad to act as your emissary in delivering it.

"I do, however, suggest you call a meeting of the syndicate and return all funds immediately and disband as quietly as possible."

Tom Larrs and Hank Tallridge looked at each other and nodded. Devin Price shook Collin Dobson's hand. "It was a pleasure meeting you. Perhaps we can work together from time to time."

"It would be my pleasure," Collin replied.

Devin started toward the door, then stopped and turned toward the two men standing in the middle of the office. "Gentlemen, may I suggest next time you decide to gamble on something, it not be anything that involves sports. I suggest you gamble on how fast it takes an iceberg to melt," Devin smiled and walked out the door.

Jack and Clay drove Tamara back to Denton to get her pickup and horse. Will and Dottie had seen to Charger's care and were waiting for them when they got back. Dottie hugged Tamara tightly as tears streamed down both of their faces. Tamara showed her the ring Clay had given her, which caused Dottie to burst into tears again. She grabbed Clay and gave him a hug.

"Ya'll quit your blubberin'," Jack said, trying to hide his embarrassment.

"Jack Lomas, you just hush up," Dottie said, wiping away the tears.

"It never fails. You get two women together and they start shedding tears," Jack said, looking at Will, who nodded in agreement.

Clay went to get Charger, saying he wanted to stay out of the line of fire. Tamara's eyes lit up when the big horse was brought out and she laughed as he nickered a greeting.

"He missed you too." Clay said, handing her the lead rope.

Tamara hugged the horse, smiling as he nuzzled her hair.

Will and Dottie said their good-byes. Dottie kissed Tamara on the cheek and congratulated her again. Will winked at Clay as he shook his hand, then turned to Jack. "We'll see you next week in Pecos?"

"We'll be there!" Jack said.

Charger was prancing around on the end of his lead rope as Tamara tried to hold him.

"I guess we better get him loaded," Jack said. "We got a ways to go before dark."

"Yep," Clay agreed. "It's a long ride home and I'm ready to get there."

Epilogue

Two weeks later, Clay returned from the mail box with an envelope addressed to him. He didn't recognize the sender but his eyes opened wide in surprise when he opened it and saw the check made out to him. The letter read:

Dear Mr. Tory,

I have been directed to send the enclosed check directly to you to cover any expenses or loss of income you may have incurred during your time of recuperation.

The persons I represent have authorized me to send their regrets for the suffering you were forced to endure

I have it on good authority that the parties responsible for your misfortune have been apprehended, and there will be no further occurrences.

Yours Truly
Devin Price

Clay almost fainted when he saw the amount of the check. He was still sitting at the kitchen table staring at it when Jack came in. Handing the letter and the check to Jack, he sat there in stunned silence waiting for him to look at both.

"This leaves a lot of questions unanswered, and brings up even more. Can you live with that?"

Clay pondered the question. "As long as it's over, I can live with it. I guess I would like to know who was behind it, but if I don't find out, it won't kill me."

"Good enough!" Jack said, giving back the check and letter. "Now you can concentrate on rodeoing and you won't have to worry about getting hijacked or kidnapped."

"That's the best news I've had in a long time. I'm sure Tamara will be relieved as well."

Jack chuckled. "I'm sure she will."

As June turned into July, Jack, Clay, and Tamara spent more time on the road. By the end of the month, Clay was sitting fourth overall in the bare-backs, second in the saddle broncs, and seventh in the bull riding. Tamara was leading the barrel racing by a narrow margin and delighted in reminding Clay and Jack of that fact any time they gave her hard time.

Tom Larrs and Hank Tallridge quickly disbanded the syndicate, returning everyone's money except for Stan Dickson's. They used a portion of his money to pay all the contestants who suffered losses because of his actions. They finally returned the rest, but only after threatening to turn him over to the authorities if he ever tried anything like that again.

Stan Dickson filed for bankruptcy shortly after everything came to a head. The FBI made several calls and even took him in for questioning, but since Crawford Lance never told who was behind Tamara's kidnapping, they couldn't tie him to anything specific, and he denied any knowledge of the incident. They finally left him alone after giving him a strong warning.

Crawford Lance pleaded guilty to kidnapping and was sentenced to ten years in prison.

Tommy Maddox was promoted to field manager with the Price Limited organization. He continues to be a valuable employee and is engaged to a barrel racer he met in Denton. He now spends his weekends traveling to rodeos and has met both Clay and Tamara personally, though he never told them of his involvement in the case.

Clay and Tamara have set May for their wedding date. They just haven't decided which May it will be, but they have assured Dottie she will be the third to know, after Jack and Tamara's parents.

The spirit of rodeo is alive and well in America. On any given weekend you will find boys and girls as young as five years of age to men and women in their sixties and seventies, competing in some fashion at a rodeo. It's this spirit that made America what it is today and will continue for as long as the spirit of the cowboy lives on.

Turn the page for the next

exciting installment of

Rodeo Riders

Final Ride

Coming in December 2000

Jack Lomas brought the pickup to a stop beside the windmill and looked up at Clay Tory, who was sitting on top of the platform by the turning vanes. Terry James was on the ground pulling the rope that ran through the block and tackle and was attached to the sucker rod in the well. Wedging a rod block against the sucker rod, he eased off the rope and let the twenty-foot length of rod settle against the block, then pulled off his hat and wiped the sweat from his brow. Clay climbed down from the platform after making sure the rod was secure.

"How's it going?" Jack asked, looking at the number of rods lying on the ground.

"We've got about half of them out," Terry stated. "We should have the rest out in about two hours and ready for the new leathers."

"I brought them with me," Jack said, reaching into the back of the pickup and pulling out a box. Looking around the pasture, he mentally cringed at the condition of his range. His eyes narrowed with concern as he looked upon the sun-baked grassland that had once been green and lush. "We sure need another rain like those we got in May." It was the end of July and there had been no rain for over a month.

"Uh-huh," Terry agreed. "I thought we were going to have a wet summer, but it sure didn't turn out that way."

"It sure didn't," Jack answered dispiritedly.

"Maybe we'll get lucky soon and get a gully washer," Terry interjected, trying to improve Jack's quickly fouling mood.

Sighing, Jack looked at the cloudless sky. "Yeah, maybe we'll get lucky."

Terry looked helplessly at Clay, who shrugged and shook his head, not knowing what to say. Thinking it might be a good idea to change the subject, he said, "We better finish getting these rods pulled, or we'll be here 'til after dark."

By the time they finished with the windmill and arrived back at the ranch house, Julie James had lunch prepared. Jack had hired both Terry and Julie two years earlier when Clay had turned pro, and he and Jack had started traveling the rodeo circuit together. Terry's official title was ranch manager, but if truth be known, Julie was the true manager, even when Jack was home. She ran an efficient household and kept all three men in line. She cooked, cleaned, played nurse, and constantly admonished both Jack and Clay on their eating habits while on the road.

"We'll be leaving Thursday for Oklahoma," Jack commented as they ate their lunch. "We should be back late Sunday night or early Monday." Looking at Clay, he sighed wearily. "If we don't get some relief from this drought pretty soon, you're going to have to travel without me." With his elbows on the table, Jack ran his hands through his gray, thinning hair in weary exasperation. "I can't afford to be away from the ranch for extended periods of time anymore. You'll be making three or four rodeos a week, which means you won't be here that often, and Terry can't do all that needs to be done by himself."

Clay reflected on what Jack was saying. For the past two years he and Jack had traveled the rodeo circuit together. It was hard to think of going alone, but he knew Jack was right—Terry just couldn't manage the entire ranch by himself. A pang of guilt flooded through him. He should be staying at the ranch and helping out, rather than traveling all over the country while Jack and Terry stayed home and did all the work.

"I think I should cut my traveling down some so I can be here to help until this drought's over."

Shaking his head, Jack replied in a voice that left little room for argument, "No you won't. You've got a good chance of making it to the finals and you need a good summer to clinch it. Terry and I can handle things here for another month, and by then you should have a good lead. You can cut back then, if need be."

Clay knew that when Jack used that certain tone of voice, there was no use in arguing with him. He sat there in silent acceptance until Julie broke in.

"Don't you worry, hon. I'll be here, and I can help out with some of the work. I can drive the hay truck to help feed, I can pull the stock trailer out to the pastures, and I sure can ride."

Clay smiled at her. "And she sure can cook, too! I swear Terry, if you hadn't already got her for yourself, I'd snatch her up and marry her right now."

"I don't believe Tamara would think too highly of that," Julie said, referring to Clay's fiancée. She and Julie had become good friends over the past few months, often teaming up against Clay in the ongoing battle between the sexes. Tamara lived in San Angelo, Texas, and competed on the Professional Barrel Racer's circuit at the same rodeos as Clay, which was about the only time they had to be together, as Clay spent the rest of his time working on the ranch. Jack had encouraged him to take off and spend time alone with Tamara, but Clay felt obligated to the ranch.

"I'll take some time off after his drought is over. Tamara understands what it's like right now," Clay stated.

Jack and Julie had tried to convince him otherwise, but he ignored their comments, feeling his place was on the range, helping out as long as conditions remained as they were.

After lunch, Terry left to check on some calves they'd put in the lower trap the day before. Julie went back to her house to do some sewing, leaving Jack and Clay to themselves. Jack sat at the table staring out the kitchen window. Clay could see the worry etched on his wrinkled brow.

"Are things really that bad?" Clay asked, concerned about this man that had become like a father to him over these past years.

Jack turned slowly to look at the young man sitting

across the table. A smile gradually replaced the look of worry. "No, things aren't that bad. I guess over the years I've grown so used to worrying when things don't go as planned that I do it more out of habit than anything else. If things get too bad, we can always sell the older cows and try to keep the young stock until conditions improve. I'd hate to have to do it. I've spent a lot of years building up the herd I've got now. But I've done it before, and I reckon if push comes to shove, I can do it again."

Clay knew how proud Jack was of his cattle herd, and with good reason. He raised some of the best beef in New Mexico, consistently bringing in top prices. He also knew it took time and careful planning to build a herd as good as his, and to lose any of them would be a setback. "How long do you think we got before we have to start selling?"

His face falling, Jack sighed. "A month, month and half. We've got enough hay to last longer, but I don't think the wells will hold out. We've lost three wells in the last month and there's two more that will probably play out shortly."

"Can we haul water in?" Clay questioned.

"I've thought about that, but I don't know where we'd haul it in from and I don't see how we could get enough to make a difference. I'm afraid if we don't get some rain in the next two to three weeks, I'm going to have to ship at least two hundred head to market."

Two hundred head was a good portion of Jack's herd. Clay was surprised by the amount. "Will that be enough to save the rest?"

Jack shrugged. "It depends on what happens. That should give us about three weeks breathing room. If we don't get some rain by then, we'll have to ship some more."

"Aren't market prices down right now, due to the drought?"

"I thought I'd ship them to Colorado—they haven't been hit by the drought. Cattle prices seem to be holding up there, but if the drought continues here I'm sure it won't be long until the market's flooded up there. It'll cost a little more for shipping, but we should still come out better than selling them anywhere around here."

They both sat in silence, each wondering the cost if the drought didn't end soon.

Rising before sunrise, they hauled hay to feed the cattle, alternating pastures so that all the stock got fed every other day. By ten o'clock the temperature had risen to ninety and by noon it had topped one hundred. The heat scorched the already dry earth until the once hearty prairie grass became brittle, breaking off at the top of the ground, leaving little to sustain the cattle.

Clay and Terry rode out each day to bring in the weaker cattle that were pushed away from the hay or couldn't make the long treks to the large trap by the house where they could be cared for and watched more closely.

Four o'clock, Thursday morning, Clay pulled out of the driveway with a reluctant Jack sitting beside him. It had taken Clay, Terry, and Julie all of the day and part of the night to convince Jack to go. He had argued vehemently that there was too much to be done for him to be gone for four days. He had finally relented, but vowed that this would be the last time until the drought was over. If it hadn't been for the fact that his old friends, Will and Dottie Hightower, were furnishing the stock at the rodeo in Ada, they might not have convinced him to go at all.

Driving east on Highway 380 in the predawn hours, Clay talked about the rodeo in McAlester to take Jack's mind off the ranch and the problems facing them. "I think Tumbleweed has become a top horse in the last few months. If he bucks like he did at Tucson, I should place in the barebacks."

"If you get to ride him!" Jack chuckled.

Clay had to smile at the remark. Jack was already beginning to sound like his old ornery self. "I plan on riding him in spite of the sorry training I've had."

A mock look of pain showed on Jack's face, causing Clay to grin widely.

"I'll have you know, big shot, that you received the best training available. Why, I know men that would have paid thousands of dollars for instructions from me."

"Name one," Clay challenged with a smile.

"Thomas Holland!" Jack shot back quickly.

"Who in the world is Thomas Holland?"

"A man who didn't get the training you did," Jack replied innocently. "And see what happened? He didn't make it."

Clay laughed heartily. "I reckon I ought to count myself lucky, then. All it cost me was a lot of aggravation, having to put up with a hardhead like you. Not to mention all the free labor you got out of me in the name of training."

"Hmmph," Jack snorted. "I don't know where you get the idea *I'm* hardheaded. You're so stubborn you make a mule look like a whipped puppy. I was just standing my ground in an attempt to keep you straight. And all that work you've claim to have done is just a small price to pay for the generosity I extended, takin' you in and givin' you the benefit of my vast knowledge and experience and all."

Once again, Clay burst out laughing. When he finally regained his composure, he said, "It'd be scary if you really believed all that bull you spread around."

Jack gave him a sly grin and pulled his hat down over his eyes. Leaning back against the seat, he said, "Just keep it between the ditches, Junior. I want to make it there in one piece."

Clay grinned and leaned over the steering wheel. It was great to be back on the road.

It was a little after seven in the morning when they entered the city limits of Abilene, Texas. Clay drove to a house on the east side of town where Tamara Allen was waiting. The house belonged to Kerry Tyler, a friend of Tamara's, and a fellow barrel racer. As they pulled into the driveway, Tamara came bounding down the porch steps and was opening Clay's door before he could bring the pickup to a complete stop. Her lithe, blond figure flew into his arms as he stepped from the cab and embraced her tightly.

"Boy, I missed you!" she said, squeezing him tighter.

"I missed you, too," he replied, picking her up and swinging her around.

Breathless, she stepped back as he set her down. She kissed him quickly before stating, "I'll get Charger and Cash ready while you hook up the trailer. Kerry's gone to Dallas with Rob Tanner. She'll meet us in McAlester tonight."

Jack smiled with glee. "Good, now I can have the entire backseat to myself so I can stretch out and sleep."

Tamara smiled back at him. "I'll have to tell Kerry how much her absence means to you."

"Now don't start spreadin' rumors," Jack said, causing Tamara's smile to widen. Jack groaned with stiffness as he got out to help Clay hook up the two-horse aluminum trailer.

After loading the horses, they were soon headed down Interstate 20 toward Ft. Worth and Dallas. Tamara and Clay, ecstatic to be together again, talked nonstop all the way to Ft. Worth, and were still gabbing away as Clay negotiated the heavy traffic in Dallas. Turning north on Highway 75, Clay was glad to see the large city fade in his side mirror.

Other than stopping for gas and a quick bite to eat, they drove straight through to McAlester, arriving at the rodeo grounds at six o'clock, an hour before the rodeo was to begin. Clay parked the pickup and trailer in the contestant parking area, as close to the arena entrance as possible. While Tamara saddled Charger to limber him up from the trailer ride, Clay got his gear bag with his bareback rigging, glove, spurs, and chaps from the camper.

"I'll see you after the bareback riding," he said to Tamara, stealing a kiss.

"You better make a good ride and win some money so you can take me out to eat after the rodeo."

Clay chuckled. "Is that the only reason you stay with me, so I can feed you?"

Smiling coyly, she stepped into the stirrup. "It's not the only reason, but it is one of the best." Reining the big horse around, she turned and was gone before he could think of an appropriate answer.

Jack and Clay walked to the chutes together, stopping to look at the stock in the holding pens. Clay had indeed drawn Tumbleweed in the barebacks, a stocky blue roan that was slowly building a reputation as a solid bucking horse in the Three T's Rodeo Company. Watching the horse through the fence, Clay felt satisfied with his draw. Not so with Gruesome, his draw in the Saddle Broncs.

"I doubt I'll place on that bag of bones," he lamented to Jack.

"Probably not, but you got two good draws with Tumbleweed and Wrangler." Wrangler, a large brindle bull with a wide horn span and lightening-quick moves, was Clay's draw in the bull riding.

"I'm looking forward to trying Wrangler again. I almost had him ridden last time, but he pulled that quick move to the left then swung right. I never saw it coming. I don't plan to let him trick me again."

Jack gave him a dubious look. "Just remember he never bucks the same way two times in a row."

Clay sighed. "Yeah, I know, but I don't plan on letting him throw me with that move again."

Clay and Jack were studying the stock when a voice from behind brought them around. "There ain't no Shetland ponies for you in that bunch, youngster."

Clay held back his smile as he looked at Billy Ettinger. "Nope, and there ain't no old wore out plow horses for you either, old man."

Billy threw back his head and laughed at Clay's ribbing—Billy being all of twenty-four. "Jack, how do you put up with this young upstart?"

"It ain't easy, but we all have our crosses to bear."

"I can only imagine," Billy said, grinning at Clay. Billy was one of the top saddle bronc riders on the circuit and was presently ahead of Clay in the overall standings, though only by a slim margin.

Glenn Timmons was standing beside Billy, smiling at the friendly sparring between the two. "Hey Clay, how's Tamara doing after her little episode last month?" He was referring to her being kidnapped and held hostage in a Dallas hotel in order to keep Clay from riding in the Denton rodeo. Though her's had been the most drastic episode, there had been other instances of cowboys' tires being slashed, batteries stolen, and even some who were knocked out and left in the boonbocks in order to keep them from competing.

"She's fine," Clay responded. "She really doesn't remember any of it, which is fortunate. I'm the one that still wakes up in a cold sweat just thinking about what could have happened."

"Too bad it wasn't you that got kidnapped," Billy said, breaking the somber mood. "I doubt if anyone would have noticed. Tamara could have found herself a real cowboy and things would have worked out better for everyone."

"Thanks!" Clay said sarcastically. "It's good to know I've got friends."

"You don't have any friends," Billy chuckled. "We just put up with you 'cause we feel sorry for you."

It was Clay's turn to laugh. "And all this time I thought you hung around me 'cause you were too old to be by yourself, and I was the only that would put up with you."

"He's got a point," Glenn chortled.

Billy gave him a sour look. "Jack, I think you and I need to get some refreshments where the air's got a better flavor. These wet-behind-the-ear youngsters are starting to give off a bad odor."

"It gets that way quite often," Jack agreed, turning up his nose. "Come on, Billy, I'll buy you a coke." Clay and Glenn followed a short distance behind.

The rodeo began with the introduction of the local dignitaries, followed by the grand entry where mounted contestants rode in single file around the arena. After the invocation and the singing of the National Anthem, it was time to ride. The bareback riding was the first event, and Clay was the seventh rider out. He stood behind the chutes with Jack, Billy, and Glenn to watch the first riders.

The horses were in great form for the evening's performance, bucking hard and showing off their moves for the audience. The first rider, Fielding Baker, had drawn Lively Liz, a strawberry roan mare. Coming out of the chute at a dead run, Liz ducked her head and cut hard to the left, then went airborne. Fielding tried valiantly to remain in the middle of Liz's back, but his right foot went over the mare's neck and he found himself with his feet in the air and his head pointing toward the ground. One more quick jump to the left loosened Fielding from his bareback rigging and sent him flying through the air. The second rider, Ross Calahan, made a qualified ride on Thunderhead, a buckskin horse that had once been a top bucking horse, but was starting to show his age. Ross scored an even seventy, which probably wouldn't be high enough to place. The third rider, Daryl Melton, rode Galloway to a score of seventy-five. Cole Dwyer missed Millie out by not having his spurs over the point of the horse's shoulders on the first jump out of the chute. Reuben Sanchez scored a seventy-one on a good horse called TWA. Jack, Clay, Glenn, and Billy all knew Reuben could have had the winning score if he'd used his spurs more.

Tumbleweed was already in the chute with Clay's bareback rigging cinched on. As soon as the sixth rider nodded and turned into the arena, Clay stepped over the chute and stood astride the horse, placing his feet on the boards.

In the arena, George Beckel was bucked off a horse named Dewey four seconds into his ride, and while the pick-up men herded the stallion out of the arena,

Clay worked his hand into the rigid suitcaselike handle of his bareback rigging and sat down gently on the horse's back.

With the arena clear, the action turned to chute number four. Clay was in position when the arena director called his name. Pulling his hat down tighter on his head, Clay leaned back, moved his spurs into Tumbleweed's shoulders and nodded.

The blue roan charged from the chute, running two lengths before sticking his head between his legs and kicking high with his back hooves.

Clay leaned back and jerked his knees upward, bringing his spurs all the way up the horse's shoulders as it lunged forward.

Tumbleweed bucked the length of the arena, twisting his body and kicking high with his back hooves. The roan horse's bucking style was perfect for a cowboy to get in time with and spur hard—and that's exactly what Clay did, scoring a seventy-seven to move into first place. He wouldn't know until the end of the week whether it would hold through the second performance.

Retrieving his bareback rigging from the derigging chute, Clay watched the remaining three riders, breathing a sigh of relief when the last rider bucked out and he retained his first-place standing.